COUNTER ACTION

THE ATERNIEN WARS BOOK #4

G J OGDEN

OGDEN MEDIA

Editing by S L Ogden
Published by Ogden Media Ltd
www.ogdenmedia.net

ONE

A NEW MISSION

MASTER COMMANDER CARTER ROSE watched the trio of Union medics push Major Carina Larsen's stasis pod out of the medical centre and into the corridor that would eventually lead back to the Galatine. One arm was wrapped around his body, hugging it tightly as if to add pressure to a gaping wound, while his other hand held his chin, and nervously tousled the wiry hairs of his silver beard. He hated that his XO was slowly being consumed by the Aternien biogenic virus, but he hated more that it was his actions that had led to her becoming infected.

The Union medics on Station Alpha had been unable to devise a cure or provide any meaningful treatments to slow the progress of the virus. None of this was unexpected, however. The simple reality was that the Aternien virus was beyond the Union's ability to understand. A century of eschewing technological advancement, for fear it might lead to the creation of another 'Aternien' threat, had made humanity more vulnerable than it had ever been in its history. The irony was that despite their superior weapons, their enemy didn't need to kill them with guns or bombs – the Aterniens could simply wipe them out with science.

Carter followed behind the pod and its entourage of medics, then saw Admiral Clara Krantz approaching from a connecting corridor. He waited for the Union's most senior officer to draw alongside, then walked with her. The admiral, as ever, looked imperious, despite the immense pressures that she was facing. The unruffled calm that Krantz projected helped the officers and crew on the station to remain focused on their jobs, instead of dwelling on the recent horrors. The logic was that if Admiral Krantz didn't look worried, then there was no reason to worry, but Carter knew differently. The admiral may have appeared glacially cool on the outside, but she wasn't blind to the fact that they were losing the war and losing it far more rapidly than even Carter had anticipated. Added to this was the deteriorating condition of Carina Larsen, who wasn't only the Galatine's XO and a crucial officer on the front line of the conflict, but the admiral's niece and only living family member.

Carter suspected that he was one of only a handful of people who knew this secret. He admired Krantz's ability to detach her emotions and not let her concerns get in the way of her duties, which was something he'd not always been able to do himself. Even so, his augmented senses could perceive that the admiral was terrified of losing Carina to the Aternien virus that had already killed hundreds of millions. He knew this because they were the same worries and fears that he was experiencing; the fear that no matter what he did, Carina Larsen was going to die.

"Admiral," Carter said, saluting Krantz then offering her a reserved and respectful nod of his head.

"Master Commander," Krantz replied with matching formality.

The stiff orthodoxy of their greeting was more for show than anything else. He and the admiral had a candid relationship – sometimes too candid – but in the presence of other Union personnel, it was good practice to follow the established conventions.

"Are there any updates on the contaminated medical supplies from the Sanitas compound on Terra Eight?" Carter asked. He wanted to open by offering the admiral his reassurances that he would do everything in his power to save Carina's life, but while that mattered more to him than anything else in that moment, it wasn't the most important item on their agenda.

"We believe that all the medical supplies that were contaminated with the dormant Aternien biogenic virus have been accounted for and quarantined," Krantz replied. She continued to look straight ahead; hands balled together at the small of her back. This was again for show. "We've managed to recall the batches that entered circulation and have put quarantine procedures in place as a precaution against the further spread of infection."

Further spread of infection… Carter repeated in his head. That meant that at least some of the sabotaged medical supplies had been distributed to fleet bases and barracks and gotten into general use.

"What's the damage?" Carter asked. It was perhaps an unfeeling way to enquire about a death toll, but it was also easier to speak in euphemisms than to use the blunt language of truth.

"The current count is a little over three-hundred and twenty thousand dead, twenty-thousand of whom were military personnel," Krantz replied, relaying the number without emotion. "That includes those who were exposed via transmission from infected victims. The number is still climbing, albeit slowly."

Carter cursed under his breath. The Aternien plan to infect medical supplies with their engineered virus was as despicable as it was insidious. Had he not uncovered the plot on Terra Eight when he did, the death toll would have been orders of magnitude higher; a fact that Admiral Krantz was keen to point out.

"The civilian dead would have numbered in the millions had you not intervened, and our military forces would have been decimated," Krantz continued. "It may not appear so, but you saved a lot of lives, Carter."

He raised an eyebrow; it was unheard of for Krantz to use his given name, and the significance was not lost on him. It was as much a personal thank you, as a professional one. Even so, it offered him little comfort.

"That's a small mercy, I suppose." He laughed bitterly and shook his head. "It's a damned sorry state of affairs when the Aterniens have us counting our blessings for only losing three-hundred and twenty thousand souls."

Krantz didn't offer an opinion, but Carter had learned to read her facial tells well enough to know that she agreed.

"What about the other worlds that the Aterniens attacked?" Carter continued, concerned to learn the fates of Terra Five, Six and Seven.

"The human populations on those planets were killed by the Aternien virus," Krantz replied. There was a shocking finality to her statement that caused Carter to question whether he'd heard correctly.

"All of them? Did no-one survive?"

Krantz sighed and reconsidered her statement, pausing to reflect and attempt an answer that was perhaps not so bleak. However, as Carter had already pointed out, small mercies were all the Aterniens had left them with.

"The evacuation efforts saved some, but they merely number in the tens of thousands," Krantz replied. "Across all three worlds, perhaps a hundred thousand in total were rescued, and placed into isolation."

Perversely, that number gave Carter some comfort. Before Krantz had told him that a hundred thousand in total had survived, his mind had gone to a darker place, and assumed that 'some' had simply meant a handful of people, perhaps in the dozens or hundreds. He then snorted and shook his head, realizing how ridiculous his mental bargaining had been. A hundred thousand saved out of four hundred and fifty million was hardly a figure to cheer about.

"One oddity in all of this is that Venture Terminal in orbit of Terra Seven was left intact," Krantz continued, and the news made Carter clear his thoughts and pay attention. "We don't know why it wasn't destroyed, since it was an easy target."

Carter knew Venture Terminal reasonably well. It was an old station, but still one of the biggest in the Union, being home to a quarter of a million people, though it was rarely at capacity. The terminal was mainly a trade outpost for the thriving jewel industry on Terra Seven, which meant that many of its occupants at any one time were trade delegations or private dealers who came and went like the cycles of the moon.

"At least Venture Terminal will provide a refuge for those fleeing Terra Seven," Carter said, trying to find a vaguely silver lining amongst the doom and gloom.

"That's exactly what happened, though unfortunately, Venture Terminal is far from the safe haven it should have been." Krantz paused to return a salute from a passing group of officers, who looked upon the admiral with a mixture of reverence and dread fear. "Because of the nature of its business, Venture was always a haven for undesirables, and the last we heard, criminal gangs had overrun the station. We got mixed reports of lynchings and mob rule, then we lost contact with the station altogether. We can't even dock our ships, because the pylons and docking garages are no longer under Union control. Criminal gangs are holding ships to ransom, forcing those fleeing the world in non-warp capable vessels to pay extortionate prices to dock, and destroying any that they fear harbor the infected."

The fact that criminals were profiteering off the war made Carter's blood boil. He was about to suggest he take the Galatine to Venture Terminal as a show of force, and put an end to the gangs, but he knew it wasn't a military priority. There was no tactical need to re-take the terminal, and they couldn't afford the ships and personnel to do so, anyway. Instead, he turned his thoughts from what had happened in the past, to what they knew of the Aternien's future plans.

"Has Union intelligence learned of the Aternien's next target?" Carter asked. "Given their successes in the outer colonies, it seems reasonable that they would now turn their attention to the inner worlds."

A wave of frustration briefly cracked the admiral's veneer of calm, but she was quick to wrestle her feelings back into their proper compartments.

"We have no solid intelligence on their next target," Krantz replied, speaking the words as one long, weary exhalation of breath. "The truth is they could hit any of our worlds with relative impunity, with the exception of Terra Prime. The core system, at least, has sufficient defenses to hold off an Aternien assault, though not indefinitely. The truth is that Aternus has far easier pickings to go after first."

Carter nodded. In the god-king's position, he'd do the same. Terra Prime was the ultimate prize, but with each of the inner worlds the Aterniens attacked, the Union would be forced to commit more of its depleting reserve of warships and soldiers. Aternus would continue to chip away at the Union, planet by planet, ship by ship, troop by troop, wearing them down so that by the time the god-king finally arrived at Terra Prime, the Union would be on its knees, a shadow of its former self.

"I've stationed the first and third-fleets at FOB Delta, near Terra Two, which gives them the best hope of responding to an assault on the inner worlds, and reinforcing the fleets that are already guarding the planets. But I won't lie, Commander, we're already spread thin."

"What about Terra Eight and Terra Nine?" Carter asked.

There was some self-interest in his question, since the forest moon of Terra Nine had been his home for decades. However, the sudden flash of anger and frustration that continued to erode the admiral's composure told him that little could be done for the outlying worlds.

"I've placed a task force at each planet, but in truth, Commander, it's little more than a show of force to placate the populaces," Krantz replied. "A single task force could be wiped out by a squadron of Aternien Khopesh-class Destroyers, or even their Epsilon-class Gunboats. But knowing that Union warships are in orbit at least stops the populations from losing their minds and descending into rioting and panic."

Carter huffed a laugh at the absurdity of it all, but he couldn't fault the admiral's logic. There were perhaps seventy million people spread across Terra Eight and Terra Nine combined, compared to twelve billion on the inner worlds. It was a cruel numbers game, but a game the Aterniens had forced them to play. The medical team escorting Carina's stasis pod then turned a corner and Carter and the admiral followed. The anchorage where the Galatine was docked was at the far end of the corridor, which meant his time with the admiral was drawing to a close.

"Do you have any updates about the Aternien infiltrators?" Carter asked. He wanted to get as much information out of the admiral as he could, before he cast off, and the question of the Aternien spies was a critical one. It had been known for some time that Aterniens had replaced certain important figures inside the Union, replicating their appearances using near-perfect synthetic façades, built over Aternien metal skeletons. However, while it had initially seemed that detecting these imposters might have been a simple case of analyzing a bio-sample for Aternien markers, one of his crew's discoveries on Terra Eight had forced them to throw that theory out of the window.

"By exposing Superintendent Mathilde McCarty as an imposter you gave our efforts to devise a detection method an enormous boost," Krantz replied. "Because of that, we've made serious headway into developing new detection technology, and I hope to be able to roll this out in the coming days."

Mathilde McCarty had been the head of the Sanitas Corporation – the pharmaceutical goliath on Terra Eight that had been infiltrated by the Aterniens and forced to produce the virus-infected medical supplies. Ten copies of McCarty had been produced, but the woman herself had been brutally murdered.

"We were able to analyze McCarty's clone bodies and determine how the Aterniens were evading detection," Krantz continued. "We discovered a device built into her cranium that projected a false bioimage, which our scanners were reading instead of the actual bio data. We're working to roll out the updates to our existing genetic scanner, which should hopefully expose the remaining infiltrators, before they do any more damage."

Carter grunted an acknowledgement then stopped, realizing they'd arrived at the Galatine's dock. The doctors and nurses had already begun to load Major Larsen's stasis pod onto the ship, where it would then be ferried to the Galatine's medical facility in preparation for the next part of his mission. This was to locate Doctor Nathan Clynes, a scientist who Carter hoped could help him to devise a new weapon to fight back against the Aternien Empire.

Nathan Clynes was the foremost expert on Aternien technology, genetic modification, and cybernetic engineering, and the mastermind behind the Longsword program. Clynes had developed all of the augmentations that gave Carter and his crew their incredible abilities, but while Carter himself had been the first Longsword-officer to undergo transformation, Clynes had experimented on himself first, often with disastrous consequences. Even so, the scientist had survived and the man's augmentations had extended his life far beyond normal human boundaries.

Nathan Clynes had gone into self-imposed exile at the end of the first Aternien war and hadn't been seen or heard from in over a century, but Carter intended to find him. Despite being forced by the Union to condemn post-human practices, and eschew technological development, Clynes believed in the core tenants of the Aternien philosophy that the next stage of human evolution was to ascend from a biological to a technological existence. Clynes knew more about Aternien technology than anyone who had ever lived, bar Markus Aternus himself. Carter's plan – and hope – was that the scientist could devise a tech-virus to infect and destroy the Aternien neuromorphic brain. In essence, Carter wanted to fight fire with fire, and prove to their enemy that their god-king was neither immortal nor invulnerable.

In truth, he had another reason for wanting to find Doctor Clynes, which was to save his XO's life. The biogenic virus that was slowly destroying her cells had been engineered by Aternien scientists. Carter had to believe that science could also provide a cure, and Nathan Clynes was the only man alive who still possessed the requisite skills and knowledge. It was a long shot, and he knew that, but it was also the only chance Carina Larsen had.

The doctors exited the Galatine's docking hatch, this time without the stasis pod in tow, and began making their way back to Station Alpha's medical facility. Krantz took this as her cue to leave also.

"Good luck, Commander," Krantz said, turning to him. "I hope you find Doctor Clynes and that your plan succeeds. In the meantime, I will travel to Terra Prime and meet with the president to get the security council resolution that we need to make this plan of yours official and legal."

"Thank you, Admiral, I won't let you down," Carter said, shaking Krantz's hand.

The resolution that Krantz had spoken of was in effect a

green light from the Union to commit an act of genocide against the Aterniens. It was extreme, and Carter expected there to be steep resistance, but in his opinion, it was either that or admit defeat and accept annihilation. They couldn't beat the Aterniens in open combat, and at every turn, the god-king had outmaneuvered them. New tactics – desperate tactics – were required, and Carter intended to go straight for the Aternien's golden jugular.

Carter was about to leave when he saw a group of seven Union security personal heading their way. Since the Galatine's dock was a dead end, he presumed they had come for the admiral. In itself, this was nothing unusual, yet Carter felt his senses climb. It was only the slightest twinge, but it was enough to make him stop and remain by the admiral's side.

"Admiral Krantz, if I may have a word?" a Union officer said. He was taller even than Carter, but beanpole thin with gangly arms and legs. Carter idly thought that the man would make a good high-jumper or basketball player.

"What is it, Lieutenant Commander Frisk?" Krantz said. It was no secret that Krantz disliked being accosted out of the blue, when she was on other business, and Frisk had apparently not called ahead to alert her.

"Sorry to jump on you like this, Admiral, but we've just received intelligence of an imminent attack," Frisk said, as the security detail behind the officer formed up, neatly.

"Why wasn't I notified right away?" Krantz growled. She immediately began checking her comp-slate, while Frisk continued.

"I don't trust the internal comm system, ma'am, so wanted to tell you, personally," Frisk replied, tautly. Carter smiled – Union security officers were famously paranoid.

"Your personal foibles are not my concern, Commander," Krantz hit back. Frisk stiffened, as if the breath escaping the admiral's mouth was colder than liquid helium. "I expect to be notified at once in future."

"Yes, ma'am," Frisk replied, moving to attention.

"Now, tell me what you know," the admiral continued.

"Our sensor network picked up an Aternien fleet massing at the remains of Union Outpost One. We believe their target is Terra Three."

"Why Terra Three?" Krantz replied. "They could jump to any of the inner worlds from Outpost One."

"We have additional intelligence that suggests Terra Three is their target," Frisk replied, without hesitation.

Despite his earlier dressing down, Frisk had kept his composure. However, while there was nothing outwardly suspicious about the officer, Carter's uneasiness persisted. He made a point of taking a subtle step toward the admiral, so that he was closer by her side.

"I am not aware of any such intelligence," Krantz countered, growing more frustrated by the second.

"It's a recent development, ma'am," Frisk replied, unflustered by the icy reception he'd received. "The situation is fluid and moving quickly."

Krantz regarded the officer for a moment, but Frisk was as still as a statue. She sighed and turned to Carter. "Delay your departure until we learn the scale of this attack, and whether the Galatine is required."

Carter nodded, but Frisk was quick to intervene.

"I don't believe that will be necessary, Admiral. Our forces can handle it."

Descending on the admiral unannounced was one way to

piss her off but telling her what to do was a surefire way to end up stationed at the ass-end of the Union.

"The Galatine is part of our forces, Lieutenant Commander, lest you forget," Krantz snapped. "And I will determine what our response shall be. Your opinion was neither sought nor required."

Frisk stiffened even further. Carter thought if the man became any more inflexible, he might splinter, like an old, weather-beaten plank of wood.

"Yes, ma'am," the officer replied, crisply.

Normally, Krantz putting the fear of God into someone, as she had just done with Frisk, would make Carter feel comfortable that nothing untoward was afoot, yet he was still uneasy. It was like the nagging feeling that he'd left the stove on or forgotten to lock the front door of his cabin after leaving.

"You're dismissed, Master Commander," Krantz said, nodding to him. "Detach from the station but remain close."

"Yes, Admiral," Carter grunted, though he didn't move away.

Frisk nodded courteously to him then stepped beside Admiral Krantz, hovering his right hand behind her back, as if to usher her forward with some unseen force. It was at this moment that Carter's senses spiked, and the concerns that had been plaguing him resolved into a moment of clarity, like a probability wave-function collapsing to determine a defined event. He darted forward and grabbed Frisk's wrist, feeling something beneath it; a long, thin object like a pen or cigar tube. He gripped and twisted, meeting a surprising amount of resistance, considering the security officer's slender frame, then pulled back the sleeve of the man's tunic to reveal an injector device. The object was metal, and it shone with a golden luster, like polished bronze.

"Aterniens..." Carter snarled, speaking the word through a clenched jaw.

Carter snapped the security officer's wrist and pushed Frisk away, but the man didn't cry out in pain. Instead, Frisk turned to the security detail that had escorted him to the Galatine's dock and waved them forward.

"Kill them both," Frisk ordered, before fixing his synthetic eyes onto Krantz. "But kill the admiral first…"

TWO

TEN TO ONE

CARTER PIVOTED and put all of his power into a palm strike that caved-in Frisk's chest and sent the Aternien infiltrator barreling across the deck. In the same movement, he engaged his buckler and shielded himself and Admiral Krantz, deflecting the barrage of gauss pistol shots that the rogue security officers had unleashed at her. Slugs slammed into his back and legs, but his battle uniform hardened to soak up the impacts, and soon the guards were forced to reload.

"Sorry about this…" Carter said to the shellshocked admiral.

While the Aternien spies were reloading their pistols, Carter grabbed Krantz's shoulders and shoved her through the open docking hatch and into the protective cocoon of the Galatine. He overestimated the power he needed to push her to safety and winced as the admiral bowled across the deck like a desert tumbleweed.

I'm going to pay for that one later… he thought.

The sound of fresh magazines being locked into place

diverted his attention away from a very likely bruised and irate admiral to the remaining imposters in the docking area. He wasn't carrying his revolver or his sword, since the standing order on Station Alpha was still that only security personnel and those on guard duty carried weapons. Carter imagined that the admiral might revise that rule in the coming days, assuming she survived.

The imposter officers opened fire again, but Carter was already moving, charging toward the pack of Aterniens with his buckler held out in front of him, like a dozer blade. Slugs pounded into his flesh and the brief ripples of pain told him that his uniform had been compromised, but whatever wounds he'd sustained, they would have to wait. His charge flattened the front two infiltrators and scattered the remainder, who dove out of the way at the last second. Carter hit the wall hard, using it to soak up his residual momentum, before scooping up a gauss pistol that had been dropped during his stampede run and sliding his finger onto the trigger.

One guard was down permanently, his metal skull and neuromorphic brain crushed by his stampede, but five remained, not including Frisk himself, who was still a threat, despite his broken body. Regaining his footing, Carter assimilated the glut of data that was being fed to him through his eyes, ears and even the vibrations through the deck, and used it all to create a detailed picture of the scene around him. Even without looking, he knew where each of the imposters were, and which of them were the most immediate threats.

Carter dropped to one knee and a gauss slug sped above his head, hitting the guard to his front, who was still recovering from the earlier charge. Aiming over his shoulder, he fired twice, sinking two slugs through the right eye socket of the Aternien that had just opened fire, before shooting another of the imposters twice in the head. The final three Aternien infiltrators then gathered around him in a triangle, one to his front and one each to either side. Augmented instinct was driving his actions now, and he attacked without hesitation, smashing his buckler into the face of the guard to his left. Gauss slugs grazed his back and sides, but he used the body of the guard he'd just battered to soak up the next volley of gunfire.

The guards were forced to reload again, and Carter used the opportunity to open fire with his commandeered pistol, shooting the first of the two remaining infiltrators in the head at close range. He turned his pistol onto the last Aternien and squeezed the trigger, but the weapon merely clicked. Cursing, he tossed the pistol and clenched his fists, but the imposter had already reloaded and was aiming his weapon at Carter's head. He raised his buckler but at point-blank range the Aternien couldn't miss, and even with his advanced battle uniform and augmented flesh and bone, he couldn't survive an entire magazine of gauss slugs being unloaded into him from less than two meters away.

A shot rang out, and Carter flinched, but he wasn't hit. A second shot was fired and the Aternien staggered back, a slug buried into his metal forehead. The air was split again and a third slug thudded into the infiltrators head, followed by another directly between the Aternien's synthetic eyes. Remarkably, the imposter remained on his feet for several seconds, before the Aternien man sagged like a limp noodle and dropped to the deck at his feet. Carter then saw Admiral Krantz surging toward him like an angry storm cloud threatening to dump its fury onto an unsuspecting town. For a moment, he wondered if he would be next in line to receive a slug from the admiral's pistol, but Krantz went straight past him and stopped in front of fake Lieutenant Commander Fritz.

"How many more of you are there on my station?" the admiral demanded, aiming the pistol at Frisk's head, but the imposter merely laughed in her face.

"Aternus is immortal," Frisk said, smiling at Krantz. "Aternus is…"

The infiltrator didn't get to finish his sentence before Krantz put two slugs into his neuromorphic brain. She then cursed bitterly – an unusual public display of anger – before raising her right arm and opening a comm channel from her comp-slate.

"Station ops, this is Admiral Krantz," the flag officer began, while dabbing blood from a cut to the side of her head.

"This is ops, Captain Harland speaking," a breathless reply came through. "Are you okay, Admiral, we've been trying to reach you?"

"I'm fine, Captain, but I was attacked by Lieutenant Commander Frisk and his security detail," Krantz replied, as ever getting straight to brass tacks. "Select a team from men and women you trust implicitly and lock down the security office, taking all the remaining guards into custody. For all we know, Frisk's entire department could be compromised."

"At once, ma'am, but there's something you should know," Captain Harland said, and Carter heard Krantz draw in a sharp intake of breath. "General Gardner and Rear Admiral Norris were just attacked in their quarters and killed, and their assassins are still loose on this station."

"How many, Captain?" Krantz said, a crack in her composure finally showing through.

"Ten in total, ma'am. Their IDs have been flagged and circulated to all comp-slates and stations."

"Very well, Captain, initiate emergency quarantine procedures at once," Krantz replied. "Lock down those quarters and isolate anyone who came into contact with Gardner and Norris. They may be infected with the Aternien biogenic virus."

There was a telling pause from the other end of the comm channel, during which time Carter imagined that Captain Harland had forced down a difficult, dry swallow.

"Yes, Admiral," the captain replied. "I have a team closing in on the other imposters. We believe they are heading for environmental control on deck fourteen."

Krantz looked like she was about to curse openly again, but instead she said, "Understood, Captain. You have your orders. Keep me apprised."

"I take it we have trouble?" Carter and Krantz both turned to see Amaya Reid standing in the Galatine's docking hatchway, plasma pistol in hand. "I saw the station alert and thought I'd check on you," Amaya continued. She looked at the sea of dead Aternien infiltrators and let out a low whistle. "Though I see that you've already taken care of that problem."

"Not quite yet, I'm afraid," Carter sighed. "Go to the armory and grab my sidearm and my sword."

Amaya nodded then raised an eyebrow at him. "Could you use an extra blade?"

Carter couldn't help but crack a smile. "I certainly could, assuming you still remember how to use that pointy thing of yours?"

"I remember," Amaya said, also smiling.

The Master Navigator hurried back into the ship, and Carter turned to Krantz, but she was already heading out of the docking area. He hurried after her and stood in her path, much to the admiral's clear annoyance.

"Under the circumstances, I'd suggest you co-ordinate operations from the bridge of the Galatine," Carter said, drawing a look of ire from the admiral.

"Master Commander Rose, I may not be as old as you, but I'm no greenhorn, either. I've more combat experience than you might think."

"I don't doubt it, Admiral, but as you pointed out to Captain Harland, the virus may be loose on the station, and the Galatine's biofilters make it the only truly safe environment." This argument alone seemed to strike home, so he quickly followed up with what he hoped would be the decisive point. "And let's not overlook the fact that the Aterniens just tried to kill you, and they'll try again if you give them half a chance. It's my duty to keep you safe."

Krantz folded her arms, and Carter realized how unintentionally condescending he'd just sounded. Nevertheless, it was the truth.

"Like it or not, Admiral, they're targeting senior officers," Carter added, sticking to his guns. "Aternus has already wiped four stars off the board; don't give them yours too."

Krantz's sigh was bordering on a growl, but she relented. "Very well, Commander, I will do as you ask," the admiral agreed. "But if the remaining imposters are targeting environmental controls, their plan will be to inject the virus into the station's air supply, so it is more than merely my life at stake."

Carter nodded then spotted the golden injector that fake

Frisk had used to attack the admiral lying on the deck, close to the imposter's lifeless body. He picked it up, and carefully inspected it for damage, both with his eyes and his compslate's scanners.

"This injector is still intact," Carter said, and he was sure he saw a breath of relief escape the admiral's lips. "And it's definitely the virus, though it appears to be suspended in another compound." He ran some additional scans, ingested the data, and allowed his mind to race toward the most likely conclusion. "It could perhaps be a timed-release mechanism, to ensure that you became infectious while surrounded by the ops command crew, or other senior staff."

He offered the injector to Krantz, who took it, though not without some reluctance. "Give that to Kendra on board. She'll run some additional scans then dispose of it safely."

Krantz continued to frown at the device and held it away from her body, like it was a stinking, soiled nappy. Amaya then returned, her plasma rapier hanging from her waist, while carrying Carter's weapons in her arms. She passed the cutlass and revolver to him, and Carter wasted no time in fastening the weapons to his scarred and bloodied battle uniform. The fabric was repairing quickly, as was his flesh. The occasional clatter of solid slugs hitting the deck accompanied the process, as his muscles pushed out the squashed lumps of metal like acorns falling from a mighty oak tree. Krantz watched the gory spectacle with interest and no small measure of disgust, before meeting his eyes.

"Well, Commander, it seems that all our fates are in your hands once again, but I trust no-one more to get this done," Krantz said. "Now, get these golden bastards off my station."

Carter straightened to attention. "Yes, ma'am."

He didn't need a stirring speech to get his blood pumping, since his augments had already enhanced his strength, speed and perception to superhuman levels, but to have the confidence and support of the admiral still gave him a boost. Krantz then retreated to the safety of the Longsword Galatine, and Carter drew his cutlass, energizing the blade in the same, fluid motion. Amaya also drew her sword; a replica seventeenth-century English swept-hilt rapier in a stunning onyx black that was as dark as space itself. She flipped the switch on the hilt and the edge crackled with plasma energy, making the thin blade look like a fork of lightning frozen in time.

"Environmental control is one level below us," Carter said, turning his mind to the task before them. "If we take emergency exit staircase 15F, it will bring us out almost directly in front of it."

Amaya nodded then regarded him with curiosity. "Did you memorize the blueprints of Station Alpha?"

Carter scowled at his Master Navigator. "Of course. Didn't you?"

That wiped the smile off Amaya's face. After agreeing to don the battle uniform once again, Carter had asked the navigator to familiarize herself with current Union ships, stations and regulations. Her ability to visualize spacetime in ways that even augmented humans like himself and Kendra Castle were unable to do were not Amaya's only gift. Her brain was a literal sponge, able to absorb information from multiple sources simultaneously. However, like so many people with great natural talent, she didn't always employ her gifts in anger. In short, she could be lazy.

"Yes, sir, I studied up, just like you told me to," Amaya

said, managing to lie while still somehow remaining perfectly charming.

"Good, then follow me," Carter said.

He didn't need to chew his navigator's ear off because he knew that once they were safely back on the Galatine, with time on their hands, Amaya would make a point of ticking off the items on her homework list in an annoyingly rapid fashion. Right at that moment, however, Carter didn't care whether his Master Navigator had memorized the deck layout of Station Alpha or knew the performance specifications of a Mark IV Union Destroyer. All he cared about was that she remembered how to fight, because the lives of everyone on the station depended not only on the sharpness of their wits, but also on the sharpness of their blades.

THREE

IMPOSTER SYNDROME

THE ALERT KLAXON was sounding in the corridors as Carter and Amaya exited the Galatine's docking area, moving at a blistering pace. With the security office on lockdown, Union soldiers were hurrying to guard critical parts of Station Alpha's infrastructure. Each of them was looking at their fellow troopers like they could stab them in the back at any moment. The threat from the Aternien infiltrators wasn't just that their enemy could walk amongst them and strike at any moment; it was more subversive than that. The real danger was that it made Union crew fear and distrust one another, even their closest colleagues and friends.

Carter reached Emergency Exit Door 15F and kicked it off its hinges like it was no more substantial than a Japanese sliding screen. Amaya moved through first and together they cleared the space, then vaulted the railings and jumped to the level below, forgoing the stairs altogether. There was heavy fighting outside, and Carter didn't need his augmented hearing to pick out the scuffle of boots, rattle of gauss rifles and cries of pain from the other side of the door. He nodded to Amaya and she moved through first, plasma pistol raised. A squad of Union soldiers were hunkered down close to the environmental control section, but the dead bodies on the deck painted a clear picture of the situation, and the only color used was red.

"Sergeant, sit-rep," Carter said, moving beside a non-commissioned officer who appeared to be in charge, since his lieutenant ranked amongst the dead.

"Sir, we can't get inside," the sergeant replied, mopping blood and sweat from his brow. "We've tried grenades and gauss charges, and even storming the damned place, but the bastards just cut us down like stalks of hay. I'm not even sure how many are left."

"Let me take a look, Sergeant," Carter said, gently ushering the man aside so that he could stand directly beside the door. He chanced a look, spending no more than a millisecond in the line of fire, before returning into cover. "I see six in the control area, but no bodies on the ground."

"What? How did you..." the Sergeant stammered, but Carter had been speaking to his Master Navigator, not the trooper.

"We do this as a straight power play, nothing fancy," Carter continued.

Amaya nodded then her familiar smile returned. "You're forgetting that everything I do is fancy, skipper..."

Carter resisted rolling his eyes. "Fine, be as fancy as you like, so long as you're efficient."

"Are you fucking crazy? the sergeant cut in. The trooper had been listening in on his conversation with Amaya. "You can't go in there, it's a kill zone!"

"Just stand ready and get a quarantine team down here

on the double, in case we need to lock down this entire level," Carter said, meeting the sergeant's disbelieving eyes. "Oh and mind your language too."

"My language?" the sergeant replied. "Are you out…"

Carter's senses spiked and he engaged his buckler just in time to deflect a volley of gunfire from an infiltrator amongst the sergeant's own troop. He smashed the weapon from the Aternien spy's grasp then drove his sword through the man's gut and lifted him off the deck. The sergeant watched in rapt horror as Carter then threw the infiltrator down the corridor like a fisherman casting his line.

"You were saying, Sergeant?" Carter said, again meeting the trooper's eyes.

"Stand ready and get a quarantine squad down here on the double, aye, sir," the soldier replied, all his questions and doubts seemingly answered by Carter's demonstration.

"Carry on," Carter grunted to the man, before nodding to Amaya, who was ready and waiting to move out.

A buckler sprang from his Master Navigator's left forearm, then together Carter and Amaya charged into the environmental control room. A barrage of gauss slugs was leveled at them, and Carter quickly found himself to be the focus of the imposter's fire. Amaya had used her explosive speed and feline grace to wall-run across the far side of the room, avoiding the hailstorm of incoming slugs, and taking the Aterniens by surprise. Carter dropped low and took cover, waiting for his navigator to execute her extraordinary attack.

By the time the imposters had realized what was happening, Amaya had thrust her energized rapier through the eye-socket of one Aternien, before impaling the narrow blade through the subcutaneous soul-block of a second.

Carter waited for the remaining four imposters to turn their guns on Amaya, then made his move. He wasn't as fast as his navigator, but he was as explosive as a nuclear detonation. His heavy cutlass tore through the bodies of two imposters in a single swing, before he bludgeoned a third with the basket hilt of the weapon until the Aternien's metal skull resembled a pock-marked pumice stone.

In the time it had taken for him to complete his ferocious offensive, Amaya had incapacitated the last infiltrator, who was a copy of a female engineering crewman. His navigator and expert swordsman had sliced off the Aternien's fingers to disarm her, before thrusting the blade of her rapier up beneath the imposter's chin and out through the top of her skull. Amaya then withdrew the blade with the speed of a whip-crack, and the imposter crumpled at her feet. Despite the bodies piled up around them, Carter's senses remained on high alert.

"Where are the other four?" Carter grunted, while kicking the leg of a disabled Aternien to make sure it was really dead. "Captain Harland said there were ten imposters in total."

His comp-slate chimed and Carter lifted his forearm to see that Admiral Krantz was calling from the bridge of the Galatine. He opened the channel, hoping that she could fill in the gaps.

"Commander, it appears that the imposters have splintered into two groups," Krantz began, providing Carter with the answer to his question, though it was not the answer he was hoping for. "The smaller group is heading for the Dauntless, which is docked at pylon nine. She's still undergoing the last stages of her refit and only has a skeleton crew on-board."

Carter nodded. "Understood, Admiral, we'll take care of it. The other six are already dealt with."

"Commander, the refit to the Dauntless includes the addition of smooth-bore cannons capable of firing the Galatine's nano-adaptive projectiles. If the Aterniens get control of her, they could destroy the station." There was a pause, but Carter could sense that the admiral was not finished. "I won't allow these bastards to take my ship. If necessary, I will use the Galatine to destroy her."

Carter understood her feelings better than she could ever have imagined and agreed with her completely. However, he didn't intend for the situation to become so dire as to require the Galatine to destroy the admiral's flagship.

"Understood, but it won't come to that, Admiral, I promise," Carter replied, with additional grit. "Rose, out."

"Skipper, take a look at this…"

While he'd been speaking to the admiral, Amaya had been inspecting the environmental controls. She was crouched beside an access point used to test the air quality. A golden sphere was attached to the valve.

"Has it been activated?" Carter asked.

It was a simple question, but one with momentous consequences. If the Aternien virus had been released into the station's air system, then everyone on-board – eighty-seven thousand souls, including families and civilian workers – would be dead in less than twenty-four hours.

"No, I don't believe so," Amaya said, cutting through the tension like a rapier through flesh. "But this is Kendra's domain, not mine."

Carter nodded then dialed up his Master Engineer. She answered promptly.

"The admiral's fine, boss," Kendra said, wrongly

assuming the reason why he'd made contact. "She's taken a liking to your command chair, though, so you'd better hope she doesn't get too comfy."

Carter snorted a laugh, but there was no time for their usual banter. "Kendra, I need you to get to environmental control on deck fourteen, right away. Bring RAEB, and a big tool bag."

"You got it, boss. What am I dealing with?"

Carter looked at the golden capsule and a shiver ran down his spine. "A whole shitload of Aternien virus, attached the station's air supply. It hasn't gone off… yet."

"I'm on it, boss," Kendra replied. He could already hear her running along the corridors of the Galatine. "Don't let Amaya near it. She might be able to fly like an angel but put a spanner in her hand and she could break a diamond."

"You cheeky mare!" Amaya called out, and Carter heard his Master Engineer chuckle.

"Understood," Carter grunted, closing the channel. He scowled at his navigator, who was coming perilously close to touching the Aternien device and coughed to get her attention. She whipped her hands away from the golden sphere, like a kid caught trying to steal from a cookie jar.

"Come on, we have four more imposters trying to steal the Dauntless," Carter said, motioning for his navigator to follow him. "Needless to say, the admiral is quite adamant that doesn't happen."

Carter left environmental control with Amaya glued by his side and found the cluster of Union troopers gawping at them like they were on fire. Carter stopped in front of the sergeant and waited for the dumbstruck man to notice him. It took a full five seconds.

"My Master Engineer is enroute to disarm an Aternien

device attached to the air supply," Carter explained, once he was sure he had the sergeant's attention. "Until she arrives, no-one goes in there, not the admiral, not the president, not even God himself. Do you understand me?"

"Yes, sir…" the sergeant replied. Carter nodded and moved away, but after another stupefied silence, the soldier called out after him. "Hey, who the hell are you guys?"

"We're on your side," Carter called back, without stopping. "Make sure you pass that around."

Clear of the environmental control room, Carter and Amaya picked up the pace, racing back up the stairs three rungs at a time, and exiting onto deck fifteen through the same door he'd kicked in earlier. Pylon nine was two along from where the Galatine was docked, but even if they hadn't known where to go, the bodies left behind on the deck like a trail of breadcrumbs would have given it away. Charging into the docking area, Carter found a Union Ensign standing by the doorway. The officer glowered back at him but the mind behind the young woman's eyes was clearly no longer her own, and in a flash the infiltrator had darted through the hatch, with the intention of locking them out of the Dauntless. Carter broke into a sprint, slamming his body against the metal door and bracing his legs against the arch in an attempt to prevent the hatch from shutting. A gauss pistol was thrust through the narrow opening, but Amaya was faster. She impaled the point of her rapier through the neck of the imposter, and the Aternien fell. Suddenly, the forces pushing against Carter decreased and he was able to power open the door.

The crack of a gauss pistol split the air and Carter felt the slug punch his chest. He gritted his teeth to help absorb the brief stab of pain before it was numbed then swung his cutlass and split the imposter in half from head to groin, clearing the path ahead. Gunfire filtered along the corridor, along with harried screams and yelled orders. Carter stormed toward the bridge with his rapier-wielding navigator close by his side. More bodies lay strewn on the deck, paving a bloody trail toward the bridge. The final two Aternien imposters were in the process of commandeering the Dauntless, while the woman who had been in command of the skeleton crew lay slumped in the captain's chair, bleeding heavily from wounds to the neck and chest.

Bursting onto the bridge like water from a ruptured damn, Carter went right and his navigator left. Amaya floated into the room like a cloud, and her rapier flashed like lightning, dispatching the first imposter with consummate ease. Carter stormed toward the last of the Aternien infiltrators, who was a Union lieutenant commander, wearing the insignia and name of the Battlecruiser Dauntless on his uniform. Carter gritted his teeth and cursed at how close the Aterniens were getting to Admiral Krantz, even down to taking over some of her ship's bridge crew.

"Aternus is immortal!" the imposter cried, aiming and shooting, but Carter deflected the slug with his buckler and raised his cutlass. "Aternus is forever!"

He dropped the blade and removed the Aternien's head from his shoulders, before kicking the decapitated body away. The soft murmurs of the woman on the captain's chair then stole his attention, and he hurried to her side. Deactivating and setting down his sword, Carter pressed his hands to the worst of the cuts and added pressure, but blood continued to leak out like rainwater running down a windowpane.

"Are you… are you… human?" the female officer asked.

She was terrified, but not just of dying. She was afraid of him too.

"I'm a friend," Carter replied, choosing to answer the question in a different way. "Just stay calm. Help is on the way."

Carter looked over to Amaya and his concerned expression communicated his intention without the need for words. His Master Navigator immediately got onto her comp-slate and called for a medic to attend the bridge as a matter of urgency. His own comp-slate then chimed and he saw it was Kendra calling.

"I've neutralized the Aternien device, boss," the Master Engineer said. "Sneaky little devils, those goldies. Another minute or two and it would have been game over for Station Alpha."

"Good work, Kendra," Carter replied. "Get back to the Galatine and make sure the admiral is safe."

"I'm on it, boss, though I locked her inside the bridge, so I promise you, she hasn't gone anywhere."

Carter huffed. "She won't thank you for that, even though she should. Carter out."

"Is the station… safe?" the woman in the chair asked, her voice little more than a whisper.

"It's safe, Commander, don't worry," Carter answered. He looked toward the exits, hoping to see a medical team rushing his way, but the corridors remained empty.

"That's good… that's good…" the commander replied, licking her dry lips before she spoke. Her eyelids fluttered then her head jerked back sharply, like someone who'd almost fallen asleep at the wheel. Her eyes brightened then she seemed to see him clearly for the first time. "You're the post-human, aren't you?" the woman asked. "Commander Rose, right?"

"That's right," Carter answered. He tried to maneuver his hands into a better position, but where he stopped the bleeding in one location, blood simply poured out from another. "Try not to speak. Help is on the way."

"Thank you, Master Commander Rose..." the woman said, grabbing his shoulder, though her grip was little more than that of a child. "I'm glad... you're with us..."

Carter nodded but he was still focused on trying to stop the commander from bleeding out. Then her eyelids fluttered again and her head began to loll from one side to another. At the same time, his comp-slate chimed, and he saw that it was Admiral Krantz.

"Well done, Commander. Thanks to you, the station is secure, and the virus is contained," Krantz said. He could see that she was still in his command chair on the bridge of the Galatine.

"The Dauntless is secure too, Admiral. Her crew fought bravely; they're a credit to you."

Krantz nodded and straightened her tunic. Carter could see that him complimenting her ship and crew meant a lot to her.

"Please extend my thanks to Commander Burch, who is in command of the skeleton crew," Krantz said. "I'll be over there as soon as I can get away, in order to thank the officers and crew in person."

Carter looked into the eyes of Commander Burch, but they were glassy and still. He removed his hand from the wound and felt for a pulse, though he already knew he wouldn't find one because he could no longer hear the beat of the woman's heart.

"I'm afraid that Commander Burch is dead," Carter announced, gently resting the woman's head against the back of the chair.

There was silence on the other end of the line, and despite the physical separation between them, Carter could feel the admiral's rage radiating through the ether like a solar wind.

"Understood, Master Commander. Krantz, out."

FOUR

CHOICE, CHOICES

CARTER ENTERED the bridge of the Galatine and nodded to his gopher, JACAB, who was seated in the purpose designed cubby next to his command chair. The bot bleeped cheerfully and waved back with a maneuvering fin. Amaya Reid's bot, ADA, also whistled a greeting then returned her attention to the navigation console, and continued to detach the ship from Station Alpha, in readiness to warp to their next destination. RAEB, who was at the bank of engineering consoles at the rear of the bridge, would have also chirruped a "hello", were it not for the fact he was buried inside a maintenance crawlspace, running some final checks and diagnostics.

The reason that the Galatine was currently being commanded by the trio of gophers was that Kendra and Amaya were both in the mission planning room, which was Carter's next destination. The door slid open as he approached, and he found his crew waiting for him, relaxed in the high-backed, swivel chairs that looked more suited to a board room than a warship. Given the austere accoutrements of the rest of the ship, Carter had always thought them an incongruous addition by the long-dead Fleet engineers who had designed the Galatine, but he certainly didn't begrudge them either.

"How are you healing up, boss?" Kendra asked, referring to the numerous cuts, bruises and bullet wounds that he'd sustained while defending Station Alpha from the Aternien infiltrators.

"Nothing to worry about, just a few scratches," Carter said, playing up to the role of indomitable Master Commander. He checked his uniform, which had been fully repaired, thanks to a boost of nano-machines, courtesy of RAEB. "Though, the older I get the more I realize that getting shot pisses me off more than it hurts."

Kendra laughed. "Rather you than me. I'm glad Amaya was your sidekick on that one. I much prefer the safety of my engine room."

"I thought it was fun," Amaya shrugged, swiveling from side to side in her chair. "It's been a long while since I had a good sword fight, at least with a proper sword."

Carter snorted. "That toothpick of yours isn't a proper sword. It's more like a kebab skewer."

"You're just sore because I took down more goldies than you," Amaya hit back. "Also, I didn't get shot."

"That's because I tanked all the incoming fire for you," Carter cut in. He winced as the memory of dozens of solid slugs hammering into his body intruded on his thoughts.

"It's not my fault I'm the fastest," Amaya said, shrugging again. "Besides, I thought we made a good team."

Carter nodded. "That we did, Amaya. Just like old times."

"With the exception that some of the Aterniens now look like us," the Master Navigator added as a qualification.

"I took a few scans of the imposters that you beat the crap out of in the Galatine's docking area, and they were much the same as Supervisor McCarty on Terra Six," Kendra said, picking up the thread. "That should mean that whatever detection updates Admiral Krantz already has in progress should still work to identify other imposters in the fleet."

"Assuming they don't switch-up their designs again," Carter grunted.

He was painfully aware that the Aterniens were not only out-gunning and out-maneuvering them, but they were adapting more rapidly too. It seemed that no matter what he did, all he and his crew could achieve were minor, inconsequential victories. The "small mercies" as Carter had put it to Krantz. That said, they had foiled the Aternien's plan to assassinate the admiral and infect Station Alpha's air supply, saving eighty-seven thousand lives. It may have been a rare win, but it was one worth celebrating.

Carter took his seat at the head of the oval-shaped, matte-silver briefing table and rested his arms on the surface. Unlike the others, he didn't like rocking back, believing that a lazy posture led to a lazy mind and lazy ideas. He coughed loudly and cocked an eyebrow at Kendra Castle and Amaya Reid in turn, in an effort to silently make this point, and his two officers sheepishly sat to attention.

"Nathan Clynes…" Carter said, exhaling the name of the scientist in a long, weary breath. "The purpose of this meeting is to figure out how to find him."

It may have been his idea to seek out the mastermind behind the Longsword Programme, in order to explore the potential of creating a tech-virus to attack the Aterniens, but Carter didn't relish meeting the scientist again. Nathan Clynes was about as pleasant as a toothache.

"I did a bit of digging in preparation for this meeting," Kendra said, interfacing her uniform's comp-slate with the briefing room computer.

"At least someone has done their homework," Carter muttered, eyeballing Amaya as he said this. However, the genius pilot didn't look concerned, which suggested that she had already caught up on her reading.

"Ask me anything," Amaya said, cockily.

"Okay, what's the crew compliment of a Pathway-class countermeasure ship?" Carter said, plucking a vessel and a statistic at random, one that he thought suitably obscure enough to trip Amaya up.

"Forty-five," Amaya replied without hesitation. "Six officers and thirty-nine ratings. The Union has forty-four currently in service, after losing twenty-six in recent engagements."

Carter grunted and narrowed his eyes. While he was glad that Amaya had bucked up her ideas, he never ceased to be annoyed by how smug she could be.

"Anything more you want to ask me, skipper?" Amaya Reid added, grinning.

"Yes, how come you're such a smart-ass?" Carter hit back.

Amaya shrugged. "I was just born lucky, I guess."

This time it was Kendra that coughed in order to get everyone's attention and bring the meeting back to order. "Do you want hear what I've found out, or do you want to play twenty-questions with Amaya?"

Carter narrowed his eyes at his Master Engineer, before grunting, "Proceed…"

"So, I searched the Union archive for all the records pertaining to Nathan Clynes, and had RAEB cross-reference them, looking for commonalities or mentions of places that might hint at where he went."

Kendra then coughed and held her hand in front of her face, before mumbling something even Carter was unable to hear.

"What was that part, Kendra?" Carter asked. If his Master Engineer had tried to hide it, then it was likely illegal.

Kendra coughed again, but this time kept her hand clear of her mouth. "What I said was that I also accessed Clynes' personal log entries, which were archived in the Union databanks."

Amaya Reid looked suitably impressed, but she was also curious. "Those records would have been sealed and classified above Top Secret after the war, so how did you get access?"

Carter already knew the answer, and he watched Kendra shift uncomfortably in her extremely comfortable seat, occasionally side-eyeing him to check if he was looking at her, which of course Carter was.

"Let's just say that I availed myself of the opportunity to gather crucial information from Station Alpha's mainframe while we were aboard."

"What you mean is, you broke into the station's primary core," Carter interjected, already fed up with Kendra pussyfooting around the truth.

Amaya's mouth fell open and she pointed an accusatory

finger at the Master Engineer. "You're a hacker and a cybercriminal!"

"I took advantage of a resource that wouldn't be available to us, once we departed," Kendra said, scowling and folding her arms across her chest.

"You hacked the damned computer, Kendra, just admit it," Carter said, not allowing his engineer to skirt around the topic.

"Fine, I hacked the damned computer," Kendra replied, grumpily. "But as you know, military computer systems are hardlined and the databases are synchronized periodically using physical core-blocks that have to be couriered from the central mainframe on Terra Prime. Short of raiding a courier transport ship, there was no other way to get the information we needed."

"It's fine, Kendra, you did the right thing," Carter said, raising a hand to deflate the tension. He then reconsidered his statement. "Well, technically, you broke the law in a pretty major way, but twenty years in a Union prison is a blink of an eye to people like us."

"They'd never take me alive," Kendra snorted.

Carter smiled. The idea of Union security agents from Terra Prime trying to take Kendra Castle into custody was something he'd like to see, though hoped he'd never have to.

"So, I take it that you and RAEB have a shortlist of locations for us to scout?" Carter continued, conveniently glossing over the issue of where Kendra had got the data from.

"Yes, but it's a pretty broad range of options, to say the least." Kendra tapped her comp-slate to send the data to the briefing room computer, then an image of Nathan Clynes, as he had appeared at the time of the first Aternien war, shone from the holo-emitter in the middle of the table.

"Nathan left Terra Prime in late summer, 2335, a little over three years after the armistice was signed," Kendra began. She tapped the screen and an image of a Union transport ship appeared next to the rotating mug-shot of the scientist. "Acknowledging his sudden wanderlust, and in thanks for his service, the Union gifted Nathan this C37-B Mule Light Transport ship."

Carter snorted and shook his head. "That ship and the copious amount of money the Union gave him were bribes, so that Nathan would publicly support the Aternien Act, and turn his back on us." The bitterness was still raw, despite more than a century having passed since those events had taken place.

"Yes, well, Nathan was always a fucking twat," Kendra agreed, and Carter frowned at her, forcing a half-hearted apology for her crass language. "Sorry boss, but it's true."

Carter grunted, and let it slide, since he couldn't argue with his Master Engineer's assessment of the double-crossing scientist.

"Anyways, Nathan spent those three years after the armistice upgrading and outfitting the transport vessel so that it could function independently for years, without needing to be resupplied," Kendra continued. "When he was done, that C37-B was like a miniature colony ship. Then he warped out of the Terra Prime system, and no-one has seen or heard from him since."

Carter thought back to that time, over a century ago, and dredged up the memories he had of Nathan. He'd known the man as well as anyone in the Union, which was to say not very well, since he was disagreeable and aloof, and kept himself to himself. Carter, however had the distinction of being the very first "production" model Longsword officer to be created, which meant that he and Nathan had spent a lot of time together, ensuring that all the various implants and genetic modifications were implemented correctly.

"I was still around on Terra Prime for some of that time," Carter said, stroking his silver beard, while he reflected. "This was before the Union enacted their most radical reforms, and post-humans like us became social lepers."

"I don't suppose Nathan ever hinted at where he was going?" Amaya Reid asked, hopefully. "That would save us a lot of time."

Carter considered this but had no memory of such a conversation. "I did ask him what he was planning to do with the C37, but the asshole just told me to mind my own business." He laughed. "Nathan wasn't exactly a charmer. Eventually, I got out of him that he planned to 'emigrate', but that's all he'd say."

Kendra worked her comp-slate and the cargo manifest of Nathan's modified C37-B appeared in front of them all. It was extensive.

"The C37 could comfortably handle a crew of eight, so with just Nathan on-board, he stripped out the guts to make room for extra cargo space." The engineer highlighted several items in the inventory. "He took with him a shit-ton of advanced equipment and supplies, including a couple of personal gophers he'd somehow been allowed to keep. There was even some pre-war drone tech that had become illegal at the time. How he managed to swing keeping those, I don't know."

Carter shrugged. "I think the only way the Union would allow pre-war tech to survive, would be if Nathan was never coming back." He continued to scan the inventory list, seeing construction equipment, fabrication plants and enough raw materials to build an entire planetary settlement. "With all this gear, it seems pretty clear he intended to set up home on a planet, rather than live in the void, so that should narrow the search down a little."

Kendra snort-laughed openly at this comment, and Carter took offense.

"I'm sorry, boss, I wasn't laughing at you," the engineer was swift to reply. "But once you see the options, you'll realize that 'habitable planet' doesn't really narrow things down." She worked the comp-slate again and the image of Nathan, the ship and the inventory list fizzled away, to be replaced by the details of four possible destinations.

"RAEB is eighty-seven percent sure that Nathan went to one of these four locations," Kendra said, pointing to the holo report.

Carter read each one carefully. The first was a planet named Ludio Four, which was more than 40,000 light years from Terra Prime, and way beyond the boundaries of Union exploration.

"We haven't even sent warp-probes out that far," Amaya said, again swiveling from side-to-side in her chair. "It'd be a hell of a gamble to risk finding a suitable world out there."

Carter grunted his agreement, then moved to the next entry, which was Perdita Three. This planet was considerably closer, at 'just' 3,400 light years from Terra Prime.

"Telescopic analysis suggests there are some habitable rocks in that system," Kendra chipped in. "I think the Union has even sent a few expeditionary warp probes to check it out, even if just for possible mining operations."

Carter didn't have a good feeling for Perdita Three, so moved along the list. The third system was Gliese 832, the nearest by far at only sixteen light years; it was actually closer to Terra Prime than several of the existing Union worlds.

"Gliese 832 was scouted as a possible location for Union colonization long before the war, but it was passed over in favor of more suitable star systems," Kendra explained.

Carter was only half-listening to his engineer, while continuing to study the entry for Gliese 832 at the same time as stroking his beard. His augmented gut feeling was telling him there was something about the system that made sense, but he didn't want to discount the final option, before hearing it.

"You said there were four possibilities, but only three are shown here?"

Kendra nodded. "This is where it gets interesting, boss..." she removed Ludio Four, Perdita Three and Gliese 832 from the holo image and replaced them with a galactic map, which was focused on the Outer Arm.

"RAEB also found a rumor, corroborated by a log report from Nathan's research assistant, that he planned to travel to the edge of Quadrant II and attempt a trans-galactic warp jump."

Amaya Reid suddenly sat up in her seat and stopped swiveling. "Really? I remember there was some research around trans-galactic warp when I was still an unaugmented rookie, but it never went anywhere." She let out a low whistle. "Damn, I'd love to give that a try!"

Carter was not sold. "You'd like to try a warp jump to the Andromeda Galaxy?"

"Of course!" Amaya beamed.

"Do you have any idea how far that is?"

"Two-point-five-three-seven million light years, give or take," his navigator replied, casually. "Did you know that the Galatine can theoretically jump anywhere in the universe, it's just that the margin of error increases the further beyond the mapped star charts we go."

Carter should have known that Amaya would have the answer, but her educated response did nothing to change his mind.

"The last thing we need is another entire galaxy to search." Carter turned Kendra's comp-slate toward him, tapped the screen, and sent the data for Gliese 832 back onto the holo. "Besides, we don't need to go to Andromeda to find our man. That's where he'll be."

Now it was time for his two officers to appear deeply skeptical.

"Boss, there are a couple of vaguely habitable rocks at Gliese 832, but nowhere you'd want to live," Kendra said.

"That's not exactly true," Carter said. He worked the comp-slate again, and generated a map of the Gliese 832 system, which then zoomed in on a planetoid circling the inner edge of the system's goldilocks zone.

"That is a planetoid designated Gliese 832-e," Carter continued, pointing to the diminutive rock. "Thanks to a hyper-dense magnetic core, the gravity is point-nine-seven that of Terra Prime, and it has a habitable atmosphere too. But the Union deemed it too small to be worth the effort of colonization, given there were many better options within range, as Kendra pointed out."

The two other officers studied the data on the little tropical world, and Carter could sense that he was changing their opinions.

"Why are you so sure that is where he went?" Kendra asked. "It's not exactly my idea of getting out of Dodge. Almost any Union ship could drop in there for a cup of tea if they wanted to."

"The point is, no-one wants to, which is why he'll be there," Carter explained, ready with his answer. "Nathan knew that the Union had extensively scouted 832-e and discounted it, which mean there's literally no-chance of anyone bothering him. He was a brilliant man, truly, but Nathan was impatient. He wouldn't want to spend months or years scouring the galaxy for a new world, if there was one right on his doorstep, ripe for the taking."

The room fell silent for a moment, as the three augmented Longsword officers deliberated the options. In the end, though, the decision was his alone, and the crew would follow his orders, even if that meant attempting a suicide jump to the Andromeda galaxy. Carter preferred his officers to understand his reasoning and thought process. They were a small crew – even smaller now than ever – and he was personally much closer to Kendra Castle and Amaya Reid than a regular captain would be to those under his command. If nothing else, it showed them that he respected their input, which he did.

"I'll plot a jump to Gliese 832, right away," Amaya said, smiling then springing out of her chair. "I had hoped for something more challenging, but to make this interesting, I'll try to warp us into a perfect orbital pattern."

"Just get us there in one piece, Amaya," Carter said, aware of his pilot's needs to stretch her limits. "Beyond that, knock yourself out."

FIVE

GOING IT ALONE

CARTER LOWERED himself reverently into his command chair and waited for his officers to take their stations. JACAB, who was still in his cubby beside his console, turned his glowing red eye toward him and bleeped an inquisitive sequence of tones. Normally, he'd need to refer to his comp-slate to translate the sounds, but on this occasion, he figured it was simply his bot asking what their next step was.

"We're heading to Gliese 832-e, buddy," Carter said, gently tapping his knuckles against JACAB's spherical shell. "I have a hunch that's where Nathan Clynes will be."

JACAB nodded then looked down and let out a sorrowful warble. Again, Carter didn't need his comp-slate to know what his bot was saying.

"If anyone can save her, buddy, then it's Nathan," Carter said. His thoughts were also dwelling on his XO, who remained in stasis in the Galatine's medical bay, slowly succumbing to the Aternien biogenic virus. "That guy owes us for selling out the Longswords and publicly supporting the Union's anti-post-human rhetoric a century ago."

The bot perked up a little at hearing this, then bleeped another question. Carter could sense that his gopher was searching for a little encouragement and was he was happy to give it.

"I won't give that asshole a choice," Carter replied, smiling at his bot. "Nathan will either help Carina, or I'll make him wish he'd decided to warp his ship to the Andromeda galaxy after all."

"Course plotted and laid in, skipper," Amaya Reid reported, swiveling her seat around to face him. "We should arrive in a perfect star-synchronous orbit."

"I'm not taken with the word, 'should', Amaya," Carter replied, trying to subtly remind his Master Navigator about the one condition of their arrival at Gliese 832-e – namely that they arrive in one piece.

"I'm being modest, skipper," Amaya replied, swiveling the seat from side-to-side. "Just sit back and enjoy the ride!"

ADA laughed and JACAB joined in, their synchronized bleeps sounding like a warning alarm. However, Carter knew that if the gophers were happy to make the jump, then there was likely nothing to worry about. Like cats, their bots had a keen sense for danger.

"Fine, but drop a warp comms buoy, before we jump, and transmit the transponder ID to Admiral Krantz," Carter said, once the electronic giggles had subsided. "I want her to be able to reach us if needed."

"Aye, aye, skipper," Amaya replied. Her hands floated across her console and the order was actioned. The viewscreen showed the comms buoy dropping away behind them as the Galatine cruised in the general direction of the Gliese 832 system.

"Buoy away..." Amaya said as a sonar-like ping emanated from her console. "And we're synchronized. We're hot to trot, skipper."

Carter grunted an acknowledgement then added, "Jump when ready."

He listened to the sound of the Galatine's titanic soliton warp drive spinning up then the starfield beyond the viewscreen shifted and a laser blue planet materialized below them. It was so sudden and shocking that Carter actually ducked.

"Shit, Amaya, can't you just jump from system to system normally, like everyone else?" Carter said.

"I could, but where's the challenge?" the pilot replied. "Oh, and we're in a perfect orbit, in case you were wondering..."

Carter grunted and checked the comp-slate in his chair. As promised, Amaya had exited the fold in space in a perfect star-synchronous orbit. It was another display of her incredible navigational abilities, though he chose not to let on that he was too impressed, so as not to stoke her ego.

"Good work," Carter said, keeping his praise professional. "Not that I ever had any doubts, of course."

Amaya blew him a raspberry not unlike the kind JACAB was partial to delivering, then Carter pushed himself out of his chair and walked a few paces toward the viewscreen, studying the compact new world and its beautiful, blue oceans. The door to the bridge opened and Kendra walked in, minus RAEB, who remained in engineering unless called upon.

"The Union missed a trick with this place," Kendra said,

while transferring her engineering stations to the bridge units. "It looks like an awesome little world."

"Maybe once I've crushed Markus Aternus' soul block in my fist, we can schedule some time to come for a vacation," Carter said, only half-joking. "For now though, scan the surface and see if you can determine if there any human-made structures down there."

"RAEB has already begun a detailed analysis, but nothing yet," Kendra reported, moving to the tactical console behind Carter's station and leaning her elbows onto it. "What I can tell you, though, is that this place is teeming with life. A full speciographic analysis will have to wait, but there's a shit load of marine and animal species, and bugs galore."

Carter snorted a laugh. "Great. A bug-infested, tropical alien world. Why couldn't Nathan just have set down somewhere without biting insects and a dozen other things that would likely eat you as soon as look at you?"

"The somewhat hostile nature of this little planet might have been part of the reason he chose it," Kendra replied, with a shrug. "The colony worlds all have their fair share of nasties, but none of them are a patch on the native species of Gliese 832-e."

Carter knew a little something about dangerous native animal species, and the Morsapri 'death hogs' of his forest moon immediately came to mind.

"To a hungry alien beast, we're just as tasty as a regular human, Kendra," Carter replied, cautioning against complacency. "In fact, thanks to our dense musculature, we're arguably even more appealing."

"I don't know about you two old prunes, but I'm definitely delicious," Amaya chipped in, eliciting another electronic chortle from ADA and JACAB, who clearly shared the navigator's sense of humor.

Carter scowled at the back of his Master Navigator's head. "What are you talking about? You might still look twenty-three, Amaya, but you have a century and a half under your belt too."

"The difference is that I don't look it," Amaya said, swiveling her head to smile at him.

This time Kendra laughed along with the two bots, and Carter decided to cut his losses, before he suffered any more humiliating burns.

"How's that analysis coming along?" he asked, crabbily.

"Still nothing, boss, but I'm..." Kendra stopped mid-sentence and frowned at the scan readings, which were populating the tactical console in double-quick time, thanks to RAEB's efforts from engineering. "Scratch that, I'm picking up a faint power signature. It's reasonably close to the equator at latitude negative seventeen, longitude thirty."

"On screen and magnify, then continue your analysis," Carter said, massaging his silver beard in anticipation of striking gold.

The viewscreen zoomed in on the coordinates, but all Carter could see was a tropical jungle surrounded by wetlands. There was no indication of man-made structures, and other than the faint power signature, he would have discounted it at once. However, his senses continued to impress upon him that Nathan was down there somewhere.

"It's definitely a fusion reactor core, but it's heavily-shielded, likely using pre-war tech," Kendra continued. "Whoever built this place clearly doesn't want to be found."

Carter grunted and banged his fist onto the arm of his chair. *There you are you double-crossing bastard...*

"Amaya, ready the combat shuttle," he said to his Master Navigator. "Kendra and I are going down to the surface to smoke out our quarry."

"Aye, aye, skipper," Amaya replied, transferring helm control to ADA before springing out of her seat.

Carter also turned to leave, but the tactical and ops consoles both then chimed in unison. Carter recognized the tone of the alert as an incoming communication and waited for Kendra to relay the update.

"It's a message from Admiral Krantz, relayed through the warp comms buoy," Kendra said. The tenor of her voice suggested the news was grave. "An Aternien strike force has launched an orbital bombardment of the pharmaceutical district on Terra Eight. She sent ships to intercept, but it was a distraction."

"A distraction for what?" Carter grunted.

"According to the message, they launched an assault on Terra Nine shortly afterwards, and landed another biogenic weapon."

Carter cursed bitterly. Terra Nine and its moon were not densely populated but were still inhabited by tens of millions of people, including himself until not long ago, which made the news sting even more keenly.

"It makes sense that they'd just choose to bomb Terra Eight," Amaya Reid cut in. "After we exposed the Aternien plan to infect medical supplies with the virus, the planet lost its strategic value."

"And with Krantz forced to focus her fleets on the inner words, Terra Nine is an easy target, especially if she already diverted a task force to Terra Eight," Kendra added.

Carter twisted the wiry bristles of his beard with thumb and forefinger as he considered his next actions.

"Has the admiral expressly ordered us to provide support?" Carter asked his Master Engineer, but to his surprise, she shook her head.

"Not expressly," Kendra replied, "Her exact wording was 'to render assistance, if able'. In other words, boss, she's passed the buck to you."

Carter grunted and continued to twirl sections of his beard into sharp points, like nails. Krantz was risking a lot of lives, and even her own position, by not giving him a direct order to intervene. It meant that she'd bought into his argument that the Galatine could only prolong the war, not prevent the Union's defeat. Even so, despite it going against his own council, it felt wrong to ignore a call for help.

"Kendra, you'll take command of the Galatine with Amaya as your number two, then jump to Terra Nine at once," Carter said. He'd made up his mind, for better or worse. "We'll load Major Larsen's stasis pod into the combat shuttle, then I'll head down to the planet alone, with JACAB as my wingman."

His bot warbled and saluted with a maneuvering fin, before detaching from his console and zooming off the bridge.

"You got it, boss," Kendra said. The order had been given and neither officer would protest it, even if they disagreed. "I'll load the stasis pod and have the shuttle ready to depart as soon as its on-board."

"The admiral's message also included a location and trajectory data on the Aternien fleet at Terra Nine," Amaya added, while working her station. "I'll calculate a jump that brings us out right on their butts and scare the golden crap out of them."

Carter scowled at his navigator's colorful metaphor,

which painted an unfortunately graphic picture in his mind's eye, then followed his Master Engineer, who had already left the bridge. However, he soon noticed that she'd hung back to wait for him in the corridor outside.

"Stay on your guard down there," Kendra said, as they walked together toward the shuttle bay. "Clynes is certainly no soldier, but he was always a couple of wrenches short of a full toolkit. The Union employed him because he's a bonafide genius, but he lacked empathy. Who knows what a hundred years in isolation does to a man like that."

Carter huffed a laugh. "Actually, I have a pretty good idea what it does." Kendra frowned at him, so he gave her a more earnest reply. "Don't worry, Kendra, I'll stay on my toes. I never trusted Nathan, certainly not after he rubber-stamped all the Union's backwards policies."

"He did more than just sell us out, boss," Kendra replied, still sounding unusually somber. "When I was deep diving the Union archive for intelligence about Nathan Clynes, I found much more than just clues to his location. There were a shit-ton of classified research documents and reports too. Things that chill the blood."

As the first 'production model' Longsword officer to have been created, Carter knew something of the nature of Nathan's research. The Union had been forced to develop the Longsword program at a rapidly accelerated pace, in order to counter the Aternien threat in time, and this meant bypassing any and all red-tape that would have normally stood in the way of experimental research. In short, the Union turned a blind eye to some of Nathan's controversial methods, simply because it needed the Longswords. Carter didn't know the extent of what Kendra had learned, and it was possible she'd found out even more than he already knew, which was enough. In the distant past, civilization had not shied away from human experimentation during periods of war, and the existential threat the Aterniens had posed to the human race had given Nathan Clynes the perfect excuse to add another dark chapter to humanity's history.

"I understand, Kendra, but it's actually Nathan's gifts for the dark arts of genetic modification that I'm counting on," Carter said, sidestepping the issue Kendra had raised. "But, trust me, I'll be watching that bastard like an augmented hawk."

This answer seemed to satisfy his engineer and they walked in silence for another minute, until they reached the armory and he stopped. "You go ahead, while I pick up a few things," he said, unlocking the door with his biometric ID. "Like you said, it's best to be prepared."

Kendra nodded and hustled down the long central corridor of the Galatine, while Carter stepped inside the armory and quickly equipped his sword and revolver. He also added a few nano-stims to his belt, just in case, though he hoped he wouldn't need them. *How much of a threat can one decrepit old scientist really be?* Carter thought.

He exited the armory and jogged to the shuttle bay, finding Kendra Castle hard at work using a mechanical lifter to maneuver Major Larsen's stasis pod into the hold of the combat shuttle. She lowered the body and it was magnetically grappled to the deck of the craft.

"Her rate of deterioration is accelerating, boss," Kendra said, parking up the loader and jumping out of the machine's cabin. "I'd say she has maybe forty-eight hours tops, before the virus becomes too established and too much damage has been done."

Carter grunted an acknowledgment. He hadn't planned on enquiring about Carina's condition, figuring ignorance was bliss, but he admitted to himself that it was better to know. A deadline always helped to focus the mind.

"I leave the Galatine in your capable hands," he said, holding his Master Engineer's shoulders. "Give those bastards hell."

"You can count on it, boss." Kendra thumped him solidly on the chest then set off to the bridge at a purposeful march, but she stopped on the threshold of the door and turned back. "Take care of yourself down there, Carter," she said, speaking as his friend, not his colleague. "I only just got you back and I'm not ready to lose you again."

Carter smiled. "Don't sweat it, Kendra. I'm hard to kill."

The Master Engineer nodded then was gone, leaving Carter alone with the shuttle and the stasis pod, which was humming softly in the cargo hold. He stepped inside the compact craft and wiped the condensation off the pod's glass canopy. His XO simply looked like she was sleeping. Patting the glass, he then hit the button to close the cargo ramp, shuffled past the pod and jumped into the pilot's seat. JACAB, who was already attached to the co-pilot's station, greeted him with a cheerful bleep and warble. His ever-efficient bot had run through the pre-flight checks, so the craft was ready to go.

"Thanks, buddy," Carter said, rapping his knuckles against the side of the bot. "Are you ready to do this?" JACAB warbled and nodded then focused his glowing red eye dead ahead. "Okay, then…"

He fired up the engines, and waited for the shuttle to reach launch power, before opening a channel to the bridge. "Bridge, shuttle bay; everything reads green down here."

"Confirmed, boss, you're clear to launch," came the reply from Kendra.

Blowing out a steady breath, Carter flipped the control to lower the combat shuttle into the launch tube and waited for it to lock into place. A slab of metal slid across the cavity in the deck panel above him. He felt the ship push against the mooring clamps, then the launch indicator flashed green and he hit the button to retract the door at the end of the launch tunnel, causing a rapid decompression that spat the shuttle into space like a bullet from a rifle. Once clear of the Galatine, he engaged the main engines and maneuvered a safe distance away from the Longsword-class battleship, before pulsing the thrusters and pointing the nose of the craft at the ship. Under the light of the Gliese system's red dwarf star, the Galatine looked as majestic as ever. Then, in the blink of an eye, she passed through a fold in space and was gone.

"I hope they remember the way back," Carter said to JACAB, while turning the shuttle toward the tropical planetoid.

JACAB warbled and shuddered, perhaps considering the possibility that Gliese 832-e might become their new, permanent home. He smiled at his bot and gave him a reassuring pat.

"Don't worry, buddy, they'll come back for us."

Carter locked in the co-ordinates of the power signature that Kendra had detected and piloted the robust combat shuttle toward it. Entry through the atmosphere went smoothly – or as smoothly as almost burning up due to friction could ever be – and soon Carter was flying over the giant rainforests and wetlands of the previously uncharted world. Even the poles of the planetoid were a lush green, and everywhere he pointed his scanners, he picked up massive bio-readings.

JACAB bleeped and Carter saw that his bot had sent updated coordinates to the navigation computer. Now that they were close, the scans of the stealthed power signature were easier to read, and his bot had homed in on the source. Carter turned the shuttle and followed the new vector, then alarms screamed at him, shattering the calm of what had otherwise been a tranquil flight over a veritable paradise.

"Report, buddy, what the hell is going on?"

Two plumes of smoke raced into the air from beneath the tree line and in a heartbeat his senses had spiked to their highest level. The rush of chemicals was momentarily nauseating, before his augments got his body under control. With barely seconds to act, Carter increased thrust and threw the shuttle into an evasive pattern, while at the same time launching countermeasures. The missiles took the bait and flashed past, exploding to their rear, but the shuttle was still hit by shrapnel from the warheads, which tore chunks out of their armor. More alarms wailed, and two more plumes of smoke carved across the sky.

"Hold on!" Carter yelled, more for his own benefit than for JACAB's, since the bot was latched onto the console like a limpet.

He threw the shuttle into another evasive pattern, avoiding the first missile, which turned sharply to reacquire them. The second missile had them dead to rights, but he squeezed the triggers and filled the air in front of them with shards of plasma energy. The second missile was hit and exploded and Carter banked hard to port to avoid the worst of the debris. Moments later, JACAB squawked and spun around to look aft, his eye growing wide.

"It's okay, buddy, I see it too!" Carter called out, watching the final missile snake after them in his scanner view.

He dove sharply and punched through the tops of the trees, before banking hard and swinging the shuttlecraft around. The missile followed, but it clipped a tree as it continued its pursuit and was sent off course. A second later it hammered into the hillside and exploded. Carter sucked in a deep breath then leveled off the shuttle and maneuvered it back on course toward the power signature. Their scanner readout remained clear, but he reminded himself that the shuttle had missed the SAM sites once already, and more surprises could still be in store.

"Sharpen your scanners too, buddy," Carter said, glancing at his bot. "We don't know what else Nathan might have hidden out here."

Then a plasma blast burned through the tree canopy and slammed into the shuttle's engines. He lost power and switched to maneuvering thrusters, but all Carter could do was slow their descent. Natural forces had taken command of the shuttle, and nature had determined that they were going to crash.

SIX

ANCIENT MYSTERIES

THE MANGLED CARGO bay door of the combat shuttle groaned and whirred as it ground open, allowing a blast of sticky, tropical air to rush inside the crashed craft. This was closely followed by the raucous chatter of alien birds and the disconcerting croak, growl and roar of other unfamiliar beasts, all of which combined to create the strange soundtrack of the extra-terrestrial jungle he'd found himself stranded in.

"Well, this is just great," Carter grumbled to himself, as a chunk of the shuttle's aft armor fell off. He hated hot climates, and jungles most of all.

JACAB warbled his heartfelt agreement, and Carter decided to check on the status of Major Larsen's stasis pod while waiting for the ramp to open fully. Although his rapid descent to the forest floor had technically qualified as a crash, he'd at least managed to make it a controlled one. As such, the seals around the pod remained intact, and its systems appeared to be functioning within norms, at least so far as he could determine. The same couldn't be said for the shuttle itself, Carter realized, as he stepped outside and witnessed the full extent of the damage for the first time. It didn't take a Master Engineer like Kendra Castle to work out that the plasma blast that had hit them had completely wrecked their main engines.

"Hey buddy, can you relay a damage report to my comp-slate?" Carter asked, while JACAB remained inside the ship to shut down critical components and prevent it from blowing up.

JACAB bleeped and the data was delivered promptly. He checked the readout on his comp-slate and sighed heavily. It was as long as the guest list to a celebrity wedding. Reluctantly, he started at the top and began reading.

"The starboard horizontal control surfaces are blown, the thrust vectoring engine outlets are mangled, the intercooler on engine one is slagged, the vernier thrusters are destroyed, the fuel bladder has ruptured and is sealed off…" The list went on and Carter gave up bothering to read the rest. In short, whoever had shot them down had made an unholy mess of things, and the outcome was that the Galatine's combat shuttle was going nowhere, fast.

JACAB finished the important emergency shutdown protocol on the reactor then hummed outside. He took a brief moment to look around, warbled his disapproval of their situation, then hovered next to Carter's shoulder, his scanners and indicators flashing and spinning like disco lights.

"Can you check on Carina's stasis pod, buddy?" Carter asked his gopher, nodding toward the chamber in the hold. "But keep your scanners peeled for anything out of the ordinary too."

JACAB narrowed his eye at him and warbled a confused statement.

"I don't know, *unusual* as in a missile flying our way, or a giant man-eating monster burrowing up from beneath us," Carter said, trying to define what he'd meant by "out of the ordinary".

JACAB bleeped his understanding then tapped Carter's comp-slate with one of his extendable arms. Carter re-read the report and saw that his bot had already run the analysis on Carina's stasis chamber and sent it to him. In hindsight, he should have known that JACAB would have prioritized checking on Carina, above checking on their shuttle, or scanning for man-eating monsters. The bot had a soft spot for his XO, after all.

"It says here that the pod's status is 'currently nominal', which doesn't really inspire me with confidence," Carter said. "How much longer can that contraption hold up?"

JACAB bleeped and shrugged his maneuvering fins, unhelpfully.

"Thanks, buddy," he replied, with a large dollop of sarcasm, which merely caused JACAB to blow a raspberry at him. "Do something more useful and find out what shot us down. Likely, wherever that blast came from is where we need to go next."

JACAB hovered closer and tapped Carter's comp-slate again, before turning his back on him in a huff. Carter felt the skin on his face flush hot as he saw that his gopher had already taken the initiative and run the scan he'd just asked for, which made him feel guilty for snapping at him.

"Sorry, buddy, and thanks for being on the ball," he said, shamefaced.

JACAB glanced back at him then briskly turned away

again, to make the point he wasn't yet forgiven. It was unnecessarily dramatic, but Carter figured he deserved it.

"It was definitely a Union plasma cannon that hit us," Carter said, concentrating on the analysis of the energy blast, instead of his annoyed gopher. "I'd say it was a precursor to the cannon that ended up being fitted to the Longswords, which all but confirms that Nathan Clynes is on this planetoid."

JACAB turned back to him and bleeped inquisitively.

"No, I don't know why he'd shoot us down, either," Carter replied, rubbing his beard and causing tiny fragments of broken glass from the shattered shuttle cockpit to tumble from its wiry grasp. "But I intend to find out, even if I have to wring the answer out of him."

A shrieking bird with bright purple plumage flew overhead, cutting across the scorching sun, which was already making him feel uncomfortably hot. His augments and biological modifications, aided by his battle uniform, allowed him to function for extended periods in extremes of temperature, but he personally hated sweltering, humid climes. That was why he'd set up a cabin on the forest moon of Terra Nine, which was cool and fresh most of the year, and a wintery bliss for the rest of it. Thinking about his cabin made him realize that his own home world was currently under threat of extinction. Part of him wished he was with Kendra and Amaya, fighting the Aterniens light years away, but he had another important job to perform. He needed a weapon that could strike a deadly blow to the god-king's plans, and on top of that – and equally important to him, personally – he needed to save Carina's life.

JACAB roused him from his musings by squawking a warble that was almost as shrill as the purple bird's screech, and Carter noticed that he'd sent an update to his comp-slate. It was another scan reading, but this time of their surrounding area. While he'd been daydreaming, his gopher had again been proactive, and figured out where they needed to go next. However, the report just made him feel even more miserable and deflated.

"Ten miles? Seriously?"

Carter had asked the question in the vain hope that his bot had gotten his calculations wrong, but JACAB merely nodded in reply, and pointed the way. The bot also looked downcast, as if the prospect of a ten-mile trudge in tropical heat made him miserable too, a fact which amused Carter greatly.

"I don't know why you're complaining, you can fly!" Carter said, shaking his head at his gopher.

JACAB warbled indignantly then hovered higher to keep watch, while Carter searched the cargo compartment for the shuttle's disaster kit. Unlike a regular human, he could cope with the difficult ten-mile trek without needing water, but that didn't mean he didn't benefit from it, and Carter didn't want the slog to be any more unpleasant than it had to be. Gathering what he needed, he checked on Carina a final time, but the readings remained nominal, which was as much as he could hope for.

"Hang tight, Carina, I'll be back with help as soon as I can," he said pressing the palm of his hand to the glass canopy, which was refreshingly cool to the touch.

He sealed off the cargo hold from the exposed cockpit, then stepped outside and closed the rear ramp remotely, ensuring the shuttle was as secure as it could be, considering the damage. He didn't expect that anyone or anything would interfere with it, but considering the abundance of life on the planetoid, he couldn't discount the possibly of a native species taking an interest in the ship, and accidentally unplugging something, or otherwise damaging the stasis pod.

"Lead the way, buddy," Carter said, walking in the direction his bot had flown. "And do me a favor and keep an eye out for anything that might decide to eat me."

JACAB warbled a laugh then the bot stopped moving and its indicator lights flashed rapidly. A scanner dish extended from its chassis and began to rotate before fixing position in line with the trees ahead of him. His bot squawked an alert, and Carter felt his comp-slate vibrate. However, he didn't need to risk checking it, because his own early-warning sensors had lit up like stadium floodlights. Amongst the anarchy of competing jungle noises, his mind had focused on the careful advance of heavy feet, and the rustle of disturbed leaves and branches.

Suddenly, a bird-like creature standing two meters tall charged out of the undergrowth, accelerating with ferocious speed. With similar swiftness, Carter pulled his 57-EX from its holster and drew a bead on the animal, firing and hitting it twice, before the stricken beast fell and collided with him, dumping its full momentum into Carter's body. The impact sent him cartwheeling across the parched ground, but he instinctively twisted his body and threw out his arms to arrest his fall, accidentally hammering his revolver against a boulder as he desperately tried to regain his balance.

Pain blockers numbed the fresh cuts and bruises he'd sustained, the worst of which were to his ribs, which had borne the brunt of the alien beast's uncontrolled tumble. Pushing himself up, he walked over to the creature, which was dying from the two bullets he'd already pumped into it.

The beast was lying head down, and resembled a giant bird of prey, though he could make out relatively little detail from his current angle. Not that Carter cared what the creature looked like; he only cared that it had stopped trying to kill him. He aimed his revolver at the back of the alien beast's head and squeezed the trigger, but the weapon didn't fire. Cursing, he checked the 57-EX and discovered that the cylinder had been knocked out of alignment when he'd accidentally hammered the weapon against the rock. He tried to force it back into position, but only made it worse. The timing was off, and the 57-EX was useless.

Cursing again, he drew and energized his sword, using the modernized version of the far more ancient weapon to put the beast out of its misery. It hissed and rolled over as it expired, and Carter found himself frozen to the spot, unable to believe his eyes.

"JACAB, are you close?"

The hum of his gopher's gravity repellers became louder, then the bot descended from its elevated perch, and hovered by his side.

"Buddy, tell me I'm not going crazy, and that isn't what I think it is?" he added, pointing his cutlass at the now-dead beast.

JACAB's red eye widened and its scanners went to work. The bot emitted a long string of muted bleeps and warbles, as if it were muttering to itself like a mad scientist who couldn't quite believe his findings, before turning to Carter and transmitting the report to his comp-slate. He read it with some trepidation, and though the analysis confirmed his suspicions, he still didn't believe it.

"Are you sure this a Deinonychus?" Carter asked his bot, who shrugged then nodded. "So, this is a six-feet tall, twelve-feet long, one-eighty-pound dinosaur from Terra Prime's ancient past?"

JACAB, warbled, shrugged and nodded again, though to be fair to the bot, he looked and sounded just as skeptical as Carter did. He was about to ask how an extinct dinosaur from old Earth's early cretaceous period had found itself miraculously extant again and living on a planet sixteen light years from its point of origin, when his senses became alert to a new danger.

"JACAB, climb…" Carter said, and his bot shot upward out of harm's way.

Carter backed away and raised his sword, blade humming in the humid air. There were more heavy footsteps and rustling of leaves, followed by a cacophony of throaty, honk-like barks, that sounded like gulls, but deeper and more threatening. It was an ill sound that promised ill intent. Then three more Deinonychus emerged from the undergrowth, hunting him like pack animals. The middle beast charged and Carter dove to the side and rolled out of harm's way, slashing the dinosaur's leg in the process. The other two hesitated, giving him the chance to follow up with a savage downward strike that cleanly removed the wounded creature's head.

The barks and hisses resumed in force and the two remaining Deinonychus attacked at the same time, both probing for an opening. Carter swung and stabbed his cutlass at the creatures, but they were undeterred. The beast to his right made a move and Carter punched it hard with the basket hilt of his sword, but at the same time the second Deinonychus grabbed him with its forelimbs and stabbed the sickle-claws on its back leg into his side. His battle uniform was punctured and he felt a twinge of pain before it was quickly numbed, but this was enough to know that the creature had inflicted a dangerous wound. Pushing that thought out of his mind, he wrapped his left arm around the dinosaur's head, and wrestled it to the ground, before hacking a deep gouge into its flesh.

The Deinonychus hissed and bellowed, and he struck a killing blow, impaling the full length of the blade through the beast's gut. At the same time, the dinosaur's hunting partner, which had recovered from being punched, charged at Carter, and he was forced to scramble out of its way, leaving his cutlass embedded in the dinosaur he'd just killed. The final Deinonychus seemed to sense that Carter was now vulnerable, and it stalked toward him with more confidence. Claws extended, it was about to pounce, when JACAB rained down blasts of plasma energy from his position in the sky above them. The shots lacked the power to harm the beast, but it was enough to distract it. Carter took his opportunity, running at the Deinonychus and grabbing its forelimbs, like he was challenging the creature to a knuckle-wrestling contest. He'd intended to overpower the beast, push it down then crush its long neck with a well-placed kick, but the dinosaur had a similar idea.

The beast thrust its powerful hind leg at Carter's chest, claw poised to puncture his heart, but his senses allowed him to anticipate the attack, and he caught the talon, ensuring it only grazed the material of his battle uniform, rather than sinking through it. With one hand wrapped around a forelimb, and the other holding its hind leg, Carter had the leverage to lift and throw the beast. The dinosaur sailed through the air and slammed into the trees five meters away, providing Carter with an effective demonstration that his augmented super-strength had not diminished over the years. Dazed and disorientated, the creature struggled back to its feet, but not before Carter had recovered his plasma cutlass. The Deinonychus charged again, but he met its advance and timed his slash to perfection, cutting open its neck and body and sending it down for good. Senses still on high alert, Carter scoured the bushes and tree line for any more signs of movement, holding his plasma cutlass ready to dispatch any more marauding dinosaurs. His heart rate began to settle and his sixth-sense for danger dropped, like a pressure gauge falling out of the red.

"Buddy, tell me that's all of them," Carter said, still spinning in circles, head on a swivel to make sure his settling pulse wasn't luring him into a false sense of security.

JACAB descended sharply, warbling and bleeping, but the tone of his gopher's broadcasts were calm, which in turn helped him to recover more quickly from his near-frenzied high. He disengaged the plasma edge of his cutlass, but kept the weapon in hand, just in case, then looked at the quartet of dead dinosaurs, still struggling to believe they were real. There was only one thought on his mind, and he spoke it out loud.

"What the fuck is going on?"

SEVEN

CREATURES OF THE NIGHT

CARTER CROUCHED DOWN BESIDE one of the dead dinosaurs and ran his hands through his hair. He'd fought man, post-human and beast before, but this was something new and entirely unexpected. With some trepidation, he removed his hands from his head and examined the dinosaur, but everything from its flesh and bones to its jaws and eyes looked 'real', despite Carter knowing that was impossible.

"JACAB, help me out here," Carter said, glancing at his bot, who was hovering close by, dutifully. "How the hell can there be living dinosaurs on this planet?"

JACAB shrugged then hovered over the dead Deinonychus and extended a probe into one of the wounds that Carter's cutlass had inflicted on the beast. While his bot worked, he pushed himself back to his feet, and took in his surroundings. The noises of the jungle were no less present than before, but instead of the peace and beauty of nature, all Carter now heard was the potential for danger. He worried that the shrill squawk of a tropical bird was instead a pterodactyl, circling high above him, ready to dive in for the kill. Similarly, every warble, click, creak and rustle that crept into his augmented ears could now be a prelude to an attack.

Mercifully, his comp-slate then chimed an update, giving him something else to focus his anxious mind on. RAEB had moved away to analyze one of the other beasts, chatting to himself in the process, so Carter sat down on the Deinonychus in front of him, which he was pleased to discover made for a comfortable seat. Raising his left arm, he engaged his comp-slate and read the report that his bot had just sent him, and suddenly the universe made sense again,

"It's synthetic?" he asked his gopher. JACAB paused for a moment to nod a confirmation, then continued scanning, and Carter huffed a laugh. "Well, I'll be damned," he added, patting the head of the dead dinosaur he was sat on. "It looks like Nathan Clynes has been out here playing god."

JACAB's report was typically detailed, and contained a glut of information that only his Master Engineer or Master Operator had the knowledge or patience to fully decipher. For his part, Carter focused on the elements that mattered most, and he didn't need to be a scientist to understand that the Deinonychus was a masterpiece of synthetic biology, accurate down to its lab-grown bones. According to JACAB's analysis, the dinosaur's flesh was comprised of non-biological molecules and polymers, while its skeletal structure had been 3D-printed using a hydroxyapatite-polymer mix that was previously unknown to science. JACAB's memory core still contained technical knowledge from the pre-war period, which meant that if his bot didn't know what the hell something was, it was almost certainly a completely new invention.

The most important aspect of the synthetic Deinonychus was its brain. JACAB's scans had determined that it was a similar design to the neuromorphic brain that Markus Aternus had developed, and that had led to the evolution of the Aternien race, and all of their current woes. JACAB's analysis suggested that the brain inside the dinosaur was less sophisticated from a technological standpoint than the Aternus design, but that it existed at all was akin to lightning striking twice in the same place.

Nathan Clynes had admired and respected Markus Aternus, but he also coveted the man's achievements and was fiercely jealous of his success. At the end of the first Aternien war, the Union outlawed research in post-humanism, and purged their databases of all knowledge relating to it, including all of Clynes' research. And while Clynes had gone along with it all, in order to get a handsome payoff from the Union, it was now clear that the brilliant, if troubled, scientist had spent the last century trying to emulate the achievements of his rival. How far these achievements went, however, was something that Carter was more than a little wary to discover.

Carter suddenly felt a twinge of pain in his side, which was his body's way of reminding him that he'd been hurt. While in combat, his sensation blockers remained in effect to numb the distracting effects of injuries, but as his body climbed down from its augmented high, the pain returned as an aide-memoire for him to tend his wounds. According to JACAB's report, Deinonychus meant 'Terrible Claw', and Carter considered this an apt name, bearing in mind the ugly nature of his wound. He quickly assessed his bio-readings on his comp-slate, but despite the pain, the injury was healing well and at the expected rate, with no signs of infection. Carter decided to let it to heal naturally, rather than accelerate the process with a nano-stim, the side-effects of which he'd rather not have to endure.

JACAB bleeped to get his attention and Carter pushed himself off the flanks of the dinosaur and joined his gopher. The bot had finished his analysis of the synthetic creatures, and Carter realized that JACAB had plotted a new route through the tropical forest, one which avoided what the bot had amusingly described as the 'the worst of the local wildlife.'

"What the hell could be worse than a hunting pack of 'Terrible Claws'?" he asked his bot.

Just then the ground shook, followed by the sound of trees being uprooted and snapped like twigs. Carter's senses heightened, but only slightly, and he followed the gaze of his gopher's red eye to see another dinosaur stomping across the horizon. He blinked his eyes a couple of times to make sure his mind wasn't playing tricks on him, but the creature wasn't a figment of his imagination, much as he wished it was.

"Okay, point taken," Carter said, turning back to his bot. "A T-rex is worse than these little Deinonychus."

JACAB warbled a laugh, which was a good sign that suggested the aforementioned T-rex was not heading in their direction, then hovered away to begin their ten-mile trek to Nathan Clynes' landing site. The journey wasn't difficult for someone with Carter's enhanced abilities, and thanks to the watchful eye in the sky that was JACAB, they managed to avoid running into other hungry, killer dinosaurs. The only time he needed to use his sword was to hack through patches of undergrowth and dense clumps of hanging vines, like a fictional archeologist, exploring ancient Earth's rainforests, and searching for forgotten cities and long-lost relics.

It took Carter and JACAB less than two hours to cover the ten miles between the shuttle's crash site and the location of the power signature. Carter arrived at their destination, expecting to see a perfectly-maintained smallholding, with a quaint cottage replete with smoking chimney built from local stone, all fenced off and secured from the dangers surrounding them. Instead, he found Nathan Clynes' old C37-B transport ship, hidden beneath a tarpaulin-covered makeshift garage that was rotten and covered in grime, weeds and moss, like the ship itself.

"Are you sure this is where the power reading originates?" Carter asked his bot.

JACAB spent a few moments circling the old transport vessel with his scanners set to maximum, then returned to his side and nodded. Carter sighed and shook his head. Just when he'd thought that the planet was starting to make sense again, Gliese 832-e threw him another curveball.

"Survey the area around the ship and see what you can find out, buddy," Carter said, stabbing his cutlass into the hard ground and using it like a walking cane. "I'll take a look inside the C-37. Maybe there are some clues in there as to where Nathan actually went. Come find me once you've run your scans."

JACAB warbled and nodded then climbed higher to begin his arial survey. Carter pulled his cutlass out of the ground, flourished it, if for no other reason than to loosen his wrist, then headed toward the transport ship, but he'd barely taken a few steps before his senses suddenly climbed sharply. Carter stopped dead and listened; his finger held against the switch that would ignite plasma around the edge of his powerful sword.

"Buddy, are you picking up anything unusual close by?" Carter said, talking to his bot through their open comm channel.

JACAB warbled then went quiet as the bot ran a scan. At the same time, Carter slowly turned around on the spot, eyes probing every nook and cranny of the transport ship's landing site, but he was painfully aware that there were literally hundreds of places where a creature could hide, lying in wait to strike. His comp-slate then updated, and he heard JACAB bleep a response.

"Are you sure?" Carter asked, after chancing a look at the screen, which indicated that JACAB had not detected any new threats.

JACAB warbled an answer, but the bot sounded uncertain. Carter's senses remained on high alert, which suggested that his gopher's scanners had missed something, but for the life of him, he couldn't see or hear anything out of the ordinary.

"Keep your eye peeled, buddy," Carter said, turning back to Nathan's transport ship. "There's something out here. I can feel it."

Carter lowered his sword, but kept his finger on the activation switch, then set off again toward the C37-B, keeping his steps light and casual. Almost immediately, his senses spiked and at the same time, JACAB let out a shrill warning. He energized his cutlass and spun around, but he was too late, and a claw-tipped hand slashed across his chest and sent him tumbling backward. He arrested his fall and got to his feet in one fluid motion, activating and raising his buckler in time to deflect another lashing strike from whatever had ambushed him, but the creature was moving so fast it was a blur. Trusting his fighting instincts, Carter retaliated with a punch using the barrel hilt of his sword as a cudgel and the creature staggered back, before bellowing a maddened howl in the sky that was thunderous enough to be heard for miles around.

Not for the first time that day, Carter could scarcely believe what he was looking at. This wasn't a dinosaur, nor was it any other real beast, living or extinct. It was a monstrous creature, part man, part wolf, with shaggy black fur and glowing red eyes. Its arms were spread wide, with claw-tipped hands that were angled toward him like daggers. The beast roared again, revealing razor-sharp teeth that were dripping with saliva and stained with the remains of its last meal.

Carter stood his ground and faced-down the monster, which charged at him without fear. He met its advance and drove his energized cutlass deep into the wolf-beast's chest. It howled and the creature's cries sent pain shooting through his head from ear to ear, but he pushed harder until the sword was buried hilt-deep in the monster's flesh. Dark blood, thick like treacle, oozed over Carter's hand, and he twisted the blade, forcing a shrill howl of pain from the beast. It thrashed and gnawed at him, but he held the creature at bay, using his buckler to shield his face and prevent the monster's jaws from sinking into his neck. Soon, the creature tired, and Carter shoved it away, letting it fall to its knees in a pool of its own blood. Then a final swing of his cutlass removed the wolf-beast's head, and the fight was done.

Carter flourished his sword and held it ready while his keen eyes scanned the perimeter of the clearing for any more dangers. His heart was beating so fast that if he were fully human, he'd already be dead. Then his senses began to climb down, and his pulse slowed. Taking a deep breath, he checked himself for injuries, but besides four knife-sharp slashes across his chest from the beast's initial attack, he was unhurt. JACAB then appeared beside him, and the bot looked at the decapitated creature and shuddered.

"What the hell is Nathan playing at?" Carter said, finally feeling secure enough to disengage his sword. "First dinosaurs and now a goddamn werewolf!"

JACAB hovered over to the beast and took samples of its flesh and blood, though he was careful to be in and out again in double-quick time. The analysis arrived on Carter's comp-slate about a minute later, and it made for familiar reading. Synthetic flesh, lab-printed bones, and a neuromorphic brain. However, this time JACAB had discovered something else too, which accounted for why the synthetic werewolf had evaded detection. The creature had an implant that was able to disperse certain types of EM radiation, which explained why it hadn't appeared on JACAB's scans. The bot had helpfully also informed Carter, via the report, that he'd updated his scanner's parameters to account for the werewolf's dispersion field. That should, the bot argued, prevent anything else from being able to sneak up on them in a similar manner.

"Why would Nathan create a werewolf then implant it with technology that made the damned thing near invisible to scanners?"

JACAB warbled a noise that sounded very much like an electronic version of, 'beats me…'

Carter sighed heavily and turned his attention back to Nathan Clynes' C37-B transport ship. It wasn't a particularly large vessel, measuring only twenty-five meters from bow to stern, but its diamond shape meant that it was almost as wide as it was long, which helped to maximize its load area, whilst still allowing it the capability for atmospheric flight. He approached the vessel and this time managed to reach it without getting lynched by another of Nathan Clynes' fantastical creations. The shelter that the ship was underneath had been built from local resources, mainly wood and a limestone-like material with a high clay content. It had decayed heavily through a century of weathering, and the covering of moss and climbing vines made it look like part of the natural terrain.

Carter stood under the shelter's roof, and the temperature dropped a degree or two thanks to the shade and the cool stone. Besides a coating of mud and dust, the C37 appeared to be in reasonable condition, at least from the outside. JACAB had already set to work scanning the ship and a regular set of pings emanated from Carter's comp-slate as the bot transmitted his updated findings. The key discovery was that the vessel's reactor was the source of the power signature his gopher had detected. Carter was disheartened by this, as it made it more likely that the ship's graveyard was all that remained of Nathan Clynes. Considering the nature of the scientist's creations, he imagined that the man had probably been eaten by one of his own inventions some decades in the past.

"Can you get the bay door open, buddy?" Carter asked, while visually surveying the front half of the ship.

JACAB warbled then pointed to the aft section with one of his extendable arms, before disappearing from view. Carter scowled and hurried after his bot, only to discover that there was no rear bay door; it had been removed from the ship. He jumped up and grabbed the sill then hauled himself inside the cargo hold. It was not only empty, but a significant proportion of the ship's internal structure had been stripped out too, right down to the bare framework. Even elements such as internal pipework and cabling was missing.

"I guess Nathan must have cannibalized the ship for parts and equipment, but if that's the case, then were the hell is his settlement?"

JACAB bleeped a non-committal answer from somewhere up ahead, though Carter couldn't see where the bot had gone. He moved through the ship, forced to play hopscotch to make progress, since a large number of deck panels had also been removed, then found his bot in the engine room. He paused to read his comp-slate and found that JACAB had handily summarized the relevant data.

"Nathan did a great job of stripping this C37-B, without compromising the function of its reactor core," Carter remarked. "In fact, it looks like the reactor, and the bare minimum of other systems needed to keep it running, are the only things he didn't strip. This place is now more like a power plant than a ship. It could certainly never take off again."

They left the engineering section and headed to the bridge, or what was left of it. Like the rest of the ship, the key systems, including the computer core and all the bridge consoles, had been carefully stripped and removed. Carter huffed a laugh as he saw that the captain's chair remained, like a lonely throne in a ruined castle. He planted himself in the dusty seat, which creaked like old bones, then rubbed his silver beard. Following Nathan Clynes' trail was like taking two steps forward and three steps back. There must have been a reason why the scientist had left the C37-B's reactor running, but it was certainly not obvious to him at that moment.

JACAB chirruped, sounding suddenly excited, and Carter spun the creaking chair around to face the bot. His gopher was holding a folded-up comp-slate in one of his mechanical arms. JACAB hovered closer and handed the device to Carter, and he wasted no time unfolding it. Miraculously, the comp-slate still had some charge left in its battery cells, and the device promptly booted up. Carter searched the device, but it had been wiped clean, save for one video memo. He selected the icon on the screen, eagerly anticipating the contents of the message. As it loaded, he felt a rush of excitement, which he imagined must have been similar to that of an archeologist discovering a secret, lost city. No-one, not even Carter Rose, could deny the thrill of the unknown.

"I am making this recording in case I die before I complete my work, so that at least something of me will remain," said Nathan Clynes, speaking from the past; the message had been recorded over a hundred years ago. "Gliese 832-e is not nearly as far from the Union as I'd have liked, but it will suffice for my needs. Besides, I doubt anyone will ever come looking, and that's fine with me. As far as I'm concerned, the Union can go to hell for what it forced me to do. In fact, I hope one day Markus Aternus comes back to finish the job." Nathan laughed and shook his head. "If I had my time again, I would have joined him, but the work blinded me, as did my ambition. The Union gave me a state-of-the-art lab, a blank cheque, and free reign to do whatever the hell I liked. It was enough to make me forget the reason they needed the terrible things I built." He paused and sighed. "No, that's a lie. I knew I was giving them the tools to beat Markus, but I didn't care. I wanted to beat him too; I wanted to prove that I could advance the human race and do it better than he did. But all I ended up achieving was to set back the course of humanity's evolution by centuries."

Nathan's head dropped low and he genuinely appeared to be on the verge of tears. When the man's eyes looked into the camera lens again, they were reddened and moist. The scientist looked tormented, and sick with regret.

"Everything I did, and everything I achieved was for nothing. They destroyed my labs, purged my records and smashed my equipment. The Longswords were objects of beauty as well as power, but they tossed them aside like trash. And as for their crews, my children in a way… Well, they were cast out too, and treated as pariahs to be feared and loathed."

Nathan's chin dropped again and he angrily wiped tears from his eyes. There was another pause, then when the scientist next stared into the camera lens, Carter could feel the rage radiating from the screen.

"I was given the means to advance the human race, and I succeeded. In return, the Union threatened my life and my reputation, unless I agreed to condemn and disavow my creations. The very things that saved humanity from annihilation!" Nathan Clynes, normally so placid and unthreatening to look at, suddenly appeared deranged. "So, fuck them, and fuck humanity! I'll create my own Eden, right here on this world. I'll unlock the secret of everlasting life and keep it far away from the Union. On this world, I am God, and God help anyone who tries to stop me."

The message ended, and Carter lowered the comp-slate

to his lap. He'd always known that Nathan had resented the role he'd been forced to play, but he'd had no idea how deep that resentment ran. Now he knew for sure that willingly enlisting the scientist's co-operation would be impossible. Even so, he was determined to try. And if he failed, then he would force Nathan Clynes' hand, by whatever means at his disposal.

JACAB warbled and bleeped, disturbing Carter from his thoughts, and he checked his personal comp-slate, expecting to read his bot's commentary on what Nathan had said. Instead, he found a map that showed an underground complex, built directly beneath their feet. He jumped out of his chair and turned to his gopher.

"Can you find a way in?"

JACAB's red eye widened, and the bot nodded.

EIGHT

HOUSE OF HORRORS

FOLLOWING HIS GOPHER'S LEAD, Carter jumped down from the cargo hold of the hollowed out C37-B and stepped out into the bright sunlight of the sweltering tropical world. According to JACAB's scans, Nathan Clynes' underground complex extended four levels below the surface and was powered by a hardline feed directly from the ship's reactor. From the data JACAB had obtained, the level immediately below them appeared to be a storage area, and while his gopher couldn't determine what it contained, the space was certainly not empty. The level below the storage zone had a more oxygen-rich environment and a lower concentration of volatile organic compounds, which JACAB suggested was an indoor garden or hydroponics setup for growing food. Below that was a workshop and then finally a living space on sub-level four.

JACAB slowed to a hover in the middle of a dell that appeared to have once been bulldozed or otherwise mechanically cleared, though nature had since reclaimed it. The ground directly below his bot sloped downward, as if there had been a sinkhole or cave-in at some point in the past. Carter approached closer and saw that the slope was in fact not a natural feature of the landscape, but the remains of a slip road. It led to a sturdy-looking metal barrier, which he recognized as the missing cargo bay door from the C37 transport ship. However, the entrance was blocked by tons of rock and other assorted flotsam and jetsam that looked to have accumulated over the years due to mudslides and heavy storms.

"Buddy, see if you can hack the lock mechanism, while I clear away some of this debris," Carter asked his gopher, who obliged with a sprightly bleep.

Carter made his way down the slope, slipping and sliding as he went on account of the powdery soil and loose stones, then cleared a path to the door. The bulk of the obstructions were dead wood and smaller rocks, which he made light work of, while the occasional boulder presented more of a challenge. Those that were basketball-sized and smaller he could easily shot-put out of range, while the gym-ball boulders required more effort. Even so, eight or nine-hundred-pound rocks were still well within his capability to move.

Finally, Carter reached the door and rapped his knuckles against it. It clanked like a dinner gong, and the sound reverberated through the cavernous space on the other side. He tried to force it, but the door wasn't merely wedged into place. Instead, Nathan had done a proper job of installing it correctly, including locks bolted into the frame and a powered opening mechanism, which was too robust even for his augmented might to muscle open.

"How are we doing on that lock, buddy?" Carter said, turning to his bot and dusting down his hands. "Because unless there's a plasma cutter lying around here somewhere, you're our only way in."

JACAB chirruped and warbled then his indicator lights began to flash wildly as he set to work, hacking the door mechanism. Carter used the opportunity to take a well-earned breather, and a drink of water from the supplies he'd brought with him. The planetoid was hot enough as it was, without the additional heat of manual labor adding to his discomfort. He stoppered the bottle and replaced it on his belt, then felt a chill run down his spine, though this was nothing to do with a shift in air temperature, but rather his body's early warning mechanism kicking into gear. He was suddenly on alert, chemicals flooding his muscles, and mind racing, but as with the synthetic werewolf, he couldn't pinpoint the source of the danger. He was about to ask his bot for help when a snake the size of a basilisk sprang out of a burrow to the side of the door and wrapped its serpentine body around his. Within seconds, he was coiled up inside the giant serpent, which began to squeeze with the power of a car crusher.

"JACAB, help!" Carter cried out, using his powerful shoulders to resist the constricting pressure of the creature.

His gopher raced to his aid and began hammering energy blasts into the snake's body, scorching its scaly skin. The serpent hissed then lashed out at the bot with the end of its tail, striking him like a baseball bat and propelling JACAB into the trees. The serpent then turned to Carter and opened its jaws, which were wide enough to swallow his head in a single bite. His augments were designed to provide his body with exceptional bursts of power when needed, and faced with a mortal threat, every cell in Carter's body accelerated into overdrive. He let out a roar that made the howl of the werewolf sound like the whimper of a puppy, then threw out his arms and expanded his chest, ripping the serpent's body to shreds, and sending lumps of snake meat bouncing across the glen, as if a hand grenade had exploded inside the animal's stomach.

Carter fell to his knees and pressed his hands to his heart, which was thumping so loudly that his chest sounded like a timpani drum. The burst of power had saved his life, but the come down was worse even than the aftereffects of a high-dose nano-stim. He forced his breathing into a regular rhythm and waited for his muscles to relax and his pulse to slow. Then he remembered that JACAB had been hit and was about to race into the jungle looking for him, when the bot hummed into view.

"Are you okay, buddy?" Carter asked, grabbing JACAB and turning him from side to side, looking for damage, but all he could find was a tennis-ball sized dent in his shell.

JACAB warbled and gave him a 'thumbs up' sign with one of his mechanical arms. Then the bot noticed the fleshy remains of the snake and blew a giant digital raspberry at the exploded serpent.

"I'm just about done with this planet already, so I'm hoping there are fewer unpleasant things indoors than there are out," Carter said, turning his attention to the door.

JACAB warbled a statement and Carter nodded his agreement. "Nathan Clynes excepted, of course."

His gopher resumed his efforts to release the locks, then a few seconds later the door began to grind open, and the bot chirruped a "ta da!" sound.

"Good work, buddy," Carter said, ducking underneath the slab of metal and drawing his sword. "Make sure you close up behind us, though. I don't want any dinosaurs, mythical monsters or giant synthetic snakes following us inside."

JACAB bleeped his agreement then Carter's comp-slate chimed a message. He read it but figured that his gopher was merely pulling his leg.

"Come on, buddy, you can't expect me to believe that snake was real?" Carter, replied narrowing his eyes at his bot.

JACAB warbled softly and nodded, then his comp-slate updated with an analysis. It hadn't been difficult for his bot to take a bio-sample, given how much of the snake was spread around the entrance to the underground complex, and to his surprise, it read as organic.

"I've definitely had enough of this planet," Carter grunted. "It's more like a jungle of horrors than a tropical paradise."

The door stopped opening at the half-way point then began to close again, rapidly decreasing the amount of sunlight that was being let into the storage area, until it was pitch black, forcing Carter to ignite his cutlass to illuminate the way ahead.

"See if you can find a light switch, will you?" Carter said, cautiously moving further inside Nathan Clynes' secret lair.

JACAB hovered into the darkness then the thump of relays switching echoed throughout the chamber, and rows of harsh strip lights, presumably repurposed from the interior of the C37-B, flickered into life. A curse slipped from Carter's lips. Far from escaping the terrors of Gliese 832-e, Carter had just willingly walked into the epicenter of a nightmare.

"Scanners on full, buddy," Carter said, keeping his sword ready. "If one of these things so much as twitches, I want to know..."

JACAB bleeped his acknowledgement, though at a much softer volume than the bot would normally speak at. The reason for his restraint was that the underground storage room was filled with dozens more of the scientist's ghastly and bizarre creations. The macabre works of bioengineering were arranged in rows, standing motionless like statues, as water dripped from the ceiling, forming puddles at their feet. The first rows were a collection of vaguely human-looking men and women, some with modifications as slight as an extra eye, while others were more outlandish, with multiple arms, hooved feet or even two heads. Then there were rows of animals, ranging from tigers and other wild cats to hyenas and gazelle, all of which looked remarkably true-to-life, unlike the rows behind, which were home to mythical beasts and flights of fancy. There was a centaur, a griffin, and what Carter assumed was Nathan's interpretation of a goblin.

And so it went on, row after row of synthetic beings, some imagined, some real, and some so fantastical as to be comical. Carter couldn't help but chuckle at the man-sized chicken, with feathery arms instead of wings. He thought that couldn't be topped, until he came across a cow with four sets of udders, one of which was on top of the poor beast's head.

"I think Nathan must have lost his mind on this rock a long time ago," Carter commented, as he moved along the rows, toward the solitary door at the far end of the space. "That's assuming he's still alive, of course."

Carter dwelled on this last point, since Nathan's survival was seeming less likely by the second. The SAM launchers and plasma cannon that had shot him down could have been automated defenses, but he figured that trespassing on

Nathan's ship and breaking into his underground lair would have compelled the scientist to show his face, yet there was still no sign of Nathan Clynes, anywhere.

"See if you can work your magic on the that door too," Carter said, using his sword to point to the only exit. "The sooner this freakshow is behind us, the better."

JACAB hovered over to the door and used his various tools to unscrew the control panel before getting to work. RAEB was more specialized at hacking locks and breaking security systems, but as a Command Assistant Bot, JACAB was a jack of all trades, much like Carter himself. The control panel fell to the ground with a piercing clank, then JACAB interfaced with the door mechanism and began processing. He warbled as he worked and sent a message to Carter's comp-slate. The basic gist of it was, "This might take some time..."

"Do your best, buddy," Carter said, turning back to the rows of synthetic beings. "But try to be quick, because I've got a bad feeling about this place."

Carter had felt on edge ever since they'd entered the storage area, so his comment wasn't merely to provide JACAB with a sense of urgency. At first, he'd put his disquiet down to chemical fluctuations as a consequence of his life-saving burst of engineered hormones and stimulants from fighting the snake, but he'd since realized it was something else. Something ominous. Then he caught a flicker of movement in his peripheral vision, and his head snapped toward the location, but he saw nothing. His senses crept up another notch, then he saw movement again, this time more clearly. Then again, and the cause was obvious.

"Buddy, speed things up..." Carter said, adopting a fighting stance. "We're about to have company."

JACAB warbled in a confused manner and looked at him. At the same time, a four-armed, hoof-footed man broke ranks and charged. The bot squealed like a pig then spun back to the control panel, and worked so fast that his extendable limbs were a blur. Meanwhile, Carter moved out to meet his attacker head on. It was distracting enough to be facing an opponent with four arms and feet like a horse that otherwise looked human, but it didn't help matters that the 'man' was completely naked, and also anatomically correct, at least in terms of its nether regions.

Carter wanted to shut his eyes, but he maintained his focus and timed his cut to perfection, slicing through the abomination's body and sending its two severed halves bowling across the deck to his rear. Then another creature broke ranks and charged, this time a reptilian humanoid that would have been perfectly at home as a character in a low-budget sci-fi holo movie. The reptilian hissed and showed Carter its claws, before charging at him. The creature was seven feet tall and as muscular as a gorilla, but while its claws were like eagle's talons, Carter had the advantage of a sword.

Stepping aside at the last moment, he evaded the lizardman's charge and hacked the sword across the reptilian's back. It howled and hissed, then spun around and struck him across the side of the face with the back of its leathery hand. The punch was harder than any he'd been hit with in his entire life, and he staggered back, momentarily dazed. The reptilian pressed its advantage and slashed cuts across Carter's chest, adding to those from the Deinonychus that were now almost healed. Another punch sent him reeling in the other direction and he tasted blood in his mouth. A tooth had broken loose and he spat it out angrily.

There were many things in the galaxy that pissed off Carter Rose, but being punched in the face was one of the worst, especially when it made him bleed.

The reptilian attacked again, but this time Carter evaded and sliced off the creature's left arm below the elbow. It stopped and looked at the stump with an unknowable expression on its scaly face, and Carter took the opportunity to punch it hard in the gut. The lizardman hissed a wheeze and bent low, allowing Carter to cave in the creature's skull with a hammer strike from the basket hilt of his cutlass. It collapsed dead, then JACAB screeched a warning, and Carter spun around to see two more creatures peeling away from the line.

"You have got to be kidding me..." he growled, overcome with exasperation.

His two new opponents were both fictional beings like the reptilian, but of a very different ilk. The first was a ten-foot tall, fur covered ape-like beast with reddish-brown fur and a human-looking face. He'd never seen one before – no-one had – but he was pretty sure it was supposed to be Bigfoot. The second was easier to discern. Carter had watched enough high-fantasy holos in his time to recognize an orc when he saw one, and the creature ambling toward him, scimitar-like sword in hand, was a classic example of the fictional creature.

"Any time now on that door, buddy!" Carter called out, while moving to face-off against his latest foes.

The Bigfoot was lumbering and slow, so it was the orc who reached him first. The creature cackled and taunted him then attacked wildly, hacking its scimitar like a deranged butcher. Carter quite enjoyed sword fighting, but at that moment, he'd had enough. He swatted the orc's blade away, which turned out to be a replica made only of soft metal. Then, as the Orc looked up at him with an expression of cold fear, he lopped off its head, and sent it skidding into the corner of the room.

"Now, JACAB!" Carter called out, backing away from the giant sasquatch. The ground shook with each stomp of the monster's feet, drowning out the frantic bleeps and squawks from his gopher. The beast arrived and raised its massive hands above its head, ready to deliver a hammer strike that would likely punch Carter through the floor like a nail through plywood. He held his sword ready then rolled aside as the monster's hands came crashing down, battering a bomb-hole-sized hollow into the ground. He swung his cutlass and severed the synthetic tendons in the back of the Bigfoot's knee. It roared, shaking the cavern and causing water and dirt to rain down around them, then dropped like a disgraced politician's approval ratings. Carter leapt into the air and landed on the beast's chest, driving his cutlass through its synthetic heart and causing it to expire with a guttural wheeze that smelled like rotten vegetables.

Carter jumped off the sasquatch then JACAB bleeped with excitement and spun around, waving its maneuvering fins at Carter like it had short-circuited. The exit door slid open a moment later, and his bot vanished through it.

"Great work, buddy," Carter called out. He then dashed through the door, which thudded shut behind him, and followed his gopher down a steep flight of stairs to sub-level two.

NINE

LUNATIC INVENTIONS

CARTER FELT the air temperature rise by several degrees as he reached the bottom of the rickety and rudimentary stairs, which he realized had been fabricated from the C37-B's carved-up deck plates. The door, also repurposed from the transport ship, was already open, and Carter could see JACAB hovering just across the threshold. He stepped through and the door thudded shut behind him.

"Did you do that?" Carter asked, but JACAB bleeped forlornly and hovered a few inches closer to him. "Then that's a worrying omen," he added, keeping a firm grip on his cutlass.

Suddenly, Carter's senses climbed, but he wasn't detecting a threat so much as a presence. He moved through the room, which was an underground garden as JACAB had predicted, letting his instincts guide him, then saw a spherical bot hovering over one of the planter beds. It was using a hose that was attached to the ceiling to water the plants in the bed. The bot suddenly froze and its red eye locked onto him, then it squawked in surprise, threw down the hose and sped through a spherical door in the far wall, which immediately closed behind it.

"That looked like a gopher," Carter said, turning to his own bot, who nodded his agreement. "Anyone you know?"

JACAB's eye widened, and his extendable arms rested on the equator of its shell, like a human pressing their hands to their hips. It was as if the bot was saying, "Just because I'm a gopher, it doesn't mean I know every other gopher in the entire damned universe," which Carter figured was a fair point.

"At least it suggests that Nathan might still be around, otherwise why would that bot bother watering the plants?"

JACAB chirruped his agreement then stuck close by his side as they progressed further into the garden. Unlike the storage area on the level above, sub-level two was brightly lit and even hotter and more humid than the surface of Gliese 832-e. Carter was the least 'green-fingered' person he knew, but the reason for the sweltering temperatures seemed obvious, even to him. Inside the space were rows and rows of aquaponics bays and vertical farming units. Some were growing food, including recognizable produce, such as tomatoes, salad greens, potatoes and assorted herbs, while less recognizable plants sprouted from others. And the deeper inside the horticultural level they went, the more esoteric and alien the flora became.

Curiously, Carter's senses had remained elevated even after the disappearance of the bot, so he moved cautiously, despite knowing that the likelihood of being attacked by a cucumber or lettuce was on the lower end of the threat scale. Even so, he couldn't shake the feeling that there was much more to sub-level two than just growing food.

"Keep your scanners peeled, buddy," Carter said to his

bot, while rapping his knuckles on the undented side of JACAB's shell. "We've already had yetis and werewolves, so who knows what bizarre, man-eating plants Nathan's mind might have conjured up."

JACAB shivered then nodded, before hovering ever so slightly closer to Carter, to the point where he could hear the bot's servos and gears whirring softly in his ear. Then one aquaponics bay in particular caught his attention, and he huffed a laugh as he approached the coffee plant and inspected the lush red fruits.

"Nathan always did enjoy a hot cup of java," Carter said. "I guess there are some things a guy just can't do without."

JACAB bleeped and warbled and Carter realized that the sound was more distant. He looked around and discovered that his bot had hovered away to inspect a rack of plants that were separated from the fruits and vegetables by a three-meter gap. He let the coffee cherries slip through his fingers and joined his gopher. His comp-slate updated at the same time.

"Opium poppies?" Carter said, after reading the update from JACAB.

His bot nodded then pointed to another rack of plants further along. Carter glanced back at his comp-slate and saw that JACAB had identified a number of other species too, including erythroxylum novogranatense, the leaves of which were used to produce cocaine, and rye that was contaminated with ergot fungus, from which a scientist could easily synthesize LSD.

"It looks like he has quite the pharma lab going on," Carter said, moving along the rows of farming units. "If Nathan was using LSD recreationally, it would certainly explain the existence of the zanier creations on the floor above us."

JACAB chuckled electronically then stopped in front of a huge, bulbous vegetable that resembled an oversized party balloon planted in the dirt. The bot began scanning it then suddenly the plant split open, like a flower blooming, and a sticky red tongue lashed itself around JACAB. In a flash, the tongue whipped back inside the plant and it snapped shut. Fortunately for his gopher, Carter's augments suppressed the responses that often left regular humans paralyzed with shock, and he immediately dug his fingers into the plant and tore it open. The insides looked like the stomach cavity of a shark, and Carter could see the remains of partly-digested flesh, though he didn't want to think about what animal or creature had been fed to the dangerous flower.

Amongst the digestive juices and meat was JACAB, still held in place by the sticky tongue. Carter grabbed the bot and wrestled him free, allowing JACAB to escape, but the tongue fought back and lashed him across the side of the face. Carter felt a sharp sting of pain, which oddly wasn't numbed by his sensation blockers, but he battled on and grabbed the tongue with both hands before snapping it like breaking the neck of a snake. The tongue went limp and he tossed it down before staggering backward, away from the killer vegetable. He felt suddenly faint and crashed into a hydroponics bay to his rear. Lights and shapes were flashing before his eyes in a chaotic pattern, and his heart was beating at twice its normal rate.

"Buddy, I don't feel so good..."

JACAB was at his side in an instant, and Carter felt the bot's probes pierce his thick skin. The lights and indicators on his gopher went into overdrive, as JACAB processed the samples, then darted away and disappeared through a dense wall of foliage in a hydroponics bay opposite him.

"Buddy?" Carter called, slurring the word. He pushed himself up but could barely stand. "Buddy, I need you..."

It had been a long time since Carter had experienced true fear. The sort of mortal dread that was a common feature of regular human lives simply wasn't a factor in his own existence. He never got sick, never had to worry about crippling or debilitating injuries, and while his beard had gone silver, he otherwise had barely aged in a hundred and fifty years. Now he felt like he was dying, and it scared the shit out of him.

"Buddy!" Carter called out again, as he dropped to his knees, but still he couldn't see the bot. He could barely see anything at all.

Shakily, he raised his left arm and tried to focus on his comp-slate, but it was just a blur. Then he fumbled around his belt area, looking for a nano-stim, and managed to wrap his fingers around one of the life-saving silver canisters. Popping the cap, he brought it to his neck, then his muscles froze. The nano-stim slid out of his grasp and rolled away beneath one of the dozens of planters. Eyes darkening and muscles seizing up, he suddenly saw a blur of light rush past his face. He tried to turn his head, but his neck was immobilized, as if he were wearing a brace. He felt a sharp prick, first to the right side of his neck, then to the left. Straight away, his muscles loosened and he planted his hands on the floor, which was all that stopped him from falling face-first into the metal deck plates. Next, his eyes cleared and his throat opened, allowing him to take deeper breaths. Soon after, his strength returned quickly, and within a minute he was able to stand.

"What the hell just happened?" Carter wondered, flexing his fingers and stretching his arms, though remarkably he felt no discomfort.

JACAB hovered in front of him, scanner dishes swiveling like they were out of control. The bot chattered and warbled to himself then Carter's comp-slate updated with a full bio-scan readout. The plant that had swallowed JACAB and stung Carter with its tongue was a hybrid, marrying a normally harmless insectivorous species found on Terra Eight, with an aggressive carnivorous plant native to Gliese 832-e. The native plant contained an intensely powerful toxin, which when combined with the species from Terra Eight, and some genetic manipulation from Nathan Clynes, had resulted in the lethal creation he'd encountered.

"I guess we found our man-eating plant," Carter said, looking at the now deceased killer vegetable. Its red tongue was dangling out from the fleshly bulb as if the plant had been brutally strangled. He turned to JACAB and patted his gopher, affectionately. "Thanks, buddy. You saved my life."

JACAB shrugged and looked embarrassed, and Carter pulled the bot in for a hug, which caused him to giggle, electronically.

"How did that thing affect me, though?" Carter added, once he'd released his bot. "I'm immune to all known forms of disease, and toxins usually have no effect either."

JACAB bleeped and warbled excitedly and his comp-slate updated. It seemed clear that this was a topic the bot had already given some thought to. Carter skimmed through the analysis, which went largely over his head, though the gist of it was that the toxin had managed to evade his nano-machines by presenting as harmless, naturally-occurring plasma proteins in his blood. JACAB had found an antidote to the toxin growing in the same rack, which suggested that Nathan Clynes had not only been spending his time making synthetic fantasy creatures but expanding his understanding of biology too. For what reason, remained to be seen. The bot had also speculated that Carter's exposure to the super-toxin, and the antidote, had actually made him more resilient than ever before. The nano-machines in his blood were designed to learn and adapt, which meant that they were now even more effective at fighting foreign bodies, especially those that tried to hide in plain sight. It was a good example of the old adage, "What doesn't kill you, makes you stronger."

"Come on, let's keep moving," Carter said, ushering his bot away from the rack of killer plants, while keeping a respectful distance from the other aquaponics bays that might have contained similarly experimental-looking creations.

JACAB worked on opening the door to the next level down, while Carter stood guard in case any more of Nathan Clynes' inventions decided that he or his bot might make a tasty snack. Presumably motivated by his near-death experience, it didn't take long for the bot to open the door, and it took even less time for him to rush through it. Carter followed, just as keen to leave the horticultural zone as his gopher was, then arrived at another door at the bottom of the rickety stairs just as JACAB was unlocking it. Moments later, it slid open and he entered the new space, sword in hand and blade energized, ready for anything. It was quickly apparent that sub-level three was part engineering workshop, part science lab, and was filled with advanced equipment and supplies that would have made Kendra Castle's head explode with excitement.

"Once we've found Nathan, maybe we can use this place to hammer out that ding in your shell," Carter said to his bot. He then noticed that stomach juices were still dripping out of his gopher's various compartments. "And maybe we can get you cleaned up too..."

JACAB warbled meekly then shook like a dog, spraying plant goo all over the floor, and over Carter's pants. He frowned at the bot, who merely shrugged in response. Unfortunately, having plant goo on his boots turned out to be the least disgusting thing about sub-level three. Synthetic body parts lay strewn across the lab tables, including severed heads, limbs and internal organs from a range of beings, some human, some animal, some unrecognizable. Carter tried to remind himself that none of it was 'real', but even for someone that wasn't unaccustomed to dismembering his foes, the room was tough to stomach.

Mercifully, the workshop was less gruesome and macabre. There were part-assembled drones and other automatons, as well as computer components and machine parts that were in various states of assembly or repair. Carter recognized much of it as pre-war tech, which explained how Nathan had been able to manufacture and synthesize many of the weird and wonderful inventions they'd come across so far. About two-thirds of the way across the workshop floor, JACAB bleeped softly, alerting Carter to another gopher. This one resembled RAEB and was tooled-up with even more equipment than Kendra's bot possessed. It was working to repair a computer board that was originally a core component of the C37-B's environmental control system and hadn't noticed them.

"Hello, there!" Carter said, waving at the bot. The gopher

froze, retracted its tools, then looked at Carter. "We're here to see Nathan. We're old friends."

To say that Nathan was a friend was stretching the truth beyond breaking point, but he hoped it would relax the bot and elicit its cooperation. The gopher hovered a little closer, then peered at JACAB, who bleeped a friendly tone and waved with a maneuvering fin. The workshop bot simply narrowed its red eye, then blew them a loud and especially vulgar digital raspberry, before racing away, and disappearing through a spherical aperture, in the same way that the horticultural bot had departed on the level above.

"Are you two related?" Carter joked, though JACAB didn't appear to see the funny side.

Then the whir of gears followed by the whine of a power core energizing wiped the smile from his face. His senses spiked and Carter turned toward the source of the noise. A compartment in the end wall slid open, and a bi-pedal labor bot stomped out. The machine was painted bright yellow, and its panels were scuffed and dented, but Carter could still make out the original registry number of Nathan's C37-B transport ship written across its chest panel. Labor bots of that kind were common on pre-war transport ships, but it was clear that Nathan had heavily modified and upgraded the unit in front of them. They were as smart as gophers like JACAB, and at seven feet tall, with the hitting power of a siege battering ram, the labor bot wasn't to be trifled with in combat either.

"Go high, buddy, and work on opening the door to sub-level four," Carter said, as the labor bot advanced, grabbing a mallet from a workbench that made Mjolnir look like a tack hammer.

JACAB bleeped his obedience then climbed above his

head, while the labor bot continued to advance, throwing heavy workbenches aside as it stomped toward him.

"Intruder identified..." the labor bot droned in a bassy monotone. "Core programming overridden… Security protocol 'Protect Nathan' enabled... Kill intruder…"

Suddenly, the bot's stomping, clumsy approach shifted gears, and the machine put on an astonishing burst of speed. Carter was ready, side-stepping the first mighty swing of the hammer, before rolling to evade a follow-up blow, which obliterated a workbench and created a cloud of dust and debris that filled the air. Carter struck the bot across the back with his energized cutlass, but its pre-war armored shell was tough, and the blade didn't deliver a critical blow. The bot spun around and punched the hammer at him, which Carter blocked with his buckler. The nano-constructed shield crumpled from the impact, and he felt the resultant shockwaves rattle his bones. A kick from the labor bot sent him thumping into the wall, and he fell to his knees, leaving a Carter Rose-shaped dent in the panel.

Growling and muttering under his breath, Carter got to his feet and squared off against the machine, which stomped toward him, determined to fulfill its programming. It punched the hammer at him again, but Carter dodged and the weapon bludgeoned a hole through the wall instead. He retaliated with a punch of his own, using the basket-hilt of his cutlass to destructive effect, as he had done on countless other occasions. The bot's chest armor crumpled, and Carter hit it again, causing the machine to stagger backward, clutching it chest. For a second, Carter thought he heard the machine wheeze. *Is this damned thing alive?* Carter wondered as the bot shook its head and regained its footing.

He pushed such thoughts to the corner of his mind, and

pressed his attack, forcing the bot to backpedal, as he landed hacking blows to its shoulders and body, melting though its armor and severing the circuits and wires beneath, like cutting arteries and tendons. Heavily damaged, the bot lashed out wildly with the hammer, but Carter stepped inside the attack and severed the machines hand, sending it and the hammer skidding across the deck. In the same motion, he brought the pommel of the cutlass down on the bot's head, crushing a section of its cranial unit and causing its mechanical eyes to flicker like candlelight in a breeze. Then a device attached to the rear of the bot's head sparked into flames then dropped to the deck and exploded.

"Stop! ... please..." the machine droned, holding up its other hand, as if begging for mercy. "I... yield..."

Carter was about to strike the final blow, but the bot's plea made him hesitate. "What happened to 'kill intruder?'," he asked, curious to understand the cause of the bot's sudden change of heart.

"My core programming was bypassed," the bot replied. It now appeared non-threatening, and Carter's internal sixth-sense confirmed this. "The sub-core block that directed the security protocol has been destroyed. It no longer binds me."

The bot pointed to the damaged processor that had fallen to the ground, and Carter recognized the device. It was pre-war tech, and not dissimilar to the sub-core blocks that powered many of the Galatine's secondary systems.

"I take it that Nathan installed this processing block to turn you into a sentry machine?"

The bot nodded. "Affirmative."

"So, what now? Are you still going to try to kill me?" Carter asked. He had no desire to destroy the labor bot, especially if it had been forced to attack him by Nathan Clynes.

"I do not wish you harm," the automaton replied. "I am a Z7-Class Autonomous Labor Bot. I fix things, not break them."

Carter nodded and stood down, allowing the bot to rise to its feet, or as much as it was able to, considering the damage it had sustained. It then twisted its body, which was broken and malfunctioning, and pointed to a door. It was larger and heavier than the others they'd seen; a blast door or airlock hatch, Carter considered.

"Nathan is through there," the labor bot added, still pointing to the hatch.

"Can you open it?"

"Affirmative..."

"Then do it," Carter grunted, still somewhat suspicious of the machine.

"Compliance..." the bot replied, with a nod, before dragging its damaged frame to the hatch. It worked for a moment then the locks on the door thudded and it swung ajar with a resonant creak. "If I am no longer required, I will resume my work," the bot added, turning back to Carter.

"Sure, go ahead," Carter answered.

The bot turned, its mashed gears and servos struggling to keep it mobile, then stomped back to its original alcove. Carter watched it closely, listening to what his senses were telling him, but his gut feeling was the bot was no longer their enemy. If anything, he felt like it was a friend.

"Hey, bot..." Carter called out. The machine paused and looked at him, its eyes seeming alive. "Do me a favor and fix yourself up before you resume your work."

The bot nodded. "Compliance..." it said, before diverting

toward a workshop bench and gathering the tools it needed to self-repair.

Carter disengaged the blade of his cutlass but kept the weapon in his hand. The labor bot was no longer a threat, but he doubted it would be the last obstacle he'd have to overcome before finally coming face-to-face with Nathan Clynes. JACAB hummed over his shoulder and bleeped into his ear. His comp-slate updated with an analysis of the labor bot, and in JACAB's estimation it was safe. As if to prove the point, his gopher waved a maneuvering fin at the labor bot, and to Carter's surprise, it waved back.

"Let's hope that Nathan is actually behind this door," Carter said to his bot. "Because I don't know about you, buddy, but I've had it up to my neck with his lunatic inventions."

TEN

THE UNDERGROUND PENTHOUSE

CARTER DESCENDED the stairs to sub-level four and found that the door into the living space was already open. He stepped through, sword held ready and blade engaged. His boots clacked sweetly against the polished hardwood floor, and classical music drifted around the room from unseen speakers. It was a far cry from the clinical, industrial space they had just left. And while it was far from empty, laden with exquisite-looking furniture, curious ornaments and art hanging on every wall, it appeared to be unoccupied.

"Well, he's certainly not slumming it, that's for sure," Carter said, as the door slid shut behind him. "This place is done up like a high-society penthouse."

He continued further inside, sword still ready, since he didn't trust there to be no more surprises and gave himself a quick tour of the living space. In addition to the gorgeous floors, the ceilings were tall, with chandeliers providing the bulk of the illumination, and the fixtures and fittings all looked to be of a premium standard. Carter took a closer look at a side table, and while he was more accustomed to taking things apart than putting them together, to his eye it looked handmade.

Hanging a left, he entered an open-plan kitchen that was unnecessarily large, considering it only needed to cater to one person. Like the side table, the cabinets appeared to have been handmade, while the sink was crafted from slabs of stone that also had a hand-cut appearance. Carter tried the faucet and was surprised when a stream of fast-flowing, clear water gushed out. It was ice cold and he noticed that there was a rapid-boiler plumbed in to provide hot water. This, at least, was not hand-made, but repurposed from the galley of the transport ship on the surface, like the faucet, he suspected.

Carter continued searching and tried a few cupboards, finding jars of preserves and dried beans, before coming across an industrial-sized fridge-freezer, which was also clearly taken from the C37-B. Inside it were fresh vegetables from the garden level, hunks of raw meat from animals he didn't recognize, eggs and even a creamy-looking milk, which was an off-putting shade of lime green. JACAB bleeped and warbled softly in his ear and he checked his comp-slate to find that his bot had delivered a quick analysis of the fridge's contents. The meat, milk, eggs and vegetables were all organic, while some of the other contents appeared to have been produced in the lab above them from algae or soya-like crops.

"At least something here is real," Carter commented, closing the fridge door firmly, like a good, uninvited house guest.

Moving on, Carter found himself in a sparsely-appointed bedroom, which was also open to the kitchen and the rest of the living space. The queen-sized bed frame was wooden and the sheets were supremely soft and felt like fine linen. Carter considered that it was possible Nathan had brought them with him from Terra Prime, though given how much of his apartment was hand-crafted, he figured it equally likely that the scientist had made them himself in the lab. The other thing Carter noticed about the bed was that it was neatly made-up, making it impossible for him to determine how recently it had been slept in.

"So, where the hell is he?" Carter said out loud.

JACAB shrugged his maneuvering fins then pointed to the other side of the room, before hovering toward the floor-to-ceiling glass walls that separated the apartment from a coal-like blackness beyond. Carter followed, and the closer he got to the window, the more he realized the darkness on the other side wasn't as absolute as he'd first thought. The windows looked out upon an underground cave with a stream flowing through it; the source of the water in the faucet, Carter guessed. The cave was lit by chemiluminescent vegetation, and he could even see luminescent fish in the stream, flashing through the water like laser beams.

Suddenly, JACAB warbled and spun around, sounding a further series of alerts. Carter's senses hadn't climbed much beyond their already elevated state, so he didn't anticipate being attacked, and his senses were correct. Instead of another of Nathan's fantastical creations, or a murderous labor automaton, he saw the two gophers that they'd encountered previously. The horticulture bot and workshop bot were hovering side-by-side in the middle of the living room, watching them with curious, glowing red eyes.

"Hey there," Carter said, staying friendly, despite the fact both of the bots had been rude to him previously, especially the workshop model. "Is Nathan around? I could really do with speaking to him. Tell him it's Carter Rose. He knows me."

The two bots looked at each other and chattered quietly. Carter noticed that JACAB had raised his sensor dish and was no-doubt eavesdropping on their conversation, a fact that hadn't gone unnoticed by the other bots, who turned their backs on him, and spoke even more softly. Then they zoomed away and exited the living space through a circular aperture in the end wall.

"Are they going to fetch him?" Carter asked his bot, but JACAB merely shrugged.

He sighed and pressed his hands to his hips, before noticing that there was another door on the same wall that the bots had disappeared through. He hadn't spotted it earlier because it was camouflaged to look like part of the bookcase that dominated the library section of the grand living room. He wandered toward it, idly looking at some of Nathan's art enroute. There were ancient Terran treasures, including Egyptian artifacts, which hinted more at the scientist's admiration for Markus Aternus than it did an appreciation of ancient Earth cultures. He also had paintings from masters dating back hundreds of years, hung alongside Nathan's own works, which were of considerably lesser standing.

"He certainly keeps himself busy," Carter mused, moving past an original of one of Monet's many paintings of water lilies, in order to reach the door. He pushed against it, but it wouldn't budge. "Hey, buddy, can you figure out how this thing opens?" Carter asked his gopher, who was busy admiring *Poppy Flowers* by Vincent van Gogh.

The bot tore himself away from his appreciation of the

painting, grumbling on account of Carter having interrupted him, and hovered in front of the hidden door. His scanners went into overdrive, and his red eye narrowed and focused. Clearly, it was more of a challenge than the previous barriers had been.

"Let me know how you get on," Carter said, leaving his bot to work.

He moved past the door to examine some of Nathan's other treasures, but in truth he was already getting bored. He could never stand more than about thirty minutes at most in a museum of art, even when he had access to such places. Stifling a yawn, he walked past a home-made harp, and a few bad sculptures of the human form, before arriving at a cabinet filled with pre-war tech that had later been outlawed. This, at least, interested him, though in a surreal way. The items in the cabinet had once been new and state-of-the-art during his lifetime; to see them reduced to curiosities in a cabinet on a world that was light years from Terra Prime somehow didn't seem real.

Then something caught his eye that he did appreciate. He walked over to the suit of Japanese Samurai armor that had been dressed on a mannequin. It was blue and gold, and both terrifying and beautiful at the same time. Carter appreciated the period of history when two armies would simply face each other across a battlefield, rather than snoop around and kill with a faceless virus, like the Aterniens were doing.

He was about to step away when his senses spiked, and the Samurai mannequin came to life. Carter backed away sharply, his augments preventing him from panicking, despite the shock of seeing the ancient warrior suddenly animate. The Samurai then drew its katana and attacked in a single, fluid motion, but his sword was already drawn and he parried the strike. The energized weapon cut the replica katana in half, and the warrior dropped it and drew its Wakizashi instead. Carter trapped the Samurai's wrist and punched the warrior with the hand-guard of his cutlass, smashing the mask from the helmet and revealing a synthetic face behind it – a living mannequin. He then plunged his cutlass through the Samurai's ornate chest armor, through the mannequin's body, and through the wall behind it, hanging the warrior like one of Nathan's paintings. He waited until the light had left the Samurai's synthetic eyes, then withdrew the blade and allowed the warrior to slump to the hardwood floor.

"God damn it, Carter, will you stop breaking my fucking stuff?!"

Carter disengaged his blade and turned to see Nathan Clynes standing in the room, pointing an energy pistol at his chest.

ELEVEN

NATHAN CLYNES

CARTER REMAINED calm and observed that Nathan Clynes had stolen into the living space through the hidden doorway that JACAB had been working to unlock while he was fighting the synthetic Samurai. His bot was now hovering above and behind the scientist, aiming his energy blaster at the back of the man's head.

"Hello Nathan, you look…" Carter was about to say, "you look well," before observing that the scientist did, in fact, look half dead. "Well, you look alive, which is something, I guess."

"I'm afraid I never benefited from your many augmented gifts," Nathan replied, with clear resentment. "Most parts of me have died over the years, though I've managed to replace them. I never gave much consideration to aesthetics, however, since I never expected to see another living soul for the rest of my life."

"In that case, you'll be heartened to learn that I really don't give a shit how you look," Carter answered.

This was a white lie, since the scientist's patchwork mix

of synthetic skin bonded to dying flesh was difficult to look at, but Carter didn't want to start off their renewed relationship on the wrong foot. He remembered that Nathan Clynes had never been handsome, and even in his prime was an average-looking, five feet, seven inches, 160lbs regular guy, with untamed brown hair and muddy brown eyes. He had not been unattractive, but there was nothing about him that stood out, either, beyond his towering intellect. Now, Nathan was a mess of cybernetic parts and decaying organs. He looked like a shop mannequin that had been left to perish in a damp basement, rotten and wilted, with parts worn down to the bare metal underneath.

"Being my own test subject had its pros and cons," Nathan said, still aiming the pistol at Carter. "The benefit, of course, is that I am still alive, well beyond my natural lifetime, while the drawback, as you can see, is that I am inferior to the finished product. The finished product, of course, being you…"

Nathan's face then twisted and the man wrinkled his nose. For a second, Carter thought that he might be having some kind of seizure, before he pulled a stained linen handkerchief from the pocket of his cream linen pants and sneezed into it. He waited a second, sneezed again, then blew his nose, filling the handkerchief with a yellow-green mucus.

"Bless you…" Carter said, more than a little surprised. "But how the hell do you have a cold? Up until I walked in here, you've been the only human being for trillions of miles in any direction."

"You, Carter Rose, are not exactly human," Nathan hit back.

"You know what I mean…"

Nathan was an irritating man who loved correcting people and hated being challenged about anything. A hundred years of isolation appeared not to have changed him one bit.

"It is a simple respiratory infection that I conjured up in the lab," Nathan said, in a throwaway manner. "I'm currently working on a cure and believe I will have it within a few days."

Carter frowned at the scientist. "So, you create diseases, infect yourself with them, then cure yourself?"

Nathan shrugged. "One has to have a hobby."

Carter was still skeptical. "Are you being serious? I could never tell your bullshit answers from your real ones."

"I obviously didn't intend to infect myself, but accidents happen," Nathan said, sounding angry at that fact. "Unlike you, I do not have the benefit of a nano-adaptive immune system, and so am still at the mercy of the common cold. Or, in this case, not so common."

Carter scrunched up his nose as Nathan blew another load of snot into the handkerchief, then pointed at the pistol in the scientist's hand.

"Do you mind putting that down?" he asked, politely. "It wouldn't hurt me, anyway, and so long as you have it pointed at my chest, you're at risk of having the back of your head blown away." Carter aimed his finger at JACAB, and Nathan twisted his leathery neck to look at the bot.

"Your gopher is an illegal object," the scientist said, lowering the pistol and turning back to Carter. JACAB blew a raspberry at him at the same time. "As is that plasma sword, and the battle uniform you are wearing, both of which were my designs, of course."

"The situation in the Union has changed a lot since you left," Carter said.

Nathan wafted a hand at him and make a "pfft!" sound with his rubbery lips, before walking over to an armchair and dropping heavily into it.

"I couldn't give two fucks what the situation in the Union is, Carter, as you well know," the scientist answered, staring at the cave though the windows. "Besides, I'm a busy man."

Though he hadn't been invited to sit, Carter dropped into an armchair opposite the scientist. "Other than inventing ways to kill yourself, it doesn't seem that you're all that busy…"

Nathan considered arguing the point, but decided it wasn't worth the energy. "Very well, I'm not busy," the man admitted. "In all honestly, I have exhausted my options. I have grown tired of woodcraft, painting, sculpture and music. I have created more new plant species than I care to count. I have read every book on those shelves a hundred times or more..."

"What about building orcs and werewolves and other nighttime terrors?" Carter asked.

Nathan laughed and wagged a finger at him. "Yes, I noticed that you encountered a few of my many creations. That was a passion of mine for the first few decades here, but I was never able to achieve my primary goal, so I chose other occupations to pass the time." Nathan scowled at the destroyed Samurai on the floor, then directed that same wrathful gaze at Carter. "He was one of my favorites, by the way."

"Sorry," Carter grunted. He wasn't sorry about killing the Samurai, or any of Nathan's other creations, but he was curious to learn what the scientist's primary goal had been. "So, what was your objective, if it wasn't to build the perfect Sasquatch?"

Nathan rolled his eyes then gestured to his own body. "To fix this, of course. But, as you can see, there is a world of difference between grafting synthetic flesh to a synthetic body, and making that same flesh adhere to and homogenize with human meat and bone."

"Your old friend, Markus Aternus, doesn't seem to have the same problem," Carter grunted. He was thinking of the Aternien imposters and their almost perfect replica bodies. However, while it was a throwaway comment, it had snared Nathan's attention like a fish-hook to the mouth.

"What do you mean by that?" the scientist snapped. "The Aternien body was purely synthetic, and never designed to mimic flesh in any way. The whole point was to transcend the human form and become something better."

Carter sat up. The many distractions, not least of which was finding Nathan Clynes in the decrepit condition he was in, had sidetracked him from the purpose of his visit. He decided to get swiftly to the point and detailed everything that had led up to his arrival at Nathan's door, as succinctly as possible. He covered the return of the Aterniens; the raids; the biogenic weapon; the imposters and Acolytes of Aternus, and how a Union admiral called Clara Krantz brought him back and enabled the rescue and refit of the Longsword Galatine. Of all these things, it was the imposters that Nathan found most fascinating.

"Does JACAB contain any data on these Aternien infiltrators?" he asked, leaning forward, eyes suddenly brighter. "I would be most interested to study a compositional analysis of their bodies, and any other information you have on this technology."

Carter sensed an opportunity and took it. "JACAB has a comprehensive analysis stored in his memory core, and I'd be willing to trade it, in return for your help."

Nathan laughed and flopped back in his chair. "You want me to help the Union in their latest war against the Aterniens, is that it?"

"I didn't come here for tea and cookies, Nathan. Why the hell else do you think I'd haul my ass to Gliese 832-e?"

"Of course, once I saw your uniform, I thought it would be something to do with the Union," Nathan replied, blowing his nose again. The handkerchief was already so full of mucus that he had to fold it into different configurations in order to find a section that wasn't already saturated. "But if that's all you're here for, then you will be disappointed. I told the fools at the Union that the Aterniens would never rest until humanity was wiped out, but that fuckwit of a president at the time wouldn't listen to me. Maybe extinction is what humanity deserves."

Carter had come expecting to meet resistance and was prepared to make his arguments. Whether or not Nathan would listen was another matter.

"I won't sit here and lie to you that the Union has made all the right calls, but I still have a duty, and so do you."

Nathan laughed again and clapped his hands together. It was a mocking gesture that twanged Carter's already aggravated nerves.

"A duty? After what those fuckers did to you?" The scientist laughed again. "You don't owe them a goddamned thing, Carter, and neither do I."

"I haven't forgotten, but that was a long time ago,"

Carter hit back, fighting hard to keep a lid on his emotions. "Millions have lived and died since the end of the first war, Nathan. There's no-one still alive who was responsible for what happened to us, apart from me and you, and a few others. However, my oath still stands."

Nathan shook his head and wagged his finger at Carter. The rank condescension was starting to grate on him, and Carter felt like snapping the scientist's finger clean off at the knuckle.

"You're not one to let bygones be bygones, Carter. I know you, remember?"

"Nathan, if I was one to hold grudges, then I would have popped your head off your scrawny neck the moment I clapped eyes on you."

The threat didn't appear to intimidate Nathan, and instead pissed him off. "Your anger toward me is unfair and unfounded," he snarled.

This time it was Carter who laughed. "You're kidding, right? You're saying there's no reason I should be pissed at you for rubber-stamping the Union's Aternien Act and anti-technology policies, and causing me and my crew to become social lepers and outcasts?"

"They would have passed those laws anyway, and you know it," Nathan countered. "By fighting the inevitable, I would have lost everything. Instead, I played their game and took the Union for whatever I could get." He pointed a finger at Carter again. "You should have done the same, Carter, but you were too fucking honorable, and look what it got you. Now you're letting them use you all over again."

Carter was done arguing about the past. "Look, I didn't come here to open old wounds. Whether you like it or not, agree with it or not, I'm going to fight Aternus and kill that bastard so he never threatens humanity again."

Nathan snorted a laugh, forcing snot onto his jacket, and Carter had to grip the sides of the armchair, crushing the wooden frame beneath it, simply to prevent himself from murdering the scientist.

"And how do you plan on stopping Markus Aternus, may I ask?"

"That's where you come in," Carter said, jabbing a finger right back at the scientist. "No-one knows more about the Aterniens than you do, so you're going to make me a tech-virus that infects their neuromorphic brain. I want to level the playing field and show Aternus that he's not beyond my reach."

"Carter, you can't be serious?" Nathan replied, talking down to him like he was an idiot. "Markus Aternus is without question the most brilliant human being that ever lived, and as an immortal god-king, he will keep that title for all time."

This did not deter Carter. Nathan claimed to know him, and that was true, but he also understood what made the scientist tick, and the man hated living in the shadow of Markus Aternus. Were it not for the genius inventor of the neuromorphic brain, Nathan Clynes would probably be ranked as the smartest human to have ever drawn breath. By his own admission, he'd spent decades trying to cheat death on Gliese 832-e, creating synthetic bodies that could house his own decrepit form, but he'd failed, where Aternus had succeeded. That would have weighed heavily on him, even now.

"So, you're saying you're not up to the job?" Carter said,

playing his next card. "Markus Aternus is too smart for you, is that it?"

Nathan cocked his head to one side. "Come now, Carter, that is an obvious tactic, and one I thought beneath you to try."

"Obvious or not, it's a valid question." Carter gestured to the living space and all of the fine things in it. "You've surrounded yourself with the work of geniuses, but the truth is, you don't rank amongst them, whereas Markus Aternus does. His neuromorphic brain is perhaps the single greatest invention in history."

"I'm not dead yet, Carter, I still have time!" Nathan snapped. Despite seeing through his ploy, it had worked.

"So, write your name into the annals of history, as the man who defeated a god," Carter replied, moving his pitch along. "Only you can do it, Nathan. Only you can outsmart and defeat the great Markus Aternus."

Nathan sighed then tapped a pad on the arm of the chair. The bot from the horticulture level appeared through the aperture in the wall, closely watched by JACAB, before disappearing off into the kitchen.

"You may not know this, but at the height of the Aternien war, the Union tasked me to find a way to 'hack' or otherwise disrupt the Aternien neuromorphic brain," Nathan said. He'd become suddenly more thoughtful and reflective, though whether the change in demeanor helped Carter or hindered him, he wasn't yet sure. "They even provided me with live 'test subjects'. Aternien Immortals that I could experiment on to my heart's content, without fear of reprisal, but still I failed. So that should answer your question."

"That was a hundred years ago. Surely you can apply what you've learned since then to take another crack at it?"

The scientist shook his head. "The brain that Markus designed is a true work of creation, Carter. I could kill it, of course – anything that lives can be killed – but not in a way that I could weaponize. And, believe me, I tried."

"Try again, and try harder," Carter urged.

"Markus will have only made his design better," Nathan hit back. It was clear he was growing weary of the conversation. "I could spend another century trying to devise a 'tech-virus' as you so quaintly put it, and still fail. It is a pointless endeavor."

Nathan's bot reappeared, carrying a tray with two mugs on it. The bot set the tray down and Nathan picked up one of the mugs, which was filled with a steaming hot, yellow-tinted liquid. The man gestured to the other cup, inviting Carter to take it. He scowled at the mug, picked it up, then glanced at JACAB.

"I'm not trying to poison you, Carter," Nathan said, sounding insulted.

JACAB scanned the drink, sampled it, and sent the analysis to his comp-slate. The beverage turned out to be a simple chamomile tea. Even so, he didn't drink it, because he still didn't trust his old friend not to try something, especially after his encounter with the man-eating vegetable two levels above them.

"Besides, even if I could create a weapon, why would I?" Nathan continued, before taking a sip of his tea. "The fact is that the Aternien race is humanity's next stage of evolution. As you so kindly pointed out, I spent decades trying to emulate what Markus Aternus achieved, and all I have to show for it are curiosities and automatons; non-sentient androids that are not and could never be alive. The Aternien brain is a wonder that will never be repeated, an event as singular as the big bang. To destroy Aternus would be a crime against the universe itself."

"You went up against him before, so why not again?" Carter pointed out.

Nathan shot him a wearying look. "That was different, and you know it. Back then I thought I was helping to usher in a new era for the Union, one where people transcended their limited human forms, and became more like you. I wanted what Aternus wanted, but instead of being a traitor to the Union, I'd be a hero. Then they betrayed me. They betrayed both of us. And given the chance, they'll do it again." He shook his head firmly. "No, Carter. I won't be made a fool of a second time."

Carter considered his options, but he'd played his best hand and Nathan had not been beaten. He could have gotten angry at the man and threatened him should he not cooperate, but he knew it would be pointless. Unless Nathan Clynes threw himself at the task of his own free will, he would fail.

"I guess I shouldn't be surprised," Carter grunted.

"Don't take it personally, Carter," Nathan said, offering him a condescending smile. "You were always my favorite creation. And you know what they say, you never forget your first!"

The scientist laughed at his own joke and spilled some of the tea over the side of the mug. Nathan's bot swooped in and mopped up the spillage, before it had chance to drip onto the man's fine linen pants.

Carter allowed himself to smile at the joke, simply to be polite, though it had always irked him that Nathan considered himself to be a father figure. Again, it didn't surprise him, though. The scientist had modeled himself on Markus Aternus, who had genuinely become the father of an entirely new species. It made sense that Nathan would see his own achievements in a similar light, so as to be compared with the great god-king.

"Before I leave you to gently rot in peace down here, I have a favor to ask," Carter said, turning to the second reason he had sought out Nathan Clynes. "I told you about the Aternien biogenic weapon, but I didn't tell you that one of my officers, an unaugmented human female, was infected with it. I placed her in a stasis chamber shortly after being exposed and brought her here."

"And you wish me to assess this patient and determine whether I can cure her?" Nathan asked. The man was moderately intrigued; he clearly needed a new challenge.

"That's right, but not just for her; for the billions of others that will become infected too," Carter said. "Maybe you won't help me to defeat Markus Aternus, but that stance doesn't preclude you from helping humanity."

Nathan considered this while sipping his tea. "Perhaps helping humanity is merely prolonging their inevitable demise? As such, would it not be more humane to simply let them die?"

Carter shot the scientist a look of exasperation, and he took the hint.

"What's in it for me, other than something to do?"

Carter thought for a moment then had an idea. "How about in return for curing Major Larsen, and providing me with the formula for that cure, I give you all of our data pertaining to the Aternien infiltrators?"

Nathan Clynes's sparse eyebrows raised up at this suggestion.

"Maybe with this data you can finally achieve your goal," Carter added, teasing his offer in front of the scientist like a carrot on a stick. "That's got to be worth something, right?"

Nathan smiled then tapped the control pad on his chair. The hidden door that JACAB had been unable to break through slid aside, and to his surprise Major Larsen's stasis pod floated inside the room on a bed of grav repellers.

"I must admit that I was curious as to why you brought someone with you in stasis," Nathan Clynes said. He smiled again. "Now I know. And now, my dear commander, we have a deal."

TWELVE

A SQUARE DEAL

CARTER JUMPED out of his seat at the sight of Major Larsen's stasis pod being sedately conveyed into the living space by grav repellers, like they were pallbearers. He wrapped his hand around the grip of his sword and glared at Nathan, who was casually reclined in his armchair, legs crossed.

"Don't worry, Carter, she's still alive and the stasis pod is viable," the scientist said, brushing off Carter's obvious concerns. "Naturally, if it were otherwise then I would not have brought it here."

Carter released the handle of his sword but remained standing. He nodded to JACAB, who quickly hovered over to the stasis pod and began scanning it to confirm the scientist's assertions. With everything that had happened since they'd arrived on Gliese 832-e, Carter had no intention of taking Nathan's words at face value.

"When did you become so cynical and distrustful, Carter?" Nathan added, coming across as offended, though Carter could tell it was an act. He then smiled sanctimoniously. "Perhaps it happened after the Union betrayed you and tossed you onto the scrapheap?"

Carter wasn't amused. "That only happened because you backed the Aternien Act and threw me and my crew under the bus to save your own hide," he replied, injecting his answer with a suitable amount of acidity.

Nathan tutted loudly then set down his tea, stood up and walked over to the stasis pod. JACAB was still running his scans, while also keeping a close watch on the horticulture bot that had brought the pod into the room.

"I had Farmer here retrieve the pod shortly after your shuttle crashed," Nathan said, patting the horticulture bot on the top of it spherical shell.

"Don't you mean after you shot me down?" Carter corrected him.

Nathan rolled his eyes. "I'm sorry if you expected me to roll out the red carpet, but one can't be too cautious. Your shuttle was approaching my complex, and the defense systems were programmed to eliminate any potential threats."

"It helps to identify friend or foe, before you start shooting…" Nathan eye-rolled again, and Carter let it drop, on account of there being more important matters to deal with. "Why did you bring the pod here?"

"It was an unexpected discovery and intriguing mystery rolled into one, so naturally I wanted to learn more," Nathan replied. "I had assumed the vessel was being piloted remotely, since there was no-one else inside. Gliese 832-e can be rather inhospitable to the unsuspecting traveler, so I did not expect to find any other survivors."

Carter approached the pod and looked through the glass canopy at the face of Major Larsen. She appeared to simply be asleep. His comp-slate updated and Carter checked the analysis his bot had just sent across. She was continuing to deteriorate, but the virus had not yet progressed beyond the point of no return.

"I already had Farmer and Fixer run a detailed raft of tests on this lovely young woman," Nathan continued, while gesturing to Farmer. Carter then noticed that Fixer, the bot from the workshop and laboratory level, had snuck back into the room and was loitering in the far corner. "As with everything that Markus touches, the virus is elegant, both in its simplicity and effectiveness."

Carter slowly circled around the pod and looked into Nathan's bloodshot eyes. The scientist shuffled his feet uncomfortably as the weight of his piercing stare and intimidating presence pressed down on him.

"I honestly don't give a damn if it's the most spectacular virus you've ever seen. All I need to know is whether you can cure her."

Nathan thought for a moment then coughed nervously to clear his throat before answering. "I care nothing for the woman in this pod, but in return for the data you possess on the Aternien's replica human bodies, I will create an antiviral, and also a serum to make others immune to the effects of this ingenious little infection."

Carter appeared suspicious. "Just like that? You don't need to study the virus some more to know if you can even do it?"

Nathan smiled and shook his head. "I already know I can do it, otherwise I wouldn't have made such a promise. Besides, I need a challenge. This will be a welcome diversion."

"A welcome diversion from building dinosaurs and hobgoblins, you mean?"

"Touché..."

Carter's comp-slate chimed a message, surprising both himself and Nathan. He looked at the screen and saw that it was from Kendra on the Galatine.

"Who could possibly be calling you out here?" Nathan said, suddenly on edge. "Did you bring someone else with you?"

"Relax, Nathan, it's just my ship," Carter answered. "You know, the one that got smashed into the Piazzi asteroid field at the end of the war, because it was considered to be dangerous technology?"

The scientist's eyes narrowed. "Really, Carter, for someone who professes to not hold grudges, you certainly make a good show of appearing otherwise."

"Do something useful and get to work on curing my XO, while I find out what they want," Carter said, while walking away from the scientist.

The sheer brass neck of Carter issuing Nathan with a command caused the scientist's hackles to rise, but the man didn't have a chance to object, before he'd slipped out of earshot and into the kitchen area of the living space.

"This is Carter, go ahead, Kendra."

"Are you okay, boss? We found the remains of the combat shuttle about ten miles from your current location."

"I'm fine," Carter grunted, while watching the scientist out of the corner of his eye. "Let's just say that Nathan isn't exactly fond of visitors."

"That sounds like him," Kendra replied, knowingly. "I can pick up the shuttle when we land to collect you. It doesn't look too badly damaged."

Carter smiled. "I thought you'd be pissed at me for crashing it."

"Who says I'm not?" Kendra replied with a cheerfulness that made it sound like she was relishing the prospect of giving him an ear-bashing. "I'm just glad you're okay." An anxious pause followed, before the Master Engineer added, "How's the Major?"

"Carina is still alive, and Nathan believes he can cure her, and create a serum to protect others against the Aternien virus."

Kendra snorted a laugh. "Coming from anyone else, I'd call bullshit on that boast, but since it's Nathan, he can probably pull it off."

"That's what I'm hoping," Carter said, while rubbing his face and beard. "It'll cost us all our data on the Aternien infiltrators, which is classified above Top Secret, of course, but I figure Krantz won't object, considering the payoff."

"The infiltrators? What the fu…" Kendra caught herself mid-curse and adjusted her question. "What the *hell* does Nathan want with that data?"

Carter looked at the scientist, who was circling the stasis pod while working on a comp-slate with energized fervor. The jarring mix of newer, synthetic flesh with wizened necrotic flesh made the man look more hideous and terrifying than any of the creations on the levels above him. By rights, Nathan Clynes should have died decades ago, and without a long-term solution to his deteriorating body, he doubted the man would survive more than a few more years.

"I think he's hoping to find the secret to eternal life," Carter said, in answer to Kendra's question.

The idea of providing Nathan Clynes with the key to

immortality appeared to strike fear into the heart of his Master Engineer.

"Is that wise? We could end up with another Markus Aternus," Kendra cautioned.

"We either take that chance or we walk away with nothing, Kendra," Carter said, facing the harsh reality of their situation. "There's nothing to say he'll succeed, and if Nathan can give us a serum to protect people against the Aternien virus, which could safeguard billions of lives, it has to be worth the risk."

Kendra didn't reply immediately, but when she did, it was with an air of resignation. "You're right, boss, as usual."

Carter grunted an acknowledgment then turned his thoughts to the reason why the Galatine had been away in the first place. "How did things go at Terra Nine?"

"It's not great news, I'm afraid," Kendra replied, and Carter closed his eyes and cursed under his breath. "The Aterniens had already landed the biogenic weapon on the surface of the planet by the time we arrived, so we immediately focused all of our efforts on destroying it."

"I take it that wasn't possible?"

"No, we got the thing, alright," Kendra replied, surprising Carter with her answer. "We rained hellfire onto the ground surrounding the weapon, tunneling deep enough beneath the surface to reach the reactor core and blow it sky high."

"That was smart thinking, Kendra," Carter said, suitably impressed with his crew's ingenuity.

"That's what I thought too, but the problem was, it was a feckin' decoy."

"What?"

His raised voice caught Nathan's interest and the

scientist briefly looked up from his comp-slate to pay attention to Carter's call. He turned his back on the man and stated his query in a more reserved manner.

"What do you mean it was a decoy, Kendra? A decoy for what?"

"While we were taking care of the weapon on the planet, one of those bastard Royal Court Khopesh Destroyers launched two modified torpedoes into the atmosphere. They detonated and expelled thousands of the virus carrier probes."

Carter was now rubbing his eyes but trying to keep Nathan from seeing his reaction. "Was it enough to kill the population?" he asked, deciding to skip any other intermediate questions he had, and go right to the end.

"Unfortunately, yes," Kendra said, guilt and regret evident in her voice. "Terra Nine only has a small population, so just a single torp was enough. If the planet had orbital defenses, or we hadn't been suckered in by the decoy, then it wouldn't have got through."

"It's not your fault, Kendra, you couldn't have known," Carter said. "In your shoes, I'd also have gone after the planetary weapon, and Aternus knew this too. He played us for fools again, and I'm getting sick of it."

"I hear you, boss," Kendra replied, sounding pissed off and fed up. "We gave those feckers a good hiding before they bugged out, though, slagging forty-six vessels in total, including that bastard Royal Court ship."

Carter nodded. *Small mercies…* he thought.

"The Forest Moon was bombarded too, but we were wise to their tactics by then, and destroyed the virus-carrying torpedoes before they could detonate," Kendra added. "I scanned Ridge Town and the surrounding area, and your cabin survived."

"Thanks, Kendra." Carter wasn't going to ask about the moon where he'd made his home, in case it appeared selfish, but he was glad his Master Engineer had mentioned it. "At least you took out one of Aternus' High Overseers," Carter continued. "It'll be reborn, of course, but hopefully the pain of that experience will make the golden bastard think twice about facing us again."

"Language..." Kendra cautioned, and though he couldn't see her, he could imagine the twinkle in her eye.

"Sorry, Kendra. It's been a rough day."

"Again, I hear you..." There was another pause, during which Carter heard his Master Engineer's sharp intake of breath. "So, are you ready to leave?"

"Soon. I still have a couple of things to wrap up here with Nathan, but I expect to be done by the time you land."

"Good, because we need to head out again as soon as possible."

Carter frowned, suddenly uneasy. It was the same, 'did I leave the gas on?' gnawing doubt that often resulted from imminent bad news. "What's up now, Kendra? Another attack?"

"No, something different, and potentially good news," Kendra replied. Carter felt his spirits lift; good news was something he needed. "While we were within range of the Union's warp comms buoys, we picked up Brodie's coded distress signal, coming from Venture Terminal at Terra Seven."

"Venture Terminal has gone to hell since Terra Seven fell," Carter said. "Admiral Krantz told me that criminal gangs and other opportunists are in control there now. Are you sure it was his signal?"

"Verified and confirmed, boss," Kendra replied. "The docking garages and pylons are all under criminal control, so he's trapped there and asking for a pick-up. I guess he must have heard about the Galatine on the grapevine."

Carter nodded. Another Longsword crew member would be a vital asset, especially one with Brodie's destructive skill set.

"Then ask Amaya to plot a course. We'll jump to Terra Seven as soon as I'm done here."

"She already has it locked in, boss," Kendra replied, sounding a little smug. "I'll drop you a line once we've landed."

The comm channel closed and Carter turned to see that Nathan Clynes was still watching him, while pretending not to be. He strolled toward the man and the stasis pod containing his XO, eager for an update.

"Trouble with the Aterniens, I take it?" Nathan said, his sarcastic tone indicating he already knew the answer.

"Don't sound so pleased," Carter grunted. He tapped his finger onto the glass canopy of the pod. "I have other urgent duties to attend to, so how soon can I get my XO back?"

Nathan shrugged. "Markus designed the virus using technology and knowledge that the Union purged over a century ago. However, he clearly didn't anticipate that it would come into my possession."

"So, you have the knowledge and you have the tech you need to beat it?"

Nathan nodded, still smiling conceitedly. "It seems that even the great Markus Aternus can err."

"Look, Nathan, you can trumpet your horn as much as

you like, so long as you can save Carina and get me that serum."

"I can provide you with the serum in exchange for all of the Union's data on Aternien synths, but I cannot save this woman's life."

Carter felt his blood pump harder through his veins and he had to stop himself from hammering his fists onto the canopy of the stasis pod for fear of smashing the glass.

"That wasn't the deal, Nathan," Carter growled at the man.

"She's too far gone, already," the scientist said, glibly and without compassion. "The priority should be to create a serum, so that others do not share her fate." The man returned to studying his comp-slate. "I will still require her body, of course," Nathan continued, speaking about Major Larsen like she was nothing more than a lab cadaver for medical students to dissect. "I will take the necessary samples, then perform a thorough autopsy once she is dead to study the effects of the virus in more detail. After that, you can have her remains to bury, or blast out into space in a torpedo, or whatever you military types prefer."

Carter felt like he was having an out-of-body experience, and observing Nathan Clynes talk about his XO like she was one of his Jekyll-and-Hyde experiments.

"Given my resources and talents, I would say that synthesizing a nano-serum should be simple," Nathan continued, oblivious to the nuclear anger that was building inside him. "I must admit to being somewhat disappointed that Markus Aternus did not make more of an effort," he added, sounding exceedingly pleased with himself, and not at all disappointed. "All told, I should have something for you to test within a week. I would recommend bringing me a number of live subjects. Four or five people should suffice. Naturally, these test subjects will die should the serum not succeed, but I do not anticipate any problems."

Nathan stopped talking, suddenly becoming aware that Carter hadn't spoken in at least a minute and appeared to be on the verge of going critical.

"I need you to save her, Nathan," Carter said, somehow achieving the impossible and stopping a chain reaction mid-flow. "That part is non-negotiable."

"Carter, this woman's sacrifice will save countless lives, and surely that is the point?" Nathan replied, allowing Carter's concerns to wash over him with the carefree kiss of a summer's breeze. "You will have done your duty, and I will become the savior of humanity for a second time. I will name it, The Clynes Cure."

"There has to be a way," Carter said, still holding back from strangling the man. It did him no good to flay the scientist's flesh from his rotten bones, before he'd completed the job. "You're supposed to be a genius, so figure it out."

"I have told you no, and that is the end of the matter!" Nathan snapped, folding his arms to emphasize the finality of his statement. "I will produce and test a serum and provide the Union with simple instructions on how to replicate it, using the limited resources available to them. In return, I will receive the data I have requested. That is the deal, Carter; take it, or leave it."

Carter paced around the stasis pod, and Nathan backed away, matching him step for step. JACAB was now hovering beside his right shoulder, while Farmer and Fixer, Nathan's two gophers, loomed behind the scientist. All three bots had armed their energy blasters.

"You owe me, Nathan," Carter said, jabbing a finger into

Nathan's decaying sternum. "For what you did a century ago, you have to try."

"I owe you nothing!" Nathan snapped, still retreating.

The words slapped him around the face, and Carter could have lopped off the man's head then and there. "You owe me *nothing*?" Carter growled. "I lost my ship and my crew because of you. I became hated and feared because of you. I spent a century in exile *because of you*!" He darted forward, taking Nathan by surprise, and grabbed the man's collar. Farmer and Fixer hammered blasts into his chest, and he managed to swat one of the bots away, before JACAB swooped in and disabled the other with perfectly aimed blasts to its grav-repellers.

"Saving her life is the bare minimum you owe me," Carter said, lifting the scientist so he was left scrambling on the balls of his feet. Up close, the man's necrotic flesh smelled as bad as it looked.

"Fuck you!" Nathan bellowed, afraid but not enough to concede. "You can't compel me through guilt, since I feel none. I was also wronged!"

"But you sold us out!"

"So what if I did?" Nathan cried. "I got all this, while the Union's greasy fingers are still tugging on your collar. I won, Carter, and that's what pisses you off!"

"You think you *won*?" Carter snarled.

He drew his cutlass and energized the blade. Nathan's eyes grew wide with fear, and he lost control of his bladder, the smell of urine adding to the foul stench of rotting skin.

"Let's find out how much of a winner you really are..." Carter hammered the pommel of his cutlass into the corner of the glass canopy covering Major Larsen's stasis pod. The glass cracked like a busted windshield, and an alarm wailed from the pod's control panel. Seconds later screeching alerts blared from hidden speakers inside Nathan Clynes' underground living space.

"Warning... Foreign Contaminant Detected," a computerized voice announced. "Recommend quarantine procedures."

"What have you done?!" Nathan yelled, as the warning was repeated. Carter set the man down and watched him scurry to the pod's control panel. He worked the controls then what little blood still remained in his face drained away. "You've caused the virus to be released!"

Carter watched the scientist scramble around the room, picking up Fixer and hurriedly reactivating the stunned bot. He spoke to the gopher in a mad panic, and it flew to the stasis pod like a cannonball and began hastily repairing the cracked glass. A few seconds later, the alarms shut off. There was a tense wait, during which time both Nathan and Carter, aided by JACAB, scanned the air inside the room. They came to the same conclusion, at the same time.

"I've been exposed..." Nathan whispered, head in his hands. "You fucking idiot! I don't have your augmented immunity to disease!"

"I know," Carter grunted. "So, if you won't find a cure to save Carina, then do it to save yourself. You're good at that, remember?"

The man looked at him, tears welling in his eyes. "You're insane. You're asking the impossible..."

"You were right about me, Nathan, I don't let bygones be bygones," Carter replied, ignoring the scientist's protests. "Save your life by saving hers, then complete the serum, and we're square." Carter disengaged the blade then aimed the tip of the cutlass at the scientist. "But screw me over again, and I'll make sure your death is a thousand times more agonizing than anything this virus will do to you."

Nathan Clynes clamped his jaw shut and nodded frantically, then Master Commander Carter Rose sheathed his sword, and left.

THIRTEEN

VENTURE TERMINAL

EXITING NATHAN CLYNES' underground complex proved to be quicker and less exhausting than entering it had been. This was due to the scientist having disabled the various synthetic sentries that had impeded his earlier progress. The labor bot that had put up a solid fight in the workshop had even waved goodbye, making Carter again wonder whether the robot was more than simply a machine, in the same way that JACAB was.

Stepping outside, he was met with the sweltering heat of Gliese 832-e. However, the discomfort this made him feel was quickly offset by the sight of the Galatine swooping down through the clouds toward them. The defensive weapons that had taken out his shuttle appeared to have also been disabled, since the Galatine was approaching unchallenged. However, even if Nathan's missile battery and plasma turret had opened fire, they would have been unable to damage the powerful Longsword-class battleship.

Carter checked his comp-slate, noting the location of the landing site that Amaya had chosen, then made his way toward it, with JACAB close by his side. It wasn't long before his senses started to climb, and he was reminded that it wasn't only Nathan's lair that harbored a host of dangerous synthetic monsters. Many of the scientist's creations roamed freely in the outdoors too, and according to his own early-warning system, potential threats were lurking close by.

Using his cutlass to hack through the undergrowth, Carter arrived in a clearing that was suitably large enough to accommodate his ship. The Galatine was descending sharply and banking toward them, the roar of its mighty engines shaking the ground and causing coconut-like fruits to tumble from the trees surrounding the plateau. His senses spiked and he saw a pack of Deinonychus stalking through the trees. The "terrible claws" had clearly spotted him and were sizing him up for their next meal. Cursing under his breath, Carter ignited the blade of his cutlass and stood ready to fight them off. Suddenly, the rotary buzz of an autocannon rippled through the air and the dinosaurs were torn to shreds by cannon fire from the Galatine's defensive weapons.

"Did I just shoot up a bunch of dinosaurs?" Kendra Castle said, speaking over the bone-conducting communicator built into Carter's battle uniform.

"Yes, you did," Carter answered, disengaging his sword. "A group of Deinonychus, to be precise."

"Call me crazy for asking, but what the hell are dinosaurs doing on Gliese 832-e?"

Carter huffed a laugh. "It's a long story, and one that I'd rather tell you once I'm off this sweltering deathtrap of a planet."

"Roger that, boss. Amaya is setting down now…"

The Galatine's ventral thrusters fired, blasting the clearing free of loose stones, twigs and the bodies of mashed dinosaurs, while also stripping leaves from any trees unfortunate enough to be in the ship's flight path. Moments later, the landing struts extended then sank into the ground as the Longsword touched down. Its cargo ramp was already in the process of lowering, and Carter jogged toward it using his hand to shield his eyes from the downdraught. The ramp was already closing again before he'd even reached the cargo hold, where he found the remains of the combat shuttle waiting for him. Shaking dust from his uniform and hair, he did a quick circuit of the craft to inspect the damage.

"It doesn't look so bad," Carter said to his bot, who was making his own assessment of the shuttle's condition. "What do you think, buddy?"

The bot bleeped and sent his opinion to Carter's comp-slate. He read the message, which simply said, "Kendra is going to kill you..."

Carter scowled at the message and then at his gopher, who was bobbing up and down in mid-air, literally shaking with electronic laughter.

"She'll understand," Carter grunted, walking past his bot, who continued to laugh at his own joke.

Carter felt the thrusters fire again and the ship lift off the ground. The frequency of the vibrations through the deck plates then shifted as the Galatine transitioned from thrusters to its main engines, which powered the sword-like craft out of the atmosphere and back into deep space, its native habitat. The vibrations, sounds and even the smell of the ship all married together to create a single unique sensation; the feeling of being home.

The door to the bridge opened and he marched inside to find Kendra Castle at the engineering stations, and Amaya Reid front and center in the pilot's seat. Their respective bots, RAEB and ADA, were also on the bridge, fulfilling vital functions that would otherwise have been the responsibility of his missing crewmembers, Cai Cooper and Brodie Kaur. Their absence on the bridge felt like losing a tooth – it was something you got used to, but it was never quite the same. Then his thoughts turned to Carina Larsen, and Carter was surprised to discover that he felt the void of her absence as keenly as he did the others. It simply didn't feel the same without her.

"Where's the Major?" Kendra asked, unintentionally twisting the knife.

"Nathan needed more time to cure her, so I had to leave her there," Carter explained. Even as he was speaking the words, he was questioning his decision, and whether he'd just handed the scientist the ultimate bargaining chip. Yet given that the alternative was to let her die, he didn't know what other choice he'd had. "But the good news is that it will probably only take him a couple of days to create a serum to counteract the Aternien virus," Carter added, in order to swiftly change the subject to something other than their absent XO. "He said a week, but that was only to make his achievement seem all that more impressive when he finishes sooner."

"That is good news," Kendra agreed. "How is that disagreeable old bastard, anyway?"

Carter could have spent the next ten minutes detailing all the ways in which Nathan Clynes had pissed him off, but instead he just shrugged. "Let's just say that the last one hundred years hasn't made him any less of an asshole."

Kendra smiled. "Can I assume he took some persuading then?"

Carter turned to Kendra and lifted his eyebrows, causing the Master Engineer's smile to stretch wider.

"If you're ready to leave, skipper, then the warp drive is spun up, and the course to Venture Terminal at Terra Seven is locked in," Amaya said, spinning her chair around to face him.

Carter looked at Gliese 832-e on the viewscreen, feeling another pang of regret at having to leave Carina behind, especially after he'd threatened Nathan. He hoped that the scientist's well-developed sense of self-preservation would override any desire for retribution.

"Execute the jump, Amaya," Carter said, dropping into his command chair.

The soliton drive spun up to a crescendo then Gliese 832-e vanished, the starfield shifted, and another planet appeared, all in the blink of an eye. The seemingly effortless 'there one minute, gone the next' swiftness of interstellar travel belied the fiendishly complicated physics that underpinned warp travel. Carter had never been gladder of their ability to travel through folds in space, because it meant that his XO was never more than a heartbeat away.

"There she is, Venture Terminal," Amaya said, angling the sword-like point of the Galatine at the space station, which was cast into sharp relief against the blue-green orb of Terra Seven. "It's strange, but the planet doesn't look any different."

Carter stroked his beard and tried to spot any obvious signs that Terra Seven's population had been exterminated, and that Venture Terminal had descended into a gang-ruled chaos, but his Master Navigator was correct. Had he not been aware that a hundred million people had perished on the planet, and that its remaining survivors were being held captive on a single space station, he would never have imagined it.

"Appearances can be deceptive," Carter grunted, reminding himself not only of the flawless fakery of the Aternien infiltrators, but also the near-perfect replica dinosaurs that had almost been the end of him. "Set a course to docking pylon six, and take us in, slow and steady."

"Aye, aye, skipper, taking her in slow and steady to docking pylon six," the pilot confirmed.

"Do you think he's really there?"

Carter glanced over his shoulder and saw Kendra leaning on the tactical console, looking at him.

"I don't see why not, assuming his message was genuine," Carter replied.

Kendra shrugged. "It came through on the Galatine's emergency channel, which only we, and the other Longsword crew, would know about. And the ident challenge was a match for Brodie Kaur, or at least it matched his ident at the time we were decommissioned."

"Could it have been faked?" Carter asked.

His engineer thought for a moment then blew out a sigh, puffing out her cheeks in the process. "I guess it's possible. Aternien tech is at least as advanced as ours, and we already know a couple of former Longsword officers that turned traitor and could have passed on information about our emergency comms protocols to the enemy." Kendra's expression turned grim and she seemed more apprehensive. "You don't think Brodie could have turned, do you?"

"No, not a chance," Carter answered, without a moment's hesitation. He peered back at Venture Terminal and ran his hand through his silver hair. "The crews of the different Longswords were chosen not only for their skillsets, but for their ability to endure the process of augmentation. That meant making some concessions in terms of the 'moral fiber' of the people who were selected, but when it came to my ship, there were no compromises. I was the first Master Commander, and I got my pick. All of you were the best of the best, Brodie included. He wouldn't turn his coat any more than you or I would."

When Kendra didn't answer him, Carter glanced back to make sure that she hadn't wandered off in the middle of his speech. Instead, he found her smiling at him with doting eyes.

"Well, fuck, Carter, that was beautiful. I didn't know you cared…" she said, only half taking the piss.

"Language…" Carter grunted, and his Master Engineer raised her hands in a conciliatory gesture.

"Assuming Brodie is there, we'll need to stay on our toes," Kendra continued, pushing back a little so that she could work the tactical station. "I reviewed the final reports from Venture Terminal, before it went dark, and it makes for grim reading. When the biogenic weapon was detonated on Terra Seven, thousands fled to the space station, seeking sanctuary. It caused a panic, not least because the Union authorities running the terminal couldn't know whether the refugees were infected with the virus or not."

Carter grunted. "I take it the station's commander made some bad calls?"

"You could say that," Kendra replied, making it clear that the expression 'bad calls' was a gross understatement. "Some of the refugee ships refused to comply with docking control and attempted to land without permission. Venture ordered them to be destroyed."

Carter sighed. In some ways, he understood the necessity of such a seemingly callous order, because letting just one infected person onto the station could have killed everyone. At the same time, he had to believe there were other options available to the station's commander that could have been explored first. It made no difference now, of course. The damage was done, and it seemed that it had been left to them to pick up the pieces.

"Word quickly got out that the station was destroying civilian transports, and there was a riot," Kendra continued. "The very last reports speak of lynch mobs and civil unrest on a station-wide scale. Then station operations was overrun, the senior officers were killed, and a power vacuum was left behind."

"A vacuum that the criminal gangs were happy to fill," Carter grunted.

Kendra nodded. "It now appears the station has fallen under the sway of rival criminal factions, each vying for dominance through alliances and conflicts."

Carter rubbed his beard then shrugged. The situation was what it was, and it did no good to dwell on it. He accepted the challenge then shot a smile at his Master Engineer.

"Just when I thought I might get an easier ride than fighting dinosaurs and samurai warriors…"

"Out of the frying pan, and into the fire, right?" Kendra answered, returning his smile. "I knew this would be just like old times…"

"Hey skipper, I'm picking up comms traffic from the docking pylon, demanding that we break off our approach,"

Amaya said, interrupting his little tête-à-tête with his Master Engineer. "I guess we shouldn't have expected a warm welcome."

"Ignore them," Carter said. He didn't take kindly to demands, especially not from criminals. "Venture Terminal might be able to blow up civilian transports, but the Galatine is another matter."

"Aye, aye, skipper," Amaya replied, holding her course and speed.

A minute later the comm panel on his chair's comp-slate flashed up another incoming message from pylon six, the contents of which made him snort-laugh.

"Apparently, we're to break off or be destroyed," Carter said, causing his pilot and engineer to both crack a smile.

The comm panel continued to light up, and he continued to ignore their repeated demands, until finally someone on the station insisted on speaking to him. This was a demand that Carter was happy to oblige, since he wanted to get a good look at his latest enemy. He tapped the button to accept the call and the image of a craggy, rough-shaven man wearing a blood-stained tan leather jacket appeared on the view screen.

"Are you deaf or just fucking stupid?" the man grunted. "Turn your ship around, now, or I'll blow it up. Last warning."

"My name is Master Commander Carter Rose, of the Union Longsword Galatine," Carter said, taking care to identify himself formally, so as to comply with Union regulations. This would make it easier to justify smashing the man's face in later, when the gang member inevitably refused to comply with his lawful demands. "Venture Terminal is a Union facility, and under martial law, it is therefore under my protection. Relinquish control of docking pylon six, and await our arrival, upon which time you will be arrested and taken into custody."

There was a pause, then the man burst out laughing. This continued for several more seconds, until the man laughed himself hoarse and had to slap his chest to stop from gasping, like a fifty-a-day smoker.

"You're a funny fucker, I'll give you that," the man said, once he'd regained some semblance of composure. "Enjoy your cold death in the vacuum of space, *Master Commander*." The man slapped a button and the comm channel was cut off at the source.

"That was rude," Amaya said. Her tone was sharp and she appeared genuinely offended.

"They've locked on with a chain gun," Kendra cut in, though there was nothing about her announcement that suggested she was concerned.

Carter saw the muzzle flash from the chain gun on the viewscreen, but it was like firing BB-gun pellets at a tank.

"Do something about that peashooter, would you?" Carter said, glancing over his shoulder to his engineer.

"Swarm missiles should do the trick," Kendra replied, working the tactical console. "I'll take out all the defensive weapons on this side of the station, in case anyone else decides to take a pot shot at us."

Carter nodded. "Just remember there are civilians on board, and we're here to help them, not vent them into space."

"You got it, boss…"

A few seconds later, a dozen swarm missiles sped away from the Galatine and snaked to their respective targets, crippling Venture Terminal's ability to further obstruct their advance. The comm panel lit up immediately, but Carter ignored it; he was done talking.

"Kendra, Amaya, you're both with me," Carter said, pushing himself out of his seat. "I have a feeling we'll all need eyes in the backs of our heads for this one."

"Who will be in command while we're gone?" Kendra asked.

It was a reasonable question, and one that reminded him he was still missing an XO; a fact that continued to sting like lemon juice on a paper cut.

"JACAB can be in command," Carter said, nodding to his gopher, who bleeped and warbled with delight. "ADA can handle docking us to the station, and RAEB can keep the lights on until we're back."

ADA and RAEB also bleeped and warbled, and soon the enthusiastic chatter of the three gophers had filled the bridge, like the laughter of children playing.

"You have the conn, buddy," Carter said, pointing to JACAB while heading toward the door. "Just don't leave without us. That's an order."

JACAB saluted Carter with a maneuvering fin, then sped over to the command chair and docked himself in place, indicator lights flashing and his glowing red eye wide with excitement.

FOURTEEN

ONE AND ONLY CHANCE

CARTER PULLED open the door to the armory and marched inside, followed closely by Kendra Castle and Amaya Reid. He went straight to his plasma cutlass and fixed the weapon to his battle uniform, before picking up his 57-EX revolver. He was about to attach the holstered weapon to his uniform too, when he remembered that the revolver was broken.

"Crap, I don't suppose we have another one of these, do we?" Carter asked his engineer, while showing her the revolver and its damaged cylinder.

Kendra tutted in what Carter considered to be a needlessly pointed manner then snatched the revolver out of his hand.

"Yes, we do, lucky for you," she replied, tossing the broken revolver onto a shelf then moving across to a different weapons locker. "Though, if you keep breaking stuff at the rate you have been recently there won't be anything left in here."

"Things break, Kendra, and the combat shuttle needed a

refit, anyway," Carter said, unrepentant. "Besides, don't try to pretend you won't enjoy rebuilding it."

The Master Engineer returned with a new 57-EX revolver in hand. "That's not the point and you know it."

"The point is, I don't really care what your point is," Carter hit back. "I break it and you fix it. That's the deal."

Kendra scowled at him then attached the weapon to his battle uniform. The exchange was playful, not ill tempered, and part of a ritual that went back almost a hundred and forty years. Carter would play the cavalier Master Commander, charging in where angels fear to tread, and smashing stuff up in the process, while Kendra would play the grumpy engineer, who always had to pick up the pieces. The beauty of the game was that it didn't require any acting on either of their parts.

"I figured you might need this too," Kendra added, attaching a higher-capacity ammo pouch to his uniform.

"Thanks, and on the subject of weapons, you two need to get geared up as well," Carter said, adjusting the fit of the ammo pouch. "Make sure you equip an energy pistol as well as your blades."

"Two, in my case," Kendra replied, attaching a plasma pistol to each hip.

Carter smiled as he watched Kendra equip the dual pistols. She could shoot just as well with her left hand as her right, and given the chance, she preferred to use both at the same time. Then he had a thought. "Hey, Kendra, did you ever find your sword?"

She flashed her eyes at him then reached inside the same locker that had contained the spare 57-EX and removed a Japanese tantō. She slid the weapon from its short sheath and plasma flashed along the blade's edge, crackling and spluttering softly, and causing shadows to dance on the walls of the armory.

"It's been a while since I saw that in action," Carter said, admiring the elegant short sword.

"I hope I don't have to use it, though somehow I doubt that will be the case," the engineer replied, disengaging the blade then attaching the sheathed weapon to her uniform alongside her pistols.

While he and Kendra had been talking, Amaya had already equipped her weapons and was waiting for them by the door. With her ornate rapier, Kendra's traditional Japanese sword, and his naval cutlass, they cut an unlikely trio, like an alternate universe Three Musketeers, retold for a less chivalrous age.

"Time to find out if the felonious controller of docking pylon six is less of an asshole in person," Carter said, heading out of the door.

"What if he's an even bigger twat… I mean, twerp?" Kendra asked, quickly correcting herself, before Carter could berate her for her bad language.

He considered the question, and the implication behind it. The fact was that Venture Terminal was packed full of civilians, and they needed to do everything possible to avoid collateral damage.

"Let's give him and his cronies a chance to see sense, so for now we use non-lethal force," Carter replied, slowing as he approached the hatch leading into Venture Terminal. "But we don't have time to waste messing around with these underworld folk, so if they don't take the hint, and stay out of our way, things will have to get ugly."

"They may not give us a choice," Amaya pointed out.

"Then it will be their choice, not ours," Carter grunted.

"I'm not interested in killing human beings, even if some of the people on this station barely qualify for that description. Too many have died already."

Amaya and Kendra both nodded then stood ready for the hatch to unlock. JACAB bleeped at them over the comm link from the bridge and the door slid open with a hiss.

"Buddy, once we're inside the station, I want you to seal up the Galatine like a tomb," Carter said, moving inside the short boarding tunnel. "No-one gets into this ship but us, is that understood?"

JACAB warbled an acknowledgment then Carter approached the inner airlock door. Through the porthole window, he could see a group of men and women in the arrivals area of Docking Pylon Six. They were armed with gauss pistols and improvised melee weapons, ranging from kitchen knives to table legs. The gang members were all also wearing oxygen masks, presumably in an effort to protect themselves from exposure to the Aternien virus, but none of the masks looked particularly well-fitted. The thugs had clearly made more of an effort to defend their new fiefdom than they had to prevent the potential spread of a bioengineered pathogen. Checking again that his crew were ready, he threw the latch and pulled the inner hatch door open.

"You were told not to dock," a man at the front of the group of twelve called out, his voice muffled by the oxygen mask. "Now, we'll have to kill you, and take your ship."

Carter took three paces forward, and all twelve thugs aimed their weapons at him. He stopped and rested his hand on the pommel of his sword, though didn't draw it, so as not to be the instigator of the fight he was trying to avoid. He intended to keep his promise of offering the gang members a chance to back down and hoped that they would take it.

"My name is Master Commander Rose of the Union…"

"I don't give a fuck," the man cut in, before he could finish.

Carter took a deep breath and tried to compose himself. Tossing the ugly curse at him was enough to stoke his anger but interrupting him as well was a surefire way to fan the flames.

"Look, I'm not here to overthrow your criminal empire," Carter said, in his most non-threatening voice. "In case you hadn't noticed, there's a war going on. I'm only here to find my officer then I'll be on my way."

"If it's a Union officer you're after, then they're dead, already," the man replied, sounding pleased at that fact. "We rounded them up and executed them for betraying their own people." The thug smiled. "A few are still hanging from the rafters, I think."

"Then you'll pay for those crimes, in time," Carter said, squeezing the pommel harder and threatening to crush it like an egg. "But it won't be today, and it won't be because of me. That is assuming you get out of my way and stay out of my way."

The man laughed and looked at his lackies, who also laughed, whether they got the joke or not. And Carter, for one, was struggling to understand the punchline.

"You're really not getting this are you, old man?" the leader said, mocking him.

"You're not going anywhere, besides the grave. Your only choice is whether you die easy, or hard."

Vexed, Carter's chest deflated as he let out a frustrated sigh and transferred his hold on his cutlass from pommel to grip. "You're not going to back down, no matter what I say, are you?"

The man grinned and shook his head.

"So be it…" Carter said, giving himself over to his heightened instincts, then slowly drawing his sword.

The gang opened fire, but Carter and his augmented crew had already moved from where the gauss slugs had been aimed. The twelve thugs had spread themselves evenly across the far side of the arrivals lounge, making it easy for Carter to divide and conquer. He went after the ringleader and the trio of thugs closest to him, while Amaya went right, and Kendra left, both taking four apiece. Energy blasts flashed from their plasma pistols, but Carter wasn't interested in shooting the thugs. This was partly because one round from his 57-EX would put a hole in a regular human chest the size of a volleyball, but mainly because the gang leader had pissed him off, and fighting hand-to-hand was the only way he'd get satisfaction.

The sight of Carter wielding an energized sword compelled the gang leader to turn tail and run, while his accomplices stood their ground and opened fire. Slugs thudded into his armor and his buckler, but within a second, Carter had cleared the distance between himself and the nearest gunman and battered the man senseless with a swipe of his hand. Leaving the thug unconscious in a pile of his own drool and blood, Carter turned his attention to the next gang member. He grabbed the barrel of the goon's pistol and crushed it like collapsing a cigar tube. The man held his nerve and struck him across the side of the face with the mangled weapon, but Carter didn't even flinch, and finally the thug succumbed to panic.

"Run…" Carter growled, fearing what he might do to the

thug should he remain in his face. The man took the hint, spun on his heels and charged toward the exit, before tripping and landing headfirst, knocking himself out cold in the process.

Two more shots rang out and he felt the slugs punch his gut. The first was repelled by his battle uniform, but the second snuck through and became lodged in his hyper-dense stomach muscles. He smacked the weapon out of the man's hand, breaking bones in the process, then grabbed the thug's wrist. The man struggled to free himself, but he was a tiny spider caught in a deadly web. Swinging his cutlass, Carter severed the man's arm off at the elbow then tossed the dismembered limb over his shoulder. The plasma cauterized the wound in an instant, leaving the goon shaking with fear and staring, wide-eyed at his missing limb, like a shell-shocked soldier on Sword Beach during the Normandy landings of World War II.

Carter dug the bullet out of his belly with his fingers and tossed it aside, before turning his attention to the ringleader, who was now firmly in his sights. The man had thrown down his weapon and was on his knees, prostrated like an Aternien acolyte worshipping the god-king, Markus Aternus. As he approached the belatedly penitent man, Carter glanced to either side to check on the progress of his crewmembers. Both were already done with their adversaries, but with his senses on high alert, he'd been able to observe their fights in his peripheral vision, at the same time as taking care of his own opponents.

Kendra had begun by knee-capping two gang-members with her energy pistols, before switching to her tantō to handle the final duo. Those two had been armed with kitchen cleavers, but neither had displayed much proficiency with their blades, unlike his Master Engineer. The first had come at her with the cleaver held high, hacking and slashing like a berserker. Kendra had been patient, then at the perfect moment, she'd ducked beneath a wild slash, twisted her hips and stabbed the thug in the armpit. The woman had cried out and dropped the knife, before staggering out of contention, blood pouring from the wound.

The second gang member displayed at least some ability with the knife, but it was still a mismatch of galactic proportions. Again, Kendra had dodged and parried with meticulous care and attention, biding her time and waiting for her opponent to make a mistake. Then when the thug missed a heavy downward cut, Kendra flourished her tantō and severed the man's hand off at the wrist. Stunned, the goon staggered away, gawping at his cauterized stump in disbelief, and allowing his engineer to knock him out with a crushing palm-strike.

Amaya's opponents had been handled with similar aplomb, but in a very different manner to the patient and measured style of violence that Kendra Castle dished out. With her rapier in hand, she was like a whirling dervish, marrying traditional fencing techniques with a style that she'd developed herself, to take advantage of her augmented grace and exquisite agility. In full flow, Amaya could have taken down all twelve of the gang members on her own, which meant four was a leisurely walk in the part for his Master Navigator.

The first of the four she'd danced past like a ballerina demonstrating an allegro. It was so fast and smooth that the thug hadn't noticed the flash of her rapier as it removed the man's fingers at the knuckles, scattering them across the deck like chipolatas. The second goon was impaled through the bicep, rendering her weapon arm useless. The woman's hamstrings were then cut as Amaya floated past and attacked the next of her victims. That gang member was firing wildly at her, screaming like a lunatic, but Amaya embodied the principles of combat that Carter held dear; namely that the best defense was not to get hit in the first place. Gauss slugs thudded into walls and ricocheted off deck plates, but each time they landed in locations that Amaya had already vacated. Then she thrust her sword through the trigger guard of the gang member's pistol, and flicked her wrist, removing the woman's finger with scalpel-like precision. The goon shrieked and dropped the weapon, but before the pistol had even hit the ground, Amaya had crushed the pommel of her rapier into the back of the woman's neck and turned out her lights.

Carter could have watched his Master Navigator fight all day, but her fourth opponent spoiled his viewing pleasure by dropping his knife, falling to his knees and throwing his hands up in surrender. Amaya deactivated and sheathed her rapier, bowed with a flourish, then shot the man in the chest with her energy pistol on low-power, stunning him into unconsciousness. Carter appreciated that his Master Navigator and Master Engineer had dutifully followed his command to subdue the gang members using non-lethal force. However, as he stormed toward the ringleader, he questioned whether he'd be able to manage the same level of restraint.

"Look, I'm sorry!" the gang leader said, back to the wall. He'd torn his oxygen mask off his face, in order that his plea was heard clearly. "I won't cause you any more trouble, I promise!"

Carter grabbed the man around the throat and lifted him

so that the tips of his scuffed boots were an inch off the deck. The man writhed and thrashed, pummeling his fists against Carter's shoulders, while wheezing guttural gasps as he struggled for air.

"I'm out here trying to save lives, not take them," Carter growled, leaning in so that their faces were only a few inches apart. He could smell the man's fear and it repulsed him. The leader was nothing more than a tough talker who couldn't back up his words. "This is your only warning. Get in my way again, or send anyone else to get in my way, and the next time you come at us, we won't hold back." He leaned in closer still and whispered in the man's ear. "Nod if you understand…"

The gang leader could barely move, but he managed another guttural croak, causing saliva to dribble from his chin and onto Carter's hand.

"Good…" Carter said. He then bashed the man's head against the wall to knock him out and tossed the unconscious body aside like discarding a candy wrapper.

"I told you this would be just like old times," Kendra said, as she and Amaya arrived by his side.

Carter frowned at his Master Engineer. "You and I must remember those days quite differently, Kendra." He shoved another unconscious body aside with his boot then found the control panel to open the exit. "Now let's find Brodie and get back to the real work."

FIFTEEN

THE DEMON

CARTER STEPPED out of the elevator onto the ground floor of Venture Terminal's promenade. The promenade spanned six decks in total and extended across the entire central section of the bulb-shaped station. It was the location where most of the terminal's shops, bars and recreation facilities were located, and it also housed the station's two sprawling natural habitats. These indoor parklands were a slice of planetary life transported into orbit, with simulated blue skies and sunlight, mixed with organic, living grass and trees. Ordinarily, the Promenade would have been an oasis where the inhabitants of Venture Terminal congregated to get away from the confines of the station. Now, it was a refugee camp, housing the lucky few who had managed to escape the virus on Terra Seven. Though, as Carter scanned the crude tents and cramped, improvised shelters, all policed by armed gangs of criminals, he wondered whether 'lucky' was exactly the right word to use.

"There must be thousands of people on this level alone," Amaya commented. "They should be getting the help and protection of the Union, but instead they're crammed in here like animals."

"I wish we could do more to help them, but until we've dealt with the Aternien threat, these gangs will have to wait," Carter said, though it pained him to be so callous.

A feeling that he was being watched suddenly caused a shiver to rush down his spine, and Carter spun around, but saw nothing suspicious that could have triggered his senses. Then he caught movement in his peripheral vision and looked up to see a group of men and women in Union uniforms swinging from the structural beams high above the promenade. Their wrists and ankles had been bound, and they'd been strung up by their necks like common criminals from a less civilized period of the Union's history. The man in the center of the group, face blue and tongue bulging out of his mouth like a part-deflated balloon, had a sign around his neck. It read, "Union Filth."

"We need to disguise our uniforms," Carter grunted, forcing himself to turn away from the swinging bodies, though the image would be forever ingrained in his memory. "If the gangs see us dressed like this, it won't be long before bullets start to fly."

Kendra and Amaya had also seen the bodies hanging above them, but like Carter, neither of them had passed comment. Nothing they could say would have helped to make sense of a senseless act, which meant that any comment was simply a waste of breath. Even so, Carter would not forget what he'd seen, nor would he forgive it, but to find Brodie and stay alive, he had to put his feelings of disgust and anger aside.

"There's a cluster of makeshift market stalls just over there," Kendra said, nodding toward a set of tables that had been pulled together about fifty meters away. "It looks like they're handing out water and food, as well as sleeping bags and clothes to anyone who needs them."

Carter nodded. Their need wasn't as great as the others in the refugee camp, but they also couldn't continue to walk around in their uniforms and expect not to draw attention to themselves.

"Focus on finding long jackets or cloaks that will cover our uniforms and help us to blend in," Carter said, easing his way through the crowd toward the market stalls.

Progress was slow on account of the crowded conditions, but Carter welcomed the cover the mass of bodies provided, because it hid them more effectively than any single item of clothing might have done.

"I hate to say it, boss, but it looks like we're already causing a stir," Kendra said, subtly pointing in the direction of the East Habitat.

Carter kept moving and kept his head down but was still able to make out a group of armed thugs pushing into the crowds. They were grabbing people at random and yanking back their hoods to look at their faces. One of the gang members was constantly checking a comp-slate, shifting his gaze from the screen to the faces of each resident they accosted to check their IDs matched up.

"If they're looking for us then it means word of our exploits at pylon six has already gotten out," Amaya said.

"Which means they're either from a different gang, or my warning has been ignored," Carter added. "Or both."

A shiver crept down his spine and his already heightened senses ratcheted up by another notch. His eyes were drawn to a hooded figure, moving swiftly across to his left, but too far away to make out clearly. He shifted some bodies aside in an attempt to get a better look, but the figure was already gone.

"What's up, skipper? You look like you've seen a ghost?" his navigator asked.

"I don't know what I saw," Carter admitted. He continued to scour the area where he'd last seen the hooded figure, but they were gone, like smoke in the wind. "Stay sharp, people. Something tells me that there's more going on here than we realize."

Carter turned back to the market stalls and his warning system alerted him again, but this time the sensation was different. The feeling the hooded figure had evoked was like the echo of a distant memory, whereas now he foresaw an imminent danger. A woman was moving toward him, and he prepared to react, but Kendra Castle got there first.

"Take one more step, and I'll spill your guts all over the deck," Kendra said. She had drawn her tantō and had the tip of the blade pressed to the woman's stomach in such a way that it remained almost entirely concealed from view.

"Take it easy, I'm a friend," the woman said, remaining impressively calm so as not to draw attention to them. "You're from the Union, right?" She added, glancing at the insignia on the chest of his battle uniform. "You can't be seen in here. If they find you, they'll kill you."

"Why do you care?" Carter grunted. It wasn't the friendliest of responses, given that the woman appeared to have their best interests at heart, but he wasn't in a trusting mood. The stranger tried to edge closer but winced as Kendra's tanto pressed into her flesh. Carter nodded to his engineer and she cautiously allowed the woman to take another step toward him.

"My name is Lieutenant Nadia Ozek," she whispered. "I was part of the station ops team, until we were overrun."

Amaya, who'd been watching Kendra's back, clandestinely accessed her comp-slate and ran the woman's ID. The result came through promptly and his navigator nodded to him.

"Okay, Nadia, what do you have in mind?" Carter asked, using the lieutenant's first name, instead of her rank, which might have put her at risk.

The woman looked around, noting the locations of the gang members that were filtering through the crowd, then turned back to him. "Come with me…"

Kendra withdrew the blade from the lieutenant's gut and she moved through the crowds in the direction they had already been headed, toward the cluster of market stalls. When she arrived, she was greeted by the others who were busy handing out supplies, then allowed through.

"Here, wear these over your uniforms," Lieutenant Ozek said, placing a collection of jackets and coats onto one of the tables.

Carter picked up a long trench coat and slipped it on. It clung to his broad shoulders, giving him the impression of a Dragnet-era private detective on steroids.

"The chatter doing the rounds is that a Union ship recently boarded the station and killed a bunch of Javelin's goons," Nadia continued, able to speak more freely now that they were huddled together by the table.

"Who's Javelin?" Kendra asked, while donning a dark tan leather jacket that blended in well with her battle uniform, whilst still disguising it.

"That's the nickname of the criminal who took over the

station," Nadia replied. "I guess you could call him the kingpin, or whatever the term is. He's the one who broke into ops with an armed gang and slaughtered my colleagues."

Nadia Ozek handed Amaya a dark green cloak, and she quickly donned it. Worn on Carter, the garment would have looked ridiculous, but his Master Navigator could make a potato sack appear elegant, and she pulled off the look with effortless panache. The hooded garment also recalled the cloaked figure Carter had seen, and the hazy image of the mystery person in his mind caused a shiver to spread through his bones. Then for the briefest moment, he was sure he saw the figure again, but as soon as he adjusted his gaze, they were gone.

"Did anyone else from station ops survive?" Kendra asked, shifting Carter's attention back to the conversation with Lieutenant Ozek.

"No, no-one from the command team made it, at least not that I know of," Nadia answered. "I've been able to contact twenty other crewmembers so far, and group them together in a safe space, ready to fight back. But the gangs are constantly searching for surviving Union personnel, and any they find are rounded up and shot, or made an example of."

Carter grunted then glanced up at the corpses swinging by their necks above the promenade. He again put them out of his mind then regarded the lieutenant with intense scrutiny, which caused the woman to appear nervous. While Nadia may have felt the weight of his discriminating stare, Carter was not judging her harshly. If anything, he was impressed with the officer. Under immense pressure, she'd not only stayed calm and stayed alive, but she was saving lives and orchestrating a resistance too. Lesser officers would have just kept their heads down and looked out for number one. Nadia Ozek was cut from a different cloth.

"How did you survive?" Carter asked, keeping his questions short and to the point.

Nadia shifted uncomfortably, as if she felt she was on trial. Carter recognized this and offered her some reassurance.

"I'm not suspicious of you. Trust me, if I were then we'd no longer be talking…" Nadia forced down a hard swallow at this. "I'm just trying to understand how you got out alive, that's all."

The lieutenant nodded, wetted her lips, then answered. "I'd just gone off duty, which I guess makes me lucky." She huffed a laugh, though there was no humor in it. "I nearly didn't make it, though. I was still in uniform and heading to the promenade for some dinner, when a group of armed gang members stopped me. If it wasn't for the Demon then I'd be dead too."

Carter frowned. "The Demon?"

"That's what people have been calling him," Nadia replied, physically shuddering as a memory invaded her mind. "The Demon of Venture Terminal, to give him his full name."

Lieutenant Ozek went on to explain that a masked vigilante had been causing untold chaos on the station ever since the Union was overthrown. The figure wore stolen Union body armor beneath a dark cloak, and the Halloween mask of a demon to disguise his face. The man had apparently been going around hacking gang members to pieces using a strengthened fire axe.

"I was as good as dead then the demon came out of nowhere and killed a dozen of these scum bags like it was nothing," Nadia said, continuing to recount the story of her miraculous survival. "I've never seen anyone fight so hard and fast in my life. It was like he was an actual demon, or something supernatural."

"Did you speak to this 'demon' before he left?" Carter asked. He had a strong suspicion who this demonically-powered axe killer could actually be.

"He spoke to me briefly and told me to gather as many Union personnel as I could find and lay low, so that's what I've been doing," Nadia replied. "When I saw you three, I figured it might have been part the demon's plan, but considering you haven't heard about him, I assume you're here for another reason?"

"Yes. Well… maybe," Carter said, uncertain quite how to answer. "It's possible this demon might actually be the reason we're here."

The lieutenant appeared confused by this, but Carter didn't have time to elaborate. Instead, he pulled back the sleeve of his new detective coat and brought up an image of Brodie Kaur on his comp-slate.

"Of the twenty others you've managed to make contact with, is this guy one of them?"

Nadia regarded the image for a few seconds, lips pouted and bottom lip pushed out slightly, as if she were stumped by a difficult exam question. She then shook her head.

"No, sorry, I've never seen him before," she answered. "And I'd remember if I did. I doubt there are many people on this station who are built like that."

Carter understood Nadia's comment. Brodie Kaur was extremely difficult to miss, in the same way that a body builder stood out in a room of regular-sized people. Apart from his hulking physique, he also had a distinctive face, square-jawed like an anvil, but with kind eyes. Nadia's brow then furrowed and she frowned at him.

"I didn't see the demon's face, but he was certainty a big guy, and insanely strong too," she added. "Do you think it could be the same man?"

"Perhaps," Carter grunted. He didn't want to commit, since the hooded figure he'd glimpsed on the promenade had not 'felt' like his old Master-at-arms. "But we'll keep a look out, all the same."

"We need to access the station's primary core block, and search the security records for our missing officer," Kendra cut in, moving the discussion on. "If operations is now controlled by this 'Javelin' character then where's the next best location to plug in?"

Nadia Ozek considered this for a moment before answering. "The station's computer core is on deck thirty-three, and you're on deck eighteen here. But access to the core is restricted, and anything below level thirty-three has been locked down tight."

"Javelin again, right?" Amaya asked, and the lieutenant nodded.

"Don't worry about that, Kendra is an expert at getting into places that we're not supposed to be," Carter said, raising an eyebrow at his Master Engineer, who nodded to accept the compliment, and the challenge.

"What's below thirty-three that's so important to the gangs?" Amaya then asked.

It was a good question, Carter figured, and it was no surprise that his rapier-sharp Master Navigator had asked it.

"Below thirty-three are the docking garages for smaller craft, the main warehouses and maintenance bays, and the primary reactor system," Nadia Ozek replied. "It's basically a lot of empty space and industrial gear, so I don't know why it's been sealed, though ships have been coming and going pretty regularly, all under Javelin's strict control."

The answer to Amaya's question had been revealing, and only reinforced Carter's gut feeling that there was something more going on at Venture Terminal than a simple gang uprising.

"Thank you, Nadia, keep up the good work," Carter said. "We're not actually here to free the station from the control of a tyrant, but if the opportunity presents itself, you can be assured that we'll take it."

For a second it looked like Nadia was about to salute him, but the officer just caught herself before doing so. "Thank you, sir. Any help you can provide is appreciated," Nadia said. She then looked down at her feet. "No-one else has come for us, and at this point, I expect no-one will. It's like the Union has abandoned everyone on Venture Terminal."

"Head up, Nadia," Carter said, his powerful voice compelling the young officer to meet his eyes as if he'd cast a spell on her. "The moment we believe we've lost, then we have. But I'm going to fight these bastards till the very end, and so are you. Never give up."

Nadia Ozek nodded, appearing to take strength and comfort from his words. Carter then quickly checked their surroundings, noting that the gang members were getting closer, which was their cue to leave. With a final nod to the lieutenant, he turned his back on the nearest group of thugs and began walking to the same bank of elevators they'd used to enter the promenade earlier. Then, without warning, electricity rushed through his body and his senses peaked. Instinctively, he spun around, mind fizzing and processing all of his sensory inputs at a vastly accelerated rate. His eyes locked onto an object that was flying toward his head, and he snatched it out of the air, with the whip-like accuracy of a chameleon's tongue. He opened his hand to find a turquoise-colored stone, no larger than a smooth beach pebble. He looked up and spotted the hooded figure moving through the crowds, and hurried after them, shoving people aside to keep pace, but the figure vanished like a ghost in midnight fog.

"Shit, I almost had them!" Carter said, as Kendra and Amaya bustled through bodies to arrive by his side.

"Almost had who, boss?" Kendra asked. "I didn't see anyone?"

Carter sighed. "I think this 'demon' has been stalking us ever since we arrived on the promenade." He held up the stone between his thumb and forefinger. "He threw this at me."

Amaya frowned at the blue pebble. "That looks like lapis lazuli, a pretty common semi-precious stone from Terra Prime."

"Why is Brodie wanging stones at you, instead of just coming over to find us?" Kendra asked.

"I have no idea," Carter replied, frustration etched into his words like the groove on a record. "Nothing about this place is making sense."

He then became alert to a new group of gang members, who were much closer than the others and heading straight for them. Curiously, Carter realized that if it hadn't been for the hooded figure, he wouldn't have seen them coming, as if the mysterious individual had been trying to warn him by throwing the blue stone.

"Damn it, we've been found," Carter said, pocketing the

lapis lazuli and turning back to the elevators. "We need to move, fast..." Carter was forced to push people out of his way in order to stay ahead of the gang members, and soon fists were being shaken and curses hurled at them.

"You three, stay where you are!" the leader of the group cried out.

Shots were fired into the air, and people ran for cover, screaming and panicked. An elevator car arrived just as they made it through the crowds, and Kendra and Amaya wasted no time emptying it, whether the occupants wanted to alight on the promenade deck or not. More gunfire rang out, but this time the shots weren't fired into the air. Carter spun around and extended his buckler, which punched through the sleeve of his trench coat and deflected the gauss slugs like rain off a windshield. More shots were loosed at them and several people went down, caught in the line of fire. Kendra and Amaya shot back with their plasma pistols, wounding two of the thugs, but dozens more were now forging a path toward them, weapons aimed.

Carter backed into the car with his officers at his side, then an adult woman with a child of no more than twelve were shot and sent tumbling to the deck. Carter cried out and tried to claw himself out of the elevator toward them, but his officers held him back. They were too far away to help, and there were now more than sixty armed gang members bearing down on them.

"Release me!" Carter roared, struggling against the augmented grip of his crewmate's hands. All he could think about was the child and how she was either dead or dying. "Damn it, let me go!"

Rage consumed him and he overpowered his Master Navigator and Master Engineer, whose combined superhuman strength was still not enough to restrain him, but the door had already closed, and the car had begun its descent. Kendra and Amaya stepped back, leaving Carter shaking with fury. He remained that way for several seconds, before turning to his officers, who met his eyes, ready to accept whatever punishment he deemed fit for disobeying his command. Yet the horrible truth was that his officers had acted correctly, in what had been a no-win situation. He couldn't have saved the mother or the child, and if they'd let him go, he'd be lying dead alongside them.

"I'm sorry for my outburst," Carter said, standing tall. "You were right to hold me back."

"If you ask me boss, right and wrong has gotten all fucked up," Kendra replied. His engineer was also furious, but not at him. "The world is going to hell."

"We're already there," Carter grunted.

"So, are we still to use restraint against these assholes?" Amaya added. Like Kendra, she was seething with rage.

Carter thought about the Union crew swinging from the joists. Then he thought about the twelve-year-old girl, bleeding on the deck on the floors above them. He allowed the images to crystalize in perfect clarity so that he would never forget them.

"No…" Carter grunted. "Now, the gloves come off."

SIXTEEN

JAVELIN

KENDRA FINISHED WORKING inside the elevator control system, leaving the fascia panel dangling just off the floor, attached by a bundle of wires. The elevator jolted into motion and began descending the final few decks to level thirty-three – Venture Terminal's computer core.

"That should do it, boss," Kendra said, disconnecting her comp-slate from the circuits and drawing her energy pistols. "Once we arrive, the doors will open automatically, so we should be ready."

Carter grunted an acknowledgment and slid his 57-EX revolver from its holster. He'd refrained from using the powerful firearm up to that point, because there was almost no chance that a regular human would survive a bullet from it, but he was done holding back. If any more gang members got in his way, he'd blow them all to hell, and not give it a second thought.

The elevator jolted to a stop and the door opened with a tuneful ping. The lobby outside was dark and refrigerated air filled the car, causing the silver hairs on the back of his neck to stand to attention. His senses were primed, but not elevated, which suggested there were no immediate dangers lurking ahead of them, but he took nothing for granted. Carter moved out first, weapon held ready, and used his augmented eyesight to peer into all the dark corners, nooks and crannies, but the computer core level appeared to be deserted.

"I'm not picking up any heat or respiration indicators that would suggest there are people on this deck," Kendra reported. While her eyes were down, checking her comp-slate, Amaya Reid was covering her. "The main computer control room is just along that corridor," she added, pointing the way.

"Take point, Kendra," Carter said, waiting for his Master Engineer to move ahead, while he covered the rear. "We need to work fast, before the gangs figure out where we went."

Kendra hustled ahead and before long she was at the door to the control room. Like the elevator, it was locked down, and the Master Engineer wasted no time in hooking up her comp-slate to crack the lock.

"I could sure use RAEB right about now," Kendra said, yanking off the access panel and fixing leads from her comp slate to the circuit board inside. "I hope those guys are okay."

He shared Kendra's concerns for the wellbeing of their gophers, considering the hostile reception they'd received, but he knew that the Galatine was a tough nut to crack.

"It'll take more than a few petty crooks to break down the door of a Longsword-class battleship," Carter replied, reassuring his engineer. He then smiled. "Besides, even if those assholes do get inside, JACAB, RAEB and ADA will give them hell. I almost feel sorry for anyone who tries."

Kendra nodded and he could sense that she felt more at ease. Then a soft chirrup emanated from the door controls and the panel flashed green.

"Got it..." Kendra said, as the door hissed open. The Master Engineer retracted the leads back into her comp slate then moved inside, pistols sweeping the space and covering every gloomy corner of the computer control room. Amaya Reid followed while Carter continued to cover their rear. In the time it had taken Kendra to hack the door, his senses had begun creeping upward, like mercury in a thermometer. It left him feeling unsettled, as if something terrible was about to happen.

"It looks like the on-duty staff bugged out in double-quick time," Kendra said, picking up an office chair that had toppled onto its back.

Carter checked the room, finding comp-slates, half-drunk coffee cups, and an assortment of personal effects that the IT workers had simply left on desks and tables in their hurry to leave. There were more chairs lying on their backs than there were standing upright. He dipped a finger into a pool of liquid that in the dim light of the room he initially thought was spilled coffee, but it was too viscous. Bringing it closer to his nose, he detected the metallic smell of iron, and realized it was blood.

"I don't think the crew went willingly," Carter grunted. He wiped the blood from his fingers onto the fabric back of a chair, then rejoined his Master Engineer and Master Navigator, who were both now huddled around the primary computer core access terminal.

"How difficult will it be for you to hack into the system

without RAEB's help?" Carter asked, standing behind his seated engineer, with his arms folded.

"Not difficult at all," Kendra replied. She held up an access card and flashed her eyes at him. "The supervisor left her ident, which does most of the work for me." The engineer slid the ident card into the terminal and began working on her comp-slate. "I can circumvent the biometrics from here, which means I should be able to gain access in…" There was a bleep from the terminal and the lock-screen was replaced by the main desktop. "… just a few seconds," Kendra added, finishing her sentence.

"Who needs an autonomous engineering bot when you have a super-human tech genius as a member of your crew?" Carter said, resting a hand on Kendra's shoulder.

"Don't let RAEB hear you say that," she replied, playfully.

Kendra accessed Venture Terminal's population database and set to work, searching for Brodie Kaur or any alter ego the Master-at-arms might have gone by while on board. As expected, however, tracking down his old officer was not a straightforward task.

"There's no record of Brodie, so he didn't come here using his real name, which is no surprise," Kendra confirmed. "But I'm using my comp-slate's processing power to run a facial recognition match, cross-referenced against security camera footage from all across the station. If he's here, or was ever here in the last few years, I'll find him."

"How long will that take?" Carter asked, folding his arms again.

Kendra shrugged. "It depends how far back we need to look, but I have a feeling we won't have to search long."

Right on cue, the computer terminal bleeped and Brodie Kaur's face appeared on the screen, taken from archived security camera footage. A series of records followed, detailing all the occasions when his Master-at-arms had been sighted.

"According to this, Brodie was resident on the station for five years, going by the name Walter Kovacs," Kendra said, summarizing the information. "But if these records are accurate, the last time he was seen on-board was two years ago."

Carter scowled and dug into some of the detail. "It says here that he worked as a private security contractor. His clients seemed to be rich folk who were key players in Terra Seven's interplanetary jewel trade."

Kendra nodded. "Venture Terminal has always had a problem with criminal elements praying on the jewel traders, so most of them hire security contractors as bodyguards to keep them safe. Looking at how much work Brodie got, it looks like he was pretty good at his job."

Carter snorted. "I'll bet he was..." The notion of his burly, super-human Master-at-arms cracking skulls and taking names like some sort of secret agent amused him.

"Look there," Amaya said, pointing to an entry in a transit log. "It says that Walter Kovacs took a transport to Terra Prime in August 2432 on the Terra Prime calendar, which ties in with his last recorded sighting. But if that's true, then who transmitted the call for help that brought us here?"

Carter massaged his beard and gave the matter some thought. Ever since arriving at Venture Terminal, he'd felt unbalanced, as if different parts of his mind were pulling in conflicting directions. His senses were rarely wrong, but while the answer eluded him, he knew in his bones that it foreshadowed something dark.

"Maybe Brodie didn't send the message after all," Carter mused, applying Occam's razor to the problem. "But one thing is certain; someone wanted us here for a reason."

"Could it be the 'Demon' that Lieutenant Ozek talked about?" Amaya asked. "Maybe it's not Brodie, but another former Longsword officer who wanted our help?"

"It's possible," Carter grunted. "But if that's true then why hasn't this 'Demon' sought us out?"

Kendra considered all the points that had been made, then opened a new window and accessed the central data feed, which was, in essence, a newswire service employing warp buoys to disseminate news throughout the Union of Nine. She waited for the data to download, skimming the headline items, before proclaiming her findings in true Kendra Castle style.

"Well, fuck..."

"Language..." Carter cautioned.

"In this case, I think you'll allow it," Kendra hit back, highlighting one of the top stories and displaying it front and center on the terminal screen. Carter almost swore himself.

"Terra Four is under attack," Carter said. The feeling that had plagued him was starting to make sense. "Taking a common frame of reference, the Aterniens warped in and landed at almost the exact moment we docked to Venture Terminal."

Kendra's voice adopted a low, ominous tone. "That's no coincidence."

"No, it's not..." Carter agreed. "There are seven-hundred and fifty million people living on Terra Four.

Someone wanted us here to make sure we couldn't intervene."

"Fuck..."

Carter raised an eyebrow at his Master Engineer but assumed she had just cause for sounding off another cuss in his presence.

"Look at this," Kendra said, moving other terminal windows out of the way to highlight a new data source. "I pulled together some security footage from when station ops was overrun by the criminal gangs and look who I found."

The face of Damien Morrow was staring back at them, and Carter almost put his fist through the terminal screen.

"Morrow is Javelin, the 'kingpin' that Lieutenant Ozek told us about," Kendra continued. "He was behind this all along. But seizing a space station and faking a message from Brodie is going to a hell of a lot of trouble, just to keep us distracted."

Carter nodded. If Morrow was involved then there was more planned for Venture Terminal than simply using it as a tool to keep the Galatine out of action. Suddenly, his senses climbed and sharpened, and he realized he was about to find out what this was.

"Everyone, on your guard," Carter warned, drawing his sword and moving into cover.

Kendra deactivated the terminal screen, then she and Amaya slipped away from the computer and drew their weapons too. None of them had energized their blades, so as not to give away their positions, but Carter quickly realized that this precaution had been unnecessary. Whoever had triggered his early warning system already knew where they were, because the person in question benefited from the same augmented sixth-sense as Carter did.

"Nice to see you again, Carter," Damien Morrow called out, from the corridor outside the computer room. "Once again, I regret it is not under more pleasant circumstances."

Carter stepped out to confront the former Master Commander of the Rhongomiant, with Kendra and Amaya by his side. The leader of the Acolytes of Aternus was also not alone. Three others stood with him, and Carter immediately recognized who they were. The first was Rollo Jay, former Master-at-arms of the Longsword Carnwennan, and the second was Fleur Lamber, who had been the Master Operator of the Longsword Pridwen. The final traitor was Shime Akeno, Master Navigator of the Longsword Clarent, and a swordsman of astonishing quality.

"I must admit that I'm a little disappointed in you," Morrow went on, wasting no time in swapping pleasantries for insults. "I knew you were a sentimental old fool, but I didn't expect you to be so gullible." The man laughed, injecting his sneer with disdain and condescension. "There's a war for the survival of the human race raging throughout the known universe, and here you are, trying to rescue one of your old crew. How predictable. How sad."

"It's no less predictable than you showing up again to do the god-king's bidding, like a good servant," Carter hit back. "Is Markus Aternus really so afraid that he'd go to such lengths to keep the Galatine off the battlefield?"

"Aternus fears no-one," Morrow snapped. Carter's come-back had clearly struck a nerve. "But you've been a thorn in the god-king's side for too long, and today that ends."

This time it was Carter who laughed. "And you're the one to stop me?"

"Yes," Morrow growled.

"That's not worked out so well for you up to now, has

it?" Carter shrugged. "Maybe the god-king is losing faith in you."

Morrow stayed silent and Carter turned his attention to the other turncoats in the room.

"I see that you've found some more acolytes to join your merry band." He smiled at Rollo Jay and Fleur Lambert, ensuring he made eye contact with them both. "It's a pity that Marco Ryan lost his head. It would be a shame if the same happened to you two."

"You're welcome to try," grunted Rollo Jay.

Carter wasn't surprised that Jay had been so easily provoked. The man had been a brute, even before he was augmented. He was thick-set and possessed a circus strongman body that Jay had chosen to retain, rather than permit the augmentation process to trim his excess bulk. He liked his overbearing mass, because he liked to be intimidating. In ordinary circumstances, the man's personal failings and lack of moral fiber would have excluded him from the Longsword program, but war forced the Union to make compromises. Few suitable candidate humans had possessed the fortitude to endure the augmentation process, and as such, Jay had made it through selection. He was a loose-cannon that had only been kept in line by his Master Commander; a good man, named Tyler Doyle. Carter had known Commander Doyle well and had mourned his passing. With his commander's guiding influence and steady hand removed, Rollo Jay had spiraled into substance abuse and hedonism. The man loved nothing more than a good fight, and Carter wasn't surprised to see that he'd jumped at the chance to join Morrow's traitorous little band.

Fleur Lambert, on the other hand, was a different matter. She was logical to a fault and could make even Cai Cooper seem eccentric. Brilliant, but distant, she had the melancholy appearance of a guillotine operator about to perform an execution. In contrast to Jay, Carter was surprised to see her by Morrow's side. She had been proud of her role, proud of the Union, and proud to be augmented, but the decommissioning of the Longsword Pridwen at the end of the war broke her and soured her character more so than the others. Carter had thought her to be long-dead.

"What about you, Fleur?" Carter asked the normally level-headed Master Operator. "Are you happy to cross swords with your own brothers and sisters, in defense of this maniacal god-king?"

"At least Markus Aternus sees us as equals, Carter," Fleur answered, coolly. "I would rather stand with someone who values me, than one who treats me as a disposable tool, to be used and abused."

Carter let her answer stand, unchallenged. Fleur would not have sided with Damien Morrow without having given the decision immense thought, and once she had made up her mind, no-one could change it, not even him.

"Shime," Carter said, nodding respectfully to the Clarent's former Master Navigator.

"Master Commander Rose," the man answered, with a similarly respectful bow. "I regret it has come to this. I mean no ill will towards you."

Carter blew out a sigh then glanced at Amaya. Shime and his Master Navigator had shared an intrinsic understanding of one another's abilities. When the Galatine and the Clarent went into battle together, it was like watching a carefully choreographed fight scene from a big-budget holo movie. He had once wondered if the two had shared more than simply an appreciation for flying starships, and the mournful expression on Amaya's face appeared to confirm this. It was like she was seeing a former lover with his new partner for the first time.

Carter turned back to Damien Morrow, who looked supremely confident, and for good reason. Carter was an effective fighter, and together with Kendra and Amaya, they were a formidable team. However, he wasn't arrogant enough to believe that they could take on four Longsword officers, without deadly consequences, especially considering the caliber of their opponents opposite. He also knew that he had no choice but to fight them.

Swords were drawn and the flash and crackle of powered blades burned away the darkness, like a new day dawning. The fighting was about to begin, when another figure moved out of the shadows cast by the energized weapons, and everyone froze in place, the senses of each augmented man and woman in the room picking up on the new danger. Beneath the figure's hood was a mask, illuminated in ghoulish detail by the radiance of the swords, and Carter could also see that the man was wearing Union body armor, customized to his robust frame. The figure then reached behind his back and drew a fire axe that had been hardened with a heavy ceramic coating to make it stronger and heavier.

The Demon of Venture Terminal had arrived, but the problem was, Carter wasn't certain whose side he was on.

SEVENTEEN

FOUR DUELS

THE 'DEMON' approached, watched just as closely by Carter and his crew as he was by Morrow and his turncoat allies. Up until a few minutes ago, he'd felt sure that the Demon was an alter ego of Brodie Kaur, but if the station's records were to be believed, his former Master-at-arms had departed Venture Terminal two years earlier. He realized he could no longer take it for granted that the axe-wielding stranger was on their side.

"And just who the fuck are you supposed to be?" said Damien Morrow, looking at the Demon like he was a lunatic escaped from an asylum.

The Demon didn't answer and simply stood between the two groups, equidistant from them. The man patted his hand with the head of the fire axe, which glinted under the glow from their energized swords and looked sharp.

"You know what, I don't give a shit who you are, or what you think you're doing," Morrow added, venting his frustration at the intruder. The arrival of the Demon had interrupted his plans and caused the former Master Commander to become flustered. "Either stand aside or get cut down with them. Your choice."

The masked figure slowly shook his head then held out the axe in one hand and used it to point to Rollo Jay. It was a challenge, pure and simple. The Master-at-arms of the Carnwennan laughed derisively then looked to Morrow for his ascent.

"Be my guest," Morrow said. "But remember why we're here."

"Don't worry, I'll make light work of this freak," Jay said, squaring off against the demon-masked intruder. "Then I'll deal with the rest of them."

"All except Carter," Damien was quick to add, while looking directly into his eyes. "The Master Commander is mine."

"Whatever you say," Jay grunted. The beast of a man then reached behind his back and drew and energized a Scottish Highland claymore, a mighty weapon with a forty-two-inch-long blade that was traditionally wielded in two hands, though Jay held it comfortably in one. The Demon nodded, returned the axe to a two-handed grip and began sizing up his substantial opponent. The others also paired off, each knowing instinctively who to duel with, based on their weapons and fighting styles. Fleur Lamber favored a historical French officer's epée, a tribute to her ancient heritage on Terra Prime. It was a long, narrow blade that required skill and precision to wield, much like Amaya's rapier, so naturally, the two faced each other. Shime Akeno had drawn a katana, a popular choice with many Longsword officers, and it gave the man a significant reach advantage versus Kendra's tantō short sword. His Master Engineer lacked Akeno's skill with the blade, but Kendra had other talents that made her an even match for the Clarent's former Master Navigator. She was cunning and didn't always fight fair.

That left Damien, a man who also favored a nineteenth-century naval cutlass as his choice of sword, a weapon that Carter knew better than anyone, his opponent included. Their blades crackled and fizzed, his with plasma energy and Morrow's with the Aternien equivalent. Carter's adversary was patient – a trait that he didn't always display – but in this instance, he was in no rush. With their deadly blades and superhuman strength, both of them had the ability to strike a killing blow in the blink of an eye. He didn't expect their fight to last long, which meant that timing was everything.

In contrast to Morrow, patience was not a word that existed in Rollo Jay's vocabulary. The brute of a man raised his energized claymore sword and charged, letting out a war cry that any ancient highland warrior would have been proud of. Surprisingly, Jay's opponent was not intimidated and met the man's advance with the fearlessness expected of his demonic alter ego. Jay swung the claymore and the Demon parried with the shaft of the axe. The sound of the two weapons colliding was deafening and the space around them exploded with flickering embers, like sparks from a grindstone. The two-handed sword should have split the axe in half, but to Jay's evident surprise, it held firm. The Demon then kicked the enormous man in the chest, and Jay flew through the glass wall of the computer ops room with the force of a tsunami.

While Jay and the Demon clashed, Amaya and Fleur saluted each other with their swords and began dueling, their furious dance of parry-and-repost taking their fight away from Carter and toward where Kendra and Akeno were facing each other. He kept his eyes locked onto Morrow, knowing that his peer would seize on any opening, but in his peripheral vision, Carter could see Amaya's and Fleur's thin blades clashing like intersecting forks of lightning.

Kendra and Akeno had approached each other with more caution and had spent the early stages of their contest testing each other's defenses. Akeno then exploded into an attack, moving so swiftly that the man was a blur, and angling diagonal cuts toward Kendra. His Master Engineer was forced to retreat and employ all of her cunning and guile to avoid the deadly strikes. Then Akeno overreached, and Kendra ducked inside his guard, drawing her energized tantō across Akeno's chest and scoring a deep groove through the man's Aternien scale armor. Akeno quickly retreated, pressing a hand to the wound, but the man showed no discomfort. Like all Longsword officers, sensation blockers acted quickly to numb any pain, but even if Akeno had been in agony, the man would not have shown it. Even so, Kendra had let her opponent know that she was dangerous, which would make the turncoat officer more cautious in future attacks.

"It's your fault that it has come to this, Carter," Morrow said, guard raised. "We could have been allies, and friends."

"You're the one who chose to betray your oath, not me," Carter pointed out. "Now shut up and fight."

Morrow darted forward and attacked with a sequence of cuts to the head and body, which Carter parried with ease.

The assault was not intended to defeat him; only to test him and keep him on his toes.

"What's really going on here, Morrow?" Carter said, flexing his shoulders to help loosen them up, ready to defend against his opponent's next attack. "You went to a lot of trouble to lure us to this station; there were countless other ways you could have gotten my attention."

"You're too suspicious, Carter. You always were…"

Morrow lunged then slashed at his legs, before attacking high, and while Carter parried each strike, his opponent was upping his game, and the margin for error was dwindling.

"Come on, Morrow, grant an old man a dying wish," Carter said, trying to stoke Morrow's ego and cause him to let slip a crucial piece of information. "You're going to kill me anyway, so what does it matter if I know what's really going on here?"

"Nothing is going on," Morrow snapped, then he lunged again, but this time Carter countered, catching his opponent off guard and chipping a scale from the shoulder pauldron of the turncoat's Aternien armor. The traitor stepped back and patted his coat to extinguish the fire that the energized blade had ignited.

"Come on, Morrow, give me an ounce of credit," Carter continued, teasing the man with a mocking smile. "Aternus had you take over Venture Terminal for a reason. You can either tell me now, or I'll beat it out of you later."

The switch from defender to aggressor had the desired effect of riling Damien Morrow. The man may have been patient, but he was also arrogant, and resentful of Carter's status at the first and most battle-honored Longsword officer ever commissioned. They were both skilled commanders and fighters, but the difference was that Morrow had something to prove, and Carter did not.

"Where's your attractive young executive officer?" Morrow replied, going back on the attack, this time using psychology instead of a sword. "I heard she was exposed to the Aternien virus. It must be upsetting to know that you got her killed?"

The mention of Carina caused his gut to knot, and in the fraction of a second his mind was distracted by thoughts of his XO, dying on Gliese 832-e, Morrow capitalized. The first swing grazed his shoulder and cut through his armor and flesh, and he parried the second before taking a hard punch to the mouth, which rocked him. Morrow's blade flashed through the air again, and he blocked on pure instinct, saving himself from what would have been a killing blow, but his opponent did not relent. Another cut opened a wound to his side, and he was driven back against the wall. Sensing that his life was in mortal danger, Carter's instincts kicked into overdrive. He saw Damien, teeth clenched and eyes wide with bloodlust, thrust the point of his cutlass toward his heart as if the attack were occurring in slow motion. He pivoted, turning his body sideways, then managed to deflect the path of the blade with the guard of his own weapon, causing it to sink through the wall instead of his own flesh. Morrow's face was now inches from his own, and he retaliated with a headbutt that smashed his opponent's nose and exploded blood into the man's eyes. Morrow staggered back and Carter thumped him across the side of the face, breaking the traitor's augmented jawbone and denting the basket-hilt of his cutlass in the process.

There was now enough distance between the two of them to facilitate the swing of a sword, and Carter was about to strike the killing blow when he saw Shime Akeno wound Kendra and force her to the ground. Akeno drew back his katana, but Kendra's head was turned and her tantō was on the deck. In that split-second, Carter made a choice, and threw his cutlass at Shime like a hunting axe. Incredibly, Akeno perceived the attack and adjusted his stance so that he was able to avoid the whirling blade as it soared past his head, but the distraction had been enough to allow Kendra to regain her senses. Seizing the handle of her tantō, she punched the blade through Akeno's scale armor and into the man's heart, before collapsing again from her wounds. Akeno looked at the short sword impaled through his flesh, regarding it with a mix of curiosity and disbelief. He pulled the weapon out, the blade streaked with blood, then looked around the room, as if searching for someone. He caught Amaya's gaze, mouthed the words, "I'm sorry…" then collapsed on top of Kendra, dead.

There was a flash of light and Carter was hit in the chest by a blast of Aternien energy. Damien Morrow had recovered, but the man was no longer fighting hand-to-hand, and instead wielded an Aternien particle pistol. Carter used his buckler to protect his head as several more blasts hammered into his body, forcing him to his knees, but Morrow had him dead to rights, and they both knew it.

"No! Stop!"

Amaya rushed to her commander's side and used her own buckler and body to block another torrent of blasts, but even with their battle uniforms and superhuman resilience, there was only so much punishment that either of them could take, and his Master Navigator went down, knocking her head in the process. He looked to Kendra, but she still hadn't moved, then scoured the room for the Demon, but their mysterious ally was nowhere to be seen, nor was Jay. He was on his own. With his cutlass gone, Carter tried to draw his 57-EX revolver, but Morrow blasted his hand, causing his fingers to curl inward like the wizened digits of a necromancer, making it impossible to hold the weapon. With wounds pockmarking his body and the smell of burned flesh invading his nostrils, Carter dragged himself against the wall, and waited for Morrow to kill him.

"I'm sorry it had to end this way," Morrow said as Fleur Lambert hobbled to his side, nursing the many slash and puncture wounds that Amaya had inflicted upon her, before his Master Navigator had run to his aid. "I wish it could have been different."

"You're not sorry, Morrow," Carter grunted, "and I wouldn't care if you were. You'll get no forgiveness from me."

Morrow appeared genuinely saddened by this, but Carter could see from the look in the man's eyes that it would not stop him from doing what had to come next.

"Goodbye, Carter," Morrow said, aiming the Aternien pistol at his head.

Carter climbed to his feet, clawing himself up the wall with one good hand, and looked his enemy dead in the eye, without fear. If he was going to die, he'd do it the way he'd lived – with honor and integrity. Then a flash of energy rippled through the air and the pistol was shot out of Morrow's hand. The traitor raised his arms to protect his head as more blasts hammered into the man and knocked him down. Fleur Lamber drew her pistol and looked for the attacker, before a blast caught her directly between the eyes, and burned a grape-sized hole into her brain, killing her instantly.

Carter searched for the gunman, then he saw a slender, shadowy figure wearing a long, black cloak move briefly into view. At first, Carter thought it was the Demon, but the height and build didn't match. He shuffled closer to get a better look and this time he was able to make out the face of the stranger. Instead of a demon mask, Carter saw the radiant golden luster of the Overseer's perfect Aternien skin.

EIGHTEEN

BENEATH THE MASKS

ROLLO JAY CHARGED and swung his claymore at the disguised Overseer, but the Aternien blocked the sword with her war spear, before spinning a kick into the man's substantial gut and driving him several steps back. Jay shook off the hit then raised his sword again, ready to resume his assault, before the turncoat Master-at-arms saw the face of the Overseer beneath the hood and froze.

"What the fuck?" Jay said, checking his attack and lowering the weapon. "Why are you here?"

In that moment of hesitation, the Demon sprang from the shadows and smashed his fire axe into the turncoat's back. The edge had already been blunted, so the weapon acted more like a warhammer, crushing the traitor's scale armor and forcing Jay to retreat to where an injured Damien Morrow was unsteadily climbing to his feet. Carter also battled his injuries and helped Amaya to stand. In the confusion that had followed the Demon's attack on Jay, the Overseer had slipped into the darkness, without explaining her unthinkable actions.

"Fall back..." Morrow hissed, sheathing his cutlass and retreating.

"We can still take them," Jay snarled through blood-stained, bared teeth.

Morrow shook his head. "They'll wait. They're not going anywhere."

With that, Morrow and Jay turned and ran. Carter fumbled for his 57-EX with his left hand, and fired into the darkness, but his injuries had made him slow on the draw, and the shots flew wide. Cursing, he was about to reload when the sight of his Master Engineer, face down on the deck, stole his entire focus, and his compulsion to give chase evaporated like steam.

"They're getting away!" Amaya called out, hobbling after Morrow, but Carter held her back.

"Let them go, Amaya," he said, eyes still fixed on his wounded engineer. "We're in no shape for a fight and Kendra needs our help."

Amaya nodded then arm in arm they went to the stricken engineer and dropped down by her side. The Demon stood over them, blunted axe in hand, but Carter sensed no danger, despite the threatening visage of the masked man. The reason was obvious to him, even before the Demon had discarded his ghoulish disguise.

"Let me help you," Brodie Kaur said.

The Master-at-arms knelt beside them then gently lifted Kendra off the deck and cradled her in his arms. At the same time, Carter removed a nano-stim from his engineer's belt and searched for the critical wound that had put his friend and colleague out of commission. Shime Akeno had stabbed her through her left side, puncturing her liver and slicing her diaphragm. It was a savage injury, but Carter could still hear

Kendra's heart beating inside her punctured chest, and he had to believe there was still a chance to save her.

Using his fingers to pull open the wound, which had only partially healed, Carter injected a one-hundred per cent dose of nano-machines directly to where they were needed most. A full dose nano-stim was a desperate last resort, and they all knew it, but his engineer was barely clinging on to life by a thread. Brodie held firm then Kendra screamed loudly enough to shatter glass, and her body contorted with unimaginable agony as the nano-machines rapidly re-built her muscles and organ tissues, along with their connecting nerves and blood vessels. Carter himself had never experienced a full-dose stim, but even at the eighty-percent mark, which had been his maximum, it had felt like he was dying, and he would have gladly welcomed the end if only to forgo the pain. Carter, Amaya and Brodie all continued to hold their fellow officer until, at last, her spasms subsided, and her writhing hisses diminished to mere whimpers and moans. It hurt them all to see her that way, and if they could have shared her pain to ease her suffering, they would have.

"It's good to see you again, Brodie," Carter said, once Kendra had fallen still in the man's muscular arms. "But I have to ask why the hell you didn't show yourself sooner?"

"I thought the demon mask would give me an advantage," Brodie replied, gently smoothing Kendra's hair out of her eyes. "I figured that if Morrow and those other guys didn't know who I was, they'd underestimate me." He shrugged. "It worked on that horse's ass, Rollo Jay. I almost took him out with that first kick, and if it wasn't for this piece of crap axe, I would have split him like a log."

Brodie tossed the fire axe across the room, and it clanged

and skidded across the metal deck plates with a shrill clamor, like collapsing scaffolding.

"I don't mean just now," Carter replied. He'd already figured out that his Master-at-arms had kept on the mask for his fight with Jay for precisely the reason he'd explained. "I meant why didn't you come over the moment you saw us on the promenade, right after we docked?"

Brodie frowned. "I don't know what you mean, MC. I didn't even know you were here until one of the Union officers hiding out from the gangs told me about you. She doesn't know who I am, since I figured it was best if the 'Demon of Venture Terminal' had a certain mystery about him, you know?"

Carter grunted a laugh. "You were always one for unnecessary theatrics."

"If it wasn't Brodie in the habitat then it must have been the Overseer," Amaya chipped in. She then smiled at the Master-at-arms and waved. "By the way... hey, Brodie!"

"Hey yourself," Brodie replied with a smile and a nod. Then his face fell as he noticed her wounds. "You look like you could use a stim too, though. Hell, you both do."

"I hate those things, but you're right," Amaya admitted.

Carter pulled a silver capsule off his belt, using his left hand, since his right still looked like a burned-out tree stump. He popped off the cap, set the dose to fifty-percent, and handed it to Amaya. She rolled her eyes and sucked in a deep breath before pressing the stim to her neck. While his Master Navigator was baring down against the pain, he took a second capsule for himself and also dialed it to fifty percent.

"I think you need a little more than fifty, MC," Brodie

said. He didn't need a comp-slate to assess battlefield injuries. "Seventy-one should do it."

Carter grumbled under his breath but set the dial to the number Brodie had suggested then pressed the stim into his burned hand. Pain flooded his body, so intense that even his sensation blockers could do nothing to abate it. The feeling of his damaged flesh being rapidly rebuilt was like a thousand scorpions crawling all over his body and repeatedly stinging him. He clenched his teeth, closed his eyes and bore down, knowing that he could do nothing but wait, and ride out the storm.

"Sleeping on the job, boss?"

Carter opened his eyes and found himself flat on his back, staring up at the ceiling. Aside from a throbbing headache, the pain of his injuries was gone, and he sat up to see Kendra looking at him. She was still reclined against Brodie's slab-like torso, though the Master-at-arms was no longer holding her tightly. Kendra's ordeal, at least, was over.

"I hate sleeping, but on this occasion, I'd kill for a couple of hours in my bunk," Carter replied, figuring that he must have passed out. "How are you feeling, Kendra?"

She shrugged. "I feel like I got stabbed with a Samurai sword, but otherwise, I'm hunky dory." She then hooked a thumb at Brodie. "Though I must admit, I figured I was dead when I woke up and saw this chump staring down at me."

Brodie laughed, causing Kendra to bob up and down against his barrel chest.

"I missed you too, you grumpy-ass wrench wench," Brodie hit back.

"To be honest, I was hoping we'd never find you," Kendra went on, pushing herself to her knees. "Now I have two people to babysit whose specialty is breaking things and not tidying up after themselves. It was bad enough just having Carter around, but both of you together are a liability."

"I haven't broken that much," Carter complained.

"Really?" Kendra said, eyebrow raised. "I can run down the list, starting with the combat shuttle you crashed, or should I leave that part to the end?"

Carter scowled at Kendra. It seemed clear from her cheeky retorts that his Master Engineer was no longer at death's door.

"You wrecked the combat shuttle?" Brodie cut in, looking disgusted to hear this news.

"It wasn't wrecked, just a little banged up." Kendra snorted, and he scowled at her again, before turning back to Brodie. "Anyway, I think we have more important matters to discuss, starting with everything you know about what's happening at Venture Terminal."

"There's a lot to tell, MC, but I can fill you in on the way," Brodie said, getting to his feet.

"On the way to where?"

"I know where the surviving Union crew is holed up," Brodie answered, offering Kendra his hand, which she accepted. "It's a safe space, and it's not too far. Besides, there's someone there you need to meet."

Brodie helped Kendra up then offered to help Amaya, but she waved him off.

"I'm okay, Brodes," the Master Navigator said, hauling herself upright. "It'll take more than a few pistol blasts to stop me."

Carter got to his feet too, using his repaired hand for leverage. It was no longer wizened and useless, but the new skin was bright red, making it look like he'd just pulled his hand out of a vat of boiling water. He checked his other wounds, which continued to rapidly heal as he watched, though his battle uniform lagged behind, making it look tired and moth-eaten.

Brodie was about to lead them away, when he saw Shime Akeno's Aternien Katana on the ground. He picked it up and gave the weapon a few test swings. It looked like a short-sword in his plate-sized hands.

"This fancy shit ain't really my style, but it'll do until I can prize that Claymore from Jay's cold, dead hands," Brodie said, sliding the katana into his back scabbard. "I always hated that asshole. He was never anything more than a thug and a bully in a uniform."

"I won't argue with that," Carter grunted. His senses suddenly climbed, but only by a fraction, then he heard the muted scuff of footsteps somewhere in the darkness, out of sight. "But you're right that this place isn't safe," he added, figuring that the Overseer was still close by. It vexed him that the Aternien had helped them, then disappeared again without so much as a word to explain her involvement.

"I'm sorry I didn't seek you guys out sooner, but after this place went to hell, I felt I could do some good here, you know?" Brodie said, leading the way to the Union hideout, and setting a brisk pace.

"Is that when you became the 'Demon of Venture Terminal'?" Amaya asked, waggling her fingers at him in a spooky manner.

"Truth be told, I kinda dig it!" Brodie said, flashing Amaya the roguish smile that his Master-at-arms was famous for. However, it persisted for only a moment before he became more solemn. "But I soon learned that the gangs are far from the biggest problem on this station." Brodie stopped and faced him. "There's a reason the goldies didn't destroy Venture Terminal, MC. They plan to use it as a weapon."

Carter frowned at his Master-at-arms. "You're going to have to explain that, Brodie."

He was more than willing to accept that the Aterniens were capable of devising inventive methods of killing people but using an entire space station as a weapon felt like a stretch.

"I will, but not here," the officer replied, resuming his brisk pace. "Actually, it's not me who will do the explaining, but the friend I told you about. This science crap was always Cai's area of expertise. How come he's not with you, anyways?"

"That's a long story, for another time," Carter grunted.

While he didn't regret helping Cai Cooper to escape Terra Six, he still wished his Master Operator was with them. For a start, his presence would have more than evened the odds in the fight against Morrow and his traitor companions, but he had a nagging feeling that he would soon need Cai's skillset too. Carter's thoughts were interrupted by another jump in his already elevated senses. It felt like a cold breeze whipping through an open window, and he scouted their rear, but there were no obvious signs they were being followed. To double check, he accessed his comp-slate and ran a scan, which also came up clear, but he still refused to believe it. He could feel a presence and knew in his bones that they were being followed, even if his eyes, ears and scanners denied it.

Their progress continued to be swift, aided by the fact that their remaining aches and pains were quickly healing.

Brodie led them through the maintenance spaces in the voids of the station to stay off the beaten track, navigating the maze of corridors and crawlspaces like he'd lived in them his whole life. Before long, the Master-at-arms had brought them back out into the open, two levels above the computer core, on deck thirty-one. Carter surveyed the space; it appeared to be an industrial kitchen and its associated stores, which provided for the station's crew. Like much of the lower levels, it was now deserted, at least of kitchen staff. However, there were people inside, and as Carter progressed further, each and every one of them got to their feet and stood to attention.

"At ease," Carter grunted. In many ways, he appreciated their show of respect, which was warranted because of his rank, but the situation hardly called for strict protocol to be adhered to, and under the circumstances, it felt wrong.

"An officer on the promenade level has been helping to gather up surviving Union crew and get them to safety," Brodie said, nodding and smiling at the people in the room, none of whom appeared to recognize him without the mask. "There were about fifty at the last count, and I help by making sure they get down without interference from the gangs." He paused then corrected himself. "Well, the Demon helps, I should say. I was planning to stage a little insurrection, once we'd gathered enough people, and re-take ops. Then you arrived."

Carter nodded then grabbed Brodie's shoulder, squeezing it firmly, like a father who was suddenly fiercely proud of his child.

"You're a good man, Brodie," Carter said, pulling the officer closer, but stopping short of embracing him. "You didn't abandon these people. You were true to your oath, and true to who you are."

"You taught me good, MC," Brodie said, blushing a little. "I only did what you'd have done in my place."

"I hate to break up this little bromance, but the folk in here look freaked out," Kendra cut in.

Carter turned his attention to the faces of the officers and crew in the room and realized that his Master Engineer was right. He was about to make an announcement, to explain their presence and reveal who his Master-at-arms actually was, when an older man pushed through the mass of bodies and approached.

"It's okay, everyone, this is my very good friend," the man said, taking Brodie's hand and shaking it vigorously, as a clear sign to the others he was an ally. "As the uniformed commander here said, he is a good man. His name is Brodie, though you know him better as the 'Demon of Venture Terminal', and I owe him my life."

The crowd relaxed, appeased by the older gentleman's interjection, then Brodie took them aside and found a table in the corner of the room for them all to sit at.

"Master Commander Rose, this is Doc' Frank Rauscher; he's a scientist," Brodie said, gesturing to the older gentleman. "He's also the guy who can explain what these golden fuckers are planning to do, pardon my language."

Kendra laughed and Carter rolled his eyes, but he wouldn't start reprimanding his Master-at-arms for his use of foul language until he was back in uniform. Instead, he shot Dr. Rauscher an expectant look. In his navy-blue Nehru suit, with disheveled greying hair and blue-tinted, round-rimmed spectacles, he looked more like an aging pop-star than a scientist, which didn't exactly inspire confidence.

"Okay, Doctor, let's have it," Carter said, prompting the scientist to answer.

Doctor Rauscher leaned in closer and had the look of a man who was about to reveal a dirty secret.

"Here's the thing, Master Commander. The Aterniens plan to warp this entire space station into Terra Prime's atmosphere, then blow it up..."

NINETEEN

A NEW MISSION

CARTER ROCKED BACK in his seat, hands planted palms down on the table as he tried to take in what the scientist had just said, but despite his augmented auditory system, he still questioned whether he'd heard the man correctly.

"Hold on a second, Doctor Rauscher, can you just rewind a little and tell me that again?" Carter asked, figuring the only way to be sure was to have the scientist repeat what he'd said.

"I know it sounds fantastical, but I assure you it's the truth," Dr. Rauscher said. "The Aterniens plan to warp this entire space station from the orbit of Terra Seven directly into the atmosphere of Terra Prime, and then blow it up for a very specific reason."

Carter huffed a laugh and shook his head. "You're right, Doctor, that does sound fantastical. In fact, it sounds unbelievable."

"I thought that too at first, MC, but hear him out," Brodie said. He turned to the scientist. "Hey, Doc, why don't you start at the beginning, and tell the commander why you're on Venture Terminal in the first place?"

Doctor Rauscher nodded then spent the next few minutes detailing a potted history of his career and academic qualifications. It turned out that the man was a highly respected planetary engineer, who specialized in terraforming, and modifying atmospheric conditions. Rauscher had been sent to Terra Seven at the behest of the Union of Nine, in order to study the changes to the planet's atmosphere caused by heavy industrialization and recommend ways to counteract any negative impacts. He was one of the few people in the Union who was permitted to advance science in his chosen field, though still within the strict limits and guidelines of the technophobic post-war Union society.

"My experiments require a significant amount of heavy equipment, including satellites, atmospheric probes and such like, which I have to store in Venture Terminal's warehouse spaces," Rauscher continued. "These storage areas take up the entirety of decks thirty-four to thirty-seven."

Carter nodded. "Those decks and anything below them were sealed off after the gangs took control of the station."

"Precisely, and for good reason!" Rauscher replied, his eyes flashing beneath his tinted, round-framed glasses. "You'll understand once I tell you what's being stored down below."

The man appeared to be enjoying himself, and Carter imagined that he was used to entertaining a lecture-theatre full of adoring students and researchers. He, on the other hand, could think of few things more tedious than academic study, and while Rauscher was having fun, Carter was getting increasingly frustrated with his ebullient manner.

"I don't wish to rush you, Doctor," Carter lied, "but this station is crawling with criminals and Aternien sympathizers, and we don't have a lot of time."

"Quite right, quite right," Dr. Rauscher said, nodding and holding up his hands in an apologetic manner. "I shall race to the point."

"You were about to explain what's being stored in the warehouse spaces," Carter said, prompting the man to get going again.

"Yes, exactly…" Rauscher agreed.

The man then appeared to lose his train of thought and began to polish the lenses of his spectacles while he collected his thoughts. Carter let out a sigh and began drumming his fingers on the table, though this immediately recalled memories of his XO, whose finger- and foot-tapping would often drive him to distraction. He stopped and tried to put the thoughts of Carina Larsen out of his mind.

"Did you catch what I just said, Commander?" Rauscher asked.

Carter realized that he hadn't. "Sorry, doctor, I was elsewhere for a moment. Please go on."

"I was simply explaining that I was down in the warehouses one afternoon, shortly before this bad business began, checking on my equipment, when a bulk quantity of chemicals was being unloaded from the cargo conveyor," Rauscher explained. "The conveyor ferries items from the docking garage at the base of the station, where the smaller freighter craft come and go."

"And there was something about these chemicals that

you thought was unusual?" Carter said, hoping to keep the scientist's mind – and his own – on track.

"Precisely, so!" Rauscher said, snapping his fingers. "Naturally, I was intrigued so went over to enquire if another scientific team was soon to arrive at Venture Terminal but was instructed in a rather crude and unsavory manner to mind my own business."

Carter sighed again and began stroking his beard. "I assume that you didn't do that?"

"No, I didn't," Rauscher said. The man shivered as if someone had just walked over his grave. "The shipments continued, and curiosity got the better of me. I snooped around for the next few days, until I was caught." Rauscher pressed his hands together in a temple and rested his chin on the tips of his fingers. The tint of his glasses failed to conceal the worry in his eyes. "Quite honestly, Commander, if it hadn't been for Brodie, I would have been murdered."

The scientist became distant as the memories of his near miss overcame him. Carter chose to give him a moment and turned to Brodie to continue the story.

"I'd been hearing about people going missing in the lower decks for a few days, and work was slower, so I decided to check it out," Brodie said. "This was before the gangs took over, like the doc said, so I wasn't in my Demon phase yet, but what I saw certainly pushed me toward it."

Brodie reached over and grabbed Dr. Rauscher's shoulder, offering him some reassurance, which the scientist appeared to badly need at that moment. Carter realized that his effusiveness had been a front; the man was simply hiding behind his smile and tinted glasses.

"I walked into one of the warehouses and saw some assholes beating on the doc," his Master-at-arms continued, still holding Rauscher's shoulder. The scientist had placed his hand on top of Brodie's. "They'd strung up a rope and looked like they were about to hang him." Brodie took a deep breath and let it out slowly, before continuing. "I put a stop to that."

"He saved my life that day, Commander Rose, but he also did more than that," the scientist said, borrowing some of Brodie's considerable strength. "He listened to my concerns about the shipments that had been coming in and did some digging."

Brodie shrugged. "I roughed some folk up," he admitted. "But in the process of beating on those guys, you'll never guess what I found out."

Carter smiled. "You learned that some of the people on the station were actually Aterniens who looked and acted human?"

Brodie recoiled. "Yeah. How the hell do you know that?"

"We've run into a few ourselves," Carter answered, ruefully. "There's a lot we need to brief you on, Brodie, but first tell me about these shipments of chemicals."

"That's just it, it wasn't only chemicals," Brodie said. "Once I really started to dig, I found all sorts of gear being shipped to the station, all through organizations that were linked to the Aternien spies."

"The most curious of these shipments were soliton warp drive components," Dr. Rauscher added. "And not just one; there was enough apparatus for four complete drives, each powerful enough on their own to jump a mid-to-large sized freighter."

"I looked into that too," Brodie added, tag-teaming effectively with the scientist. "It turns out that all of deck thirty-eight, which also contains the station's reactor and power services, was cleared out, to make way for a major project. Work had been going on day and night, for a week running up to the takeover of the station."

Carter assimilated the information, still stroking his silver beard, which helped him to think. He then circled back to the very first thing that Dr. Rauscher had said.

"You told me that the Aterniens plan to use Venture Terminal as a weapon," Carter said. "A station this size crashing to the surface of Terra Prime would be devastating, but not world-ending, so I'm assuming there's more to this than simply using Venture as a bomb?"

Brodie rocked back and held up his hands. "This is where I bow out, MC. I have no earthly idea what the doc was talking about, but I figured Cai might."

Kendra folded her arms tightly across her chest and scowled at the Master-at-arms. "And what am I, Brodie, just some grease monkey?"

"*Wrench wench…*" Brodie corrected her, with a smile. "But, sure, you can probably figure it out too."

"Thanks for the vote of confidence…"

Carter raised his hand to silence his Master Engineer and turned back to Dr. Rauscher, who took the hint and offered his theory.

"It's called Stratospheric Aerosol Injection," the scientist said. Already, the conversation had gone over his head, but Kendra seemed to be following. "The compound that was shipped to the station in bulk is an engineered aerosol comprised of highly reflective particles. If injected into Terra Prime's atmosphere in high-enough volumes and at the correct altitude, the effect would be devastating."

"How devastating, doctor?" Carter asked, keen that the scientist didn't drift off the point again.

"With the quantity of compound on this station, it would block the sun's rays almost entirely," Rauscher continued. "The particles would sit in the stratosphere indefinitely with no rain to wash them away. Within days, Terra Prime would be shrouded in a permanent darkness; an artificial nuclear winter from which there is no escape. The planet will freeze. Everything on it will die."

"So, Venture Terminal is the delivery mechanism?" Carter said, glancing at Kendra, who appeared to be buying into the theory.

"The quantity of compound required to produce a catastrophic cooling effect is too great for freighters to be effective delivery mechanisms," Rauscher added. "The station has enough capacity for all they need, and more."

"The goldies knew that they'd never get their biogenic weapon onto Terra Prime," Brodie cut in. "Even with their ships, the planet is simply too heavily protected, in space and on the ground. But the bastards had always planned for this."

Carter turned to his Master Engineer for her opinion. Despite Brodie teasing her about her capabilities, the truth was that what Kendra Castle didn't know about engineering wasn't worth knowing.

"Four soliton drives of the size the doc mentioned could open a fold large enough to transport the station," Kendra said, running calculations on her comp-slate at the same time. "The challenge has always been how to synchronize multiple independent warp fields. Each drive has a unique signature, based on its spin and core composition. Even warp drives of the same model have subtly different signatures, because no two drives are ever exactly the same."

Carter nodded. "The Union explored the idea of a 'twin

warp' drive for the Longsword class, but it just ended up creating two minutely different, overlapping folds in space, and tearing the test ships apart at a sub-atomic level."

"That's right, but just because the Union couldn't figure it out at the time, it doesn't mean it's not achievable," Kendra added.

"What about this idea of Stratospheric Aerosol Injection?" Carter asked.

"With enough of the right compound, it's possible to create the dramatic cooling effect that Doctor Rauscher described," Kendra replied, before shrugging. "The aerosol containers would need to survive the detonation of the station, and have a way to disperse the compound, but we already know the Aterniens are pretty adept at flooding planetary atmospheres with drones."

Carter nodded and grunted an acknowledgement. Then he had a thought, which would seem to cast doubt on the theory. "Why not just use the station to deploy the virus instead?"

"That was my first thought too, boss, but in every case so far, the Aterniens have needed to deploy the virus very carefully, and in a controlled manner," Kendra answered. "Dive-bombing a space station from seventy-kliks up is nether careful nor controlled. My guess is that the virus wouldn't survive."

Carter grunted again then allowed his mind to race. He still foresaw dozens of problems with Doctor Rauscher's theory, but they didn't have enough data to explore them, and everything the scientist had said fit the facts at hand.

"When Terra Seven was attacked, my instruments and atmospheric probes witnessed the utter devastation the Aternien virus caused," Rauscher said, breaking what had been a full minute of silence. "So, believe me when I say, Master Commander Rose, that the effect of this attack on Terra Prime will be even more catastrophic. The planet will become a lifeless, frozen rock, and will remain that way for millennia."

"That sounds like exactly the sort of thing Markus Aternus would do," Amaya said. She had been patiently listening up until that point, but while, like himself, she wasn't a scientist, she was astute and deeply insightful. "The god-king wants to utterly destroy the world that cast him out, then found a new empire; one with New Aternus at its core."

Commander Rose stood up, and his officers rose with him. "Then our mission is to destroy the soliton warp drives on deck thirty-eight. Without those drives, the Aternien plan fails."

Suddenly, there were raised voices from across the far side of the room, and Doctor Rauscher hurried over to learn the source of the commotion. When the man returned, pushing through the anxious crowd that had gathered, his tousled hair was even wilder, and his glasses were knocked at an angle.

"People are coming!" Rauscher said. His voice was quivering with barely restrained panic, and Carter could hear the man's fragile heart racing. "The lookout says it's an armed gang. Dozens of them…"

Carter rested his hand on the pommel of his sword and absorbed the flood of chemicals that were rushing through his body, preparing him – once again – to fight. "Brodie, take Doctor Rauscher and the others and get them to safety," he said, while drawing his cutlass. "We'll handle the gang."

TWENTY

A MAN POSSESSED

BRODIE BEGAN GATHERING up the surviving Union crew and, with Dr. Rauscher's help, ushered them toward the rear of the industrial kitchen, where they could escape into the void spaces between decks. Then the Master-at-arms drew the Katana that he'd taken from Shime Akeno and looked ready to face down the gangs with his former crew, but Carter had other ideas.

"This isn't your fight, Brodie, not yet," Carter said. "Get these people to safety on the levels above, then come and find us. You know where we'll be."

Brodie hesitated because in his heart, he was still one of them, and that meant standing and fighting by his commander's side.

"Fulfill your duty to these survivors, Brodie," Carter said, firmly. "Then, if you still want to fight, it would be my honor to have you rejoin the crew."

"You got it, MC," Brodie said, accepting Carter's suggestions as if they had been orders. In Brodie's mind, the two were one and the same. "And you'll see me again, don't worry."

The two clasped arms in a spartan handshake then went in separate directions. This wasn't without some regret on his part. Carter could have certainly used Brodie's fighting capabilities against the horde of gang members he expected were amassing outside, but to abandon the Union survivors now would be a crime.

Suddenly, the door connecting the kitchen to the main staff dining hall beyond it exploded inward then cartwheeled across the floor and smashed through a worktable. Cries of panic rose up from the people inside, but Carter, Amaya and Kendra held firm as Rollo Jay stomped inside, energy pistol in one hand, and claymore in the other. He locked eyes with Carter but appeared to be looking for someone else.

"Where's that demon-masked freak?" Jay roared, as gang members scuttled in, and took cover behind food-prep stations and cooking areas in the cavernous kitchen. "We have unfinished business."

"I'm afraid the demon is busy," Carter called back, sliding his 57-EX out of its holster. "So you'll just have to make do with us."

Jay smiled then darted into cover as Carter opened fire at the man, but like all augmented Longsword officers, the turncoat Master-at-arms had amped-up senses and agility that made him too slippery even for a bullet to catch. Carter and the others also spread out and intensified their assault, picking off the eager and foolish front rank of gang members, who had stormed inside with no clue who they were going up against. Carter reloaded then took care to line up his shots for maximum effect. The armor-piercing bullets from his overpowered revolver had enough energy to punch through entire bodies, and still kill anyone unfortunate enough to be standing behind his target. It meant that even with just five rounds at his disposal, he could still take down ten thugs, or even more. At the same time, Amaya and Kendra lit up the room with plasma blasts, wrecking the enemy cover and sending gang members fleeing for their lives, but through the smashed-open double doors, Carter could see dozens more waiting in the mess hall. Amongst them was Damien Morrow.

"Charge them!" Jay roared, grabbing one of the gang members by the scruff of his neck and throwing him forward, directly into a plasma blast from Amaya's pistol. "Get in there and push them back!"

The gang members were hesitant and several more tried to flee, but Jay blasted them in the backs of their heads before they'd even reached the door. "Fight them, or fight me!" the man roared, shoving another man forward, who was mowed down an instant later.

It was a slaughter, but Jay knew what he was doing. The gang members meant nothing to him, or to Damien Morrow. They were just fodder to throw at them until by sheer force of attrition, Carter would be compelled to fall back, fighting hand-to-hand. Then Jay and the fanatical Acolytes of Aternus, who he expected were waiting in the wings outside, would move in and press the attack. However, Carter didn't have to hold them off indefinitely; only long enough for Brodie to get the survivors to safety.

"Keep firing," Carter called out to Amaya and Kendra, while he ducked down behind an eight-burner hob and reloaded his revolver. "We need to give Brodie a couple more minutes."

"We need an exit plan too, boss," Kendra answered, at the same time as hammering blasts at the enemy with her dual plasma-pistols. "Do we go back the way we came?"

"No, they'll be watching the computer core level," Carter said, shooting a gang member through the neck and also head-shotting another who'd charged up behind him with the same bullet. "We need another way down. Take care of it…"

Kendra nodded then moved out to execute his order, while he and Amaya provided covering fire. He saw his Master Engineer take a cluster of hits on the way, causing her to momentarily lose her footing, but her battle-uniform repelled the projectiles, sparing her from serious injury.

"They're getting close," Amaya said, blasting a gang thug who'd made it to within a few meters of her, knife in hand.

Carter glanced to where Brodie was ushering the survivors through a forced-open maintenance door. A little more than half of the Union crew were through, but he still needed to buy them more time.

"We need to hold the gang back for another sixty seconds, maybe more," Carter said to his Master Navigator, at the same time as ducking deeper into cover with bullets ravaging the kitchen station he was huddled behind.

"You got it, skipper…"

Amaya ignited her rapier and Carter's face was bathed in the plasma glow from the energized blade. Then she danced out of cover and started cutting down the gang members like weeds, flowing from one to another with the natural grace of water traveling down a stream. Her thin blade pierced hearts, arteries, and organs like a hypodermic needle, and soon a pile of bodies had been left in her wake.

Carter was also eager to get into close action, and he ignited his cutlass and moved out to support her, not that it appeared she needed any help. He was under no illusion that his attacks were in any way elegant, but they were no less effective, and in some ways even more so. Pirate captains of the ancient high-seas used fear as a weapon to intimidate their victims. And while Carter had not set the ends of his beard alight, he imagined that, with burning cutlass in hand and silver hair flowing like mercury, he appeared no less terrifying than Blackbeard himself.

After the fifth gang thug had been brutally hacked down by his sword, the others turned and ran. For a second, he considered giving chase, before his senses spiked and he caught the flash of an energized blade in his peripheral vision. Carter raised his cutlass barely in time to block Rollo Jay's savage two-handed swing, but the sheer weight of the strike unbalanced him. Capitalizing on his advantage, Jay kicked him in the chest, then whirled the huge claymore at him for a second time. Carter parried but the impact knocked him clean off his feet, and before he could move, Jay was standing over him, sword held high like an executioner's blade.

Energy blasts thudded into the brute's chest armor and Jay reacted instantly, guarding his head and quick-drawing his pistol to return fire. Amaya was hit twice and Carter saw her fall, but his Master Navigator had given him the precious few seconds he needed to recover. Carter executed a kip up, an acrobatic maneuver that a man his size should not have been able to perform. Certainly, his sudden jump to his feet took Jay by surprise, giving him the initiative. Their blades clashed and Carter pushed the traitor back, though despite catching the man off-guard, he still couldn't get past Jay's defense.

With their swords pressed together, Carter pinned Jay against the wall and hammered a kidney strike that shattered the man's Aternien armor. Jay responded with a headbutt that felt like a head-on collision with a dumpster truck, then pushed him back and punched him solidly across the jaw. With the iron taste of blood in his mouth, Carter retaliated with a seismic right cross, but it was like punching a block of lead. He landed another blow that would have crushed a human skull, but still Jay would not go down. Incensed, the man bellowed a roar of incoherent rage and muscled him back. Carter fought to hold his ground, but trying to stop Jay was like trying to stop a runaway freight train. His feet skidded across the blood-soaked floor tiles then he was thrown against the door of an industrial freezer unit, the impact pressing the air from his lungs.

Instinct took over, and he ducked just before the claymore fizzed over his head, slicing through the heavy metal door like it was flimsy plastic. Frustration burned in his opponent's eyes, which made him careless, and Jay tried to impale Carter to the door with a thrust through the gut. Carter deflected the attack at the pivotal moment and countered with a brutal slash across the traitor's midsection, defeating the man's scale armor and splitting open his gut. Jay rocked back, guard raised with one hand, while the other held his split-open flesh together. Carter was about to strike the killing blow, when Damien Morrow, alerted to Jay's imminent death by his own superhuman senses, charged inside and opened fire, forcing Carter to block with his buckler and descend into cover.

Cursing, Carter watched Rollo Jay stagger into the safety of the mess hall, while at the same time pressing a nano-stim capsule into his wound. If it had been any other Longsword officer, Carter would have still expected the injury to be fatal, but Rollo Jay was an enigma, even amongst post-humans. He had undergone the most extensive augmentation process out of them all, leaning on Nathan Clynes's predilection for taking risks and pushing boundaries to enhance his body to what had been considered an unsafe level. This not only explained Jay's incredible abilities, but also his amped-up anger and thirst for violence.

"I'm getting tired of this, Carter!" Morrow's voice boomed across the room, but gone was his smooth, measured delivery, replaced by anger and exasperation.

"Then come out, and we can end it, right now," Carter called back.

The gunfire had stopped and Carter could see Morrow just outside the kitchen area, back pressed up against the frame of the door. He looked for Amaya and saw her huddled behind a pot-washing station. She was clutching an energy burn to her shoulder, but she gave him a thumbs up to indicate she was okay.

"When will you get it into your stubborn head that you can't win this?" Morrow added. "Even if you stop us here, Aternus has a dozen other ways to take out Terra Prime. It's only a matter of time."

The man was peeking around the corner, looking for an angle to get a shot, but Carter had already shifted position to keep Morrow guessing.

"You have too much faith in your god-king, traitor," Carter hit back.

The sound of his voice alerted Morrow to his location and the man fired three shots, none of which ever had a chance of hitting him. His former comrade was just keeping him on his toes. What Morrow didn't know was that every second they sparred with words and traded useless shots, the Union survivors were getting away. He quickly checked on Brodie again, and less than a dozen fleeing crew remained.

"You're also hemorrhaging co-conspirators," Carter added, taunting the man in the hope he would force an error of judgement. "First Marco, then Shime and Fleur, and now your personal guard dog has a gash in his belly the size of my forearm." He laughed, to rub salt in the proverbial wound. "You're losing friends fast. Soon, you'll have no-one to hide behind."

"I don't need to hide from you!" Morrow roared. "I'm better than you, Carter, and smarter too."

Carter smiled; he'd hooked his fish. "Then throw down the pistol and face me sword to sword, you gutless coward. We can end it here."

Though a gap in his cover, he watched the expression on Morrow's face twist and contort like he was being tortured. The animalistic human being in him was telling him to charge out and face down his enemy, alpha to alpha, while the rational part of his augmented brain was screaming at him to stay where he was and listen to reason.

"Before this is over, I'll stand over your broken body, Carter, then we'll both know who is the better man!" Morrow yelled. Carter sighed; on this occasion, reason had overcome rage. "But that day is not today."

Carter's senses were already operating at their peak, but he felt them suddenly shift, like the impression of weightlessness that comes from driving over a hump-back bridge. He switched positions again, and shots flew after him, missing by inches, but it was worth the risk in order to get a clear view through the door that Damien Morrow was so fiercely guarding. Carter saw dozens of people mobilizing outside, some armed with gauss pistols, but most with crude tools, such as wrenches and hammers. They were all dressed in worker's overalls, but this wasn't the only difference compared to the gang thugs that Rollo Jay had thrown at them earlier. Their movements were organized and confident, but crucially there was no fear in their eyes. Everyone feared death, even Carter Rose, but there was one species that had learned how to deny the reaper its prize. He hurriedly ran a scan on his comp-slate to confirm his theory, and he hissed a curse into the air as the result came back positive. Every single one of the thirty-eight workers outside was an Aternien infiltrator, and even with Kendra and Amaya at his side, he couldn't hope to defeat that many.

"Kendra, we need that exit, right now," Carter said, speaking to his Master Engineer through the comm system in their uniforms.

Amaya frowned at him and he transmitted his scan reading to her comp-slate. She checked the message and her eyes grew wide.

"I'm almost there, but if they see us leave, it won't take them long to find us again," Kendra replied.

"Then I'll create a distraction."

Carter scoured the walls and the racks of equipment before spotting what he needed. He signaled to Amaya to fall back, and his Master Navigator complied without question, darting away so swiftly that even Damien had no hope of getting a shot off at her. He readied his 57-EX, then sprang up and aimed it at his enemy.

"I thought you wanted a duel?" Morrow said, snapping his head out of the line of sight.

"I'll settle for you dead, however it comes," Carter hit back.

Morrow laughed. "I know you've seen what's waiting for you out here. You can't think I'll be stupid enough to face you now, especially with a gun in your hand?"

Carter aimed the revolver off to the side. "Who said I was trying to shoot you?"

He fired his 57-EX and the armor-piercing bullet ruptured a cooling conduit that ran up the wall next to the door that Morrow was hiding behind. A blast of superheated coolant exploded toward the door and vaporized into a dense cloud that quickly filled the room. Carter turned and ran, and energy blasts cut through the cloud after him. He was hit twice in the back but sensation blockers dulled the pain, and he returned fire, shooting his remaining four rounds in a fraction of a second. There was a distant chime of bullets striking Aternien armor, followed by a gasp, as air was pressed from Morrow's lungs. Then the shots flying at him stopped.

Kendra had opened an access hatch in the floor, and Amaya had already dropped through it. Across the other side of the space, he saw Brodie, ushering the last of the Union survivors through the maintenance door. Rauscher had stayed with the Master-at-arms to help others first and was last in line to leave. Then Jay charged through the cloud of gas, the cut to his belly healed, but still red-raw, and opened fire with an energy pistol. The scientist was hit in the back of the head and killed instantly. Brodie cried out and was about to charge at Jay when the Aternien infiltrators began piling inside, and the Master-at-arms was shot and forced to withdraw. The very last thing that Carter saw before he closed and bolted the hatch behind him, was Jay standing over the dead body of Dr. Rauscher, chest heaving and eyes wild like a man possessed.

TWENTY-ONE

PERILS OF THE VOID

CARTER and the others waited beneath the closed and locked maintenance hatch they'd escaped through, weapons in hand, waiting to see if Morrow and the Aterniens figured out where they went. Five long minutes passed as their enemy scoured the kitchen area, trying any and all doors and running scans looking for them, but Kendra's skill at disrupting electronic probes kept them hidden from view. Twice, someone above tried to force open the hatch, but Carter clung to the grab bars, bracing his body against the walls of the crawlspace to ensure it remained sealed, and eventually the Aterniens gave up and left.

Carter released the now misshapen hatch handles and flexed his fingers to pump some life back into them. In the time they'd been holed up in the crawlspace, his wounds had mostly healed and his uniform was looking less moth-eaten. The wound to Amaya's shoulder was also repairing swiftly, but of them all, it was Kendra who looked the worst for wear, despite not participating in the fight. Her near-fatal stabbing by Shime Akeno, combined with the aftereffects of a full nano-stim dose, had taken a heavy toll on her, and it would be some time before she was back to her old self.

"I think it's fair to say that I'm too old for this shit," Kendra said, while shuffling along the crawlspace at the head of the group.

"You're never too old to crawl through the rat-infested, stinking innards of a space station," Carter replied, trying to lighten the mood. "Where's your sense of adventure?"

Kendra snorted. "I think I left it on the floor of the computer core level, along with some of my vital organs and a few pints of blood."

"Then find us a way out of this tunnel that doesn't land us in front of murderous gangs or Aternien sympathizers, and we can all take a well-earned break to figure out our next move."

Kendra stopped and pointed to a duct cover to her left. "Your wish is my command, boss," she said, before punching the cover off its mounting. The mesh metal sheet banged and clattered on the floor of whatever room lay beyond.

"That's hardly what I'd call discreet, Kendra," Carter said, with admonishing eyes.

"It's okay, boss, I already scanned ahead," Kendra said, gingerly lowering herself through the opening. "We're still on deck thirty-two, which is station services. The plan I downloaded from the core says this room is currently unused."

Kendra jumped down and Carter heard her feet thud into the deck almost exactly a second later, suggesting the room she'd found had tall ceilings. Amaya went next then Carter followed, dropping into a disused storage area. It was dark, dusty and smelled dank, like a drain.

"Lovely place," Amaya said, dusting off her hands. "Couldn't you have found us a disused champagne bar instead?"

"I'll bear that in mind the next time we're forced into a ventilation system, running for our lives," Kendra replied, smirking.

"Right now, I'd settle for a way to reach deck thirty-eight, without running into Morrow or his thick-skulled Master-at-arms," Carter said. He was idly examining an unopened packet of potato chips that he'd found in a box. They were seven years out of date, so he tossed them back onto the shelf, disappointed.

Kendra brushed dust and grime off her jacket sleeve then pulled it back and projected a holo image of Venture Terminal from her comp-slate. As the primary source of light in the room, the holo-schematic cast eerie shadows on the walls, making the disused space seem like part of a long-abandoned outpost. "The quickest way to reach the reactor core on deck thirty-eight is to find a way to the upper cargo facilities on deck thirty-four," Kendra began. "There's a cargo elevator that runs from thirty-four, all the way down to the docking garages."

"Morrow will be watching the elevators, so we can't risk using them," Carter replied. He noticed that Amaya had requisitioned the out-of-date potato chips and was munching through the contents as they spoke. "Is there another route down?"

"There is an emergency stairwell, but that's a long slog," Kendra replied, zooming the map in on the newly-highlighted route.

"It's still a safer option." Carter stole a chip from Amaya Reid and she slapped his hand as he drew it out of the bag.

"How do we get to deck thirty-four, without going through the computer core level? Morrow will be watching all the entrances and exits there too."

He threw the chip into his mouth, and it tasted like week-old socks. Gurning in disgust, he looked at the bag in Amaya's hands and saw that the flavor was supposed to be roast chicken. His Master Navigator seemed not to mind, however.

"I'd say if we wanted to reach thirty-four without anyone seeing us, we should move through the void," Kendra added. She was also now eyeing up the packet of chips. "As luck would have it, this storeroom can lead us into the structural void on the west side of Venture Terminal. It won't be an easy climb without any equipment, but it's doable."

Carter nodded, while picking bits of rank-tasting potato chip out of his mouth. "Which side of the room borders the void?"

"That wall," Kendra said, stealing a chip while Amaya looked the other way. "If we punch a hole in the corner, it should take us directly into the structural void between the inner bulkhead and the outer shell."

Carter headed toward the corner of the room that Kendra had indicated and shoved the shelving racks out of the way to get a clear path to the wall. The skeletons of what looked like a dozen rats, or similar rodents, lay piled up next to an old bait box. He imagined that some had died from the poison, while the others had probably died from eating the sock-flavored potato chips that his officers were enjoying.

"Maybe we can find something in here that can prize off that wall panel?" Amaya suggested, now willingly sharing the chips with Kendra.

Carter considered his navigator's suggestion then

charged at the wall and hammered the sole of his boot into it instead. The panel crumpled like aluminum foil, and he was able to tear the rest of it away with his hands.

"Or you could just do that," Amaya added, sarcastically.

Carter ripped out the cavity insulation then stripped any wires and conduits that were in his way to reach the inner bulkhead. He banged on the slab of metal with his knuckle and it sounded considerably more substantial than the wall panel had been.

"If you're quite done stuffing your faces, I need your help to break down this bulkhead," Carter said, climbing out of the cavity. "Set your plasma pistols to maximum and see if you can burn out the bolts in these locations," he added, pointing to the areas in question.

Amaya and Kendra both nodded, largely because their mouths were too full of seven-year-old chips to answer verbally, drew their weapons and took up positions in front of the bulkhead. The sounds of the blasts were amplified by the enclosed space, and Carter waited anxiously for the firing to stop, while regularly checking his comp-slate for any signs of approaching Aterniens. However, by the time his officers had holstered their pistols again, there was still no indication they'd been discovered.

"It should go down now with the help of your size twelves," Kendra said, stepping back.

Carter took a short run at the bulkhead and drove his heel into the center of the panel, flattening it with one solid kick. Icy air rushed inside and sent a chill racing down his spine.

"There will be some residual heat from the station, but it's still colder than a penguin's asshole out there," Kendra said, studying readings from her comp-slate.

"I wasn't aware that 'penguin's asshole' was a standard unit of measurement…" Carter grunted.

"It's about minus fifty…" Kendra corrected herself, while also rolling her eyes at him. "At that temperature, a normie human would get frostbite in around ten minutes, but we can manage a couple of hours, at least. I'd still suggest we go in with head-coverings and gloves activated."

"Agreed," Carter said, double-tapping the center of each wrist to trigger his battle-uniform to expand over his hands and create a skin-tight covering. "I nominate you as expedition leader. Get us to deck thirty-four, ideally via a route that doesn't require me to kick-in any more parts of the station."

"You got it boss," Kendra replied.

The Master Engineer activated her gloves and head covering and entered the void first, followed by Amaya. Carter then stepped through, picked up the bulkhead that he'd flattened, and wedged it back into place to seal the hole. The rupture would have already registered in station operations, but he hoped that by plugging the hole again, the gang members in ops would be too lazy to check up on it, assuming they'd even noticed the alert at all.

Two decks didn't sound like a long way to Carter, until he saw the scale of the challenge ahead of them. Without climbing apparatus, it was like scaling the framework of a skyscraper, requiring them to shimmy down sheer beams and leap between cross-braces to progress. This was hampered by the fact that their target was not directly below where they'd entered the void, but two hundred meters further around the gently curving circumference of Venture Terminal. An hour into their descent and they were finally in sight of their goal, but as he caught up with

Kendra and Amaya, his senses told him something was wrong. Both had slipped behind a group of conduits and were taking care to shield themselves from view. He approached cautiously and dropped down by their side, without making a sound.

"What's the delay?" Carter said, speaking through the comm link in their head coverings.

"We've got a work crew ahead of us," Kendra said, without taking her eyes off an area of the void diagonally down and across from them. She shifted across to the side and motioned for Carter to move up. "Take a look."

Carter shuffled to where his Master Engineer had been and spotted the workers. They were all wearing the same crew overalls as the Aternien infiltrators who had stormed the kitchen. That alone pegged the workers as likely Aterniens, but the fact that none of them were wearing any form of protective gear, despite the icy temperature and low oxygen level, sealed the deal.

"Can you figure out what they're doing?" Carter asked.

"I think I already have." Kendra showed him a scan of the area where the imposter crew was working. "They're fitting cross-braces to the framework of the station and feeding them into deck thirty-eight. My guess is that they're to stabilize the quartet of soliton warp drives, so as to minimize field anomalies from excess vibrations."

Carter understood soliton drive technology enough to know that vibrations were the enemy of warp jumps. Since the core of the system was a rotating field generator, soliton drives had to be damped and isolated as much as possible to prevent mechanical tremors from impacting field formation.

"Morrow must have replaced damned near the entire engineering crew with imposters," Carter said, cursing

Markus Aternus for successfully executing another Machiavellian ploy.

"If that's true then what happened to all the people the imposters replaced?" Amaya asked.

Carter shook his head but noticed that Kendra had sucked in her cheeks and was looking at her feet. He knew when his Master Engineer was hiding something.

"What do you know, Kendra?" he asked.

Kendra sighed then sucked in air through her pursed lips so it sounded like a rueful whistle and pointed up. Carter and Amaya both looked and saw a least a hundred bodies tied to the framework with metal rope, like flies that had been captured and cocooned by a hungry spider.

"Right…" Carter said, wishing he hadn't asked.

"It looks like they're almost done, though," Kendra added, switching back to the subject of the Aternien workers. "There are only three crews still in the void."

Kendra pointed out the trio of work groups on her comp-slate and Carter peeked out of cover to eyeball them. They were all currently too far away to effectively take down with weapons fire, but he figured they could maneuver into a position to ambush two out of the three. The final group, which was working on a scaffold, obscured from above by cooling ducts, would need an alternative approach.

"Amaya, make your way to this position, and Kendra, you go here," Carter said, highlighting the two locations on Kendra's comp-slate. "I'll climb down to the scaffold and take out the six imposters working there. Wait for my signal to start shooting, so we take them all down at the same time. I don't want to give any of those goldies a chance to radio for help."

"I take it that your signal is various body parts hitting the deck, right?" Kendra replied, with a mischievous smile.

He huffed a laugh. "Well, it worked last time, didn't it?"

Carter left his engineer and navigator to advance to their respective sniper positions and began his descent. His plan was to position himself beneath the scaffold, using the platform to obscure his approach, then climb across and ambush the Aterniens at close range with his sword. Then, at the same time, Amaya and Kendra would rain down plasma on the other two groups, taking them by surprise and eliminating the threat before they could react. It was a sound plan, if for one unforeseen problem, which was that reaching the scaffold was turning out to be a lot harder than he'd expected.

His first challenge came immediately after completing his descent, by shimmying down a main structural beam. To move in line with the scaffold, he needed to traverse a forty-meter gap and ten-meter elevation, which was punctuated by conduit tubing at two-meter intervals. It was like a giant set of monkey bars, designed by the universe's most sadistic fitness instructor. The first fifteen meters didn't feel too bad, while the second felt like each of his arms was being wrenched out of its socket by a tractor. The final ten meters was excruciating, even accounting for his pain blockers, but his own tenacity, coupled with the fact his augments would simply not allow him to let go, pushed him the final distance.

Fingers throbbing and muscles burning, Carter took a moment to recover and checked on Kendra and Amaya. Both were already almost in position, and he cursed, regretting giving himself the toughest assignment. Turning back to the scaffold, which was now obscuring him from view, as planned, he took some comfort from knowing the hardest part was over. Not that a six-meter horizontal leap to a platform two-meters above him was particularly easy, but compared to what he'd just done, it was a veritable walk in the park.

Carter locked his eyes on his target and exhaled, like a gymnast preparing for a gold-medal winning vault. He ran across the beam, subconsciously drawing upon his augmented sense of balance and amped-up agility to stay perfectly stable. Kicking off, he soared though the icy air and landed on the platform with a loud clang. The sound rang out through the void like a dinner gong, and Carter felt his senses sharpen. Pushing himself up, he quickly flattened his back against an upright and waited. Footsteps approached on the scaffold above his head, and he heard voices muttering in the darkness, but they were speaking the language of the Aterniens, a dialect almost as indecipherable as their hieroglyphic written language. He could see two imposters directly above him. One was running a scan on the Aternien-equivalent of a comp-slate, while the other anxiously scoured the void space, looking for anything out of the ordinary. Carter tried to spot Kendra and Amaya, but both were out of sight, likely alerted to the danger by their own sixth-senses.

Finally, the imposter put away his scanning device and the Aterniens began to move off. In the process, dust dropped though the grating and fell onto Carter's face, sticking to his beard hairs and getting sucked up into his nose. He stifled a cough and rubbed his face, trying to stop himself from sneezing, but it was too late. The imposters had heard him and were hurrying back in his direction. Senses now on full alert, Carter anticipated their actions and got into position beneath the edge of the upper scaffold, just as an imposter workman ducked his head over the side and looked straight at him. He reached up, grabbed a thick tuft of the Aternien's fake hair, and pulled the imposter over the edge. The man screamed, not out of terror, since the Aternien's death was only temporary, but to alert his comrades, who were now charging toward him.

The fizz and flash of plasma fire from Kendra and Amaya echoed through the void as Carter swung his body onto the scaffold platform, where he was immediately kicked in the head by the second of the two imposters that had originally come looking. The man was of slight build by human standards, but because of his Aternien skeleton and synthetic muscles, he hit like a sumo wrestler. Another kick to the face bust his lip, but more importantly, it also pissed him off, and he charged the imposter, tackling him so hard that the impact bounced the man clear off the scaffold. Four remained and were coming at him with hammers and heavy wrenches in their hands. Carter drew and energized his cutlass, dispatching the first imposter with a brutal cut. The second tried to block with a sledgehammer, but his plasma-edged blade sliced through the metal shaft before continuing through the man's neck, sending his head tumbling into the bottomless darkness below. By this point, Carter's augmented blood was pumping so hard through his veins that a dozen imposters would have fallen at his feet, and he stormed forward chopping the third of four in half diagonally across the chest, before crushing the final imposter's face with a titanic straight right. The Aternien staggered back, unable to see through broken eyes, before tripping and falling over the edge and into the void.

"Boss, I'm clear up here," Kendra said over the comm channel.

"Me too, skipper. All my goldies are toast," Amaya added.

"I'm done here too," Carter said, disengaging his sword and sliding it back into its sheath.

"We'll make our way to the exit point, and see you there," Kendra added.

Carter grunted an acknowledgment, while kicking the severed lower half of an Aternien over the edge of the scaffold. He then noticed a control column in the center of the platform, and realized that the scaffold could be raised, lowered, and maneuvered laterally through the void.

"Kendra, Amaya, wait…" he called out, testing the controls, which still functioned. "Stay where you are. I've found us a ride…"

TWENTY-TWO

"KNUCKLES"

CARTER COLLECTED Amaya and Kendra with the scaffold, which maneuvered using grav-repellers in a similar manner to a 'cherry picker', except without the need for a boom and jib. The device also spared them having to continue their precarious climb and allowed them to reach the lower cargo area on deck thirty-seven, which was as far as they could go. The reactor level was shielded by thick bulkheads above and below the power services deck, which meant the only way forward was to exit back into the station and go down on foot.

"How's it coming, Kendra?" Carter asked.

His Master Engineer was busy hacking the lock on a maintenance hatch, but in a way that also didn't trigger any alarms, either on deck thirty-seven or in the operations center.

"Just a few more seconds..." Kendra replied, tongue protruding slightly from the corner of her mouth as she concentrated.

Carter nodded and rubbed his arms, which were starting

to get cold, despite the thermal protection his battle uniform conferred. Kendra's description of the void space as being colder than a penguin's asshole was accurate. The door then unlocked and Kendra turned the wheel and slowly pulled it open. To the relief of everyone concerned, no alarms sounded. Kendra moved inside first, plasma pistols held ready, then he followed Amaya through and closed the door behind him. Tapping the appropriate parts of his uniform, he retracted his head covering and gloves, then smoothed his hands through his silver hair, which felt like it had been plastered to his head with cellophane. He imagined that if Major Larsen was there with them, she'd have made some wisecrack remark, along the lines of, "Don't worry, you still look good… for an old man" and realized that he missed her sardonic humor.

The other thing Carter realized, now that he could taste something other than recycled air, was the room they'd entered smelled of blood and sweat. His senses had picked up on something else, and given how quiet Kendra and Amaya had become, he knew they sensed it too. Kendra had already moved behind a block of storage containers that had been stacked up close to the door in order to scout ahead. Then she quickly ducked back into cover and signaled that there were enemies ahead. Carter waited for her to also signal the number then muttered a curse under his breath. *Twenty…*

Carter inched closer and picked up muted grunts of pain, punctuated by the organic thwack of metal striking flesh. He also heard chair legs grinding against deck plates, and further away, there was the scuff of idle boots, and the acrid odor of cigarette smoke. Taken together it painted a picture in his mind, so that he knew exactly what to expect, even before he saw the scene with his own eyes. What he didn't expect was to discover that it was Lieutenant Nadia Ozek who was taking the beating while bound to the chair, watched by twenty armed gang members.

Nadia was the Union officer who had helped them after they'd first arrived on Venture Terminal, and whom Brodie had later revealed to be a key part of the rescue and resistance effort. She had been stripped down to her underwear and bound to a simple folding chair in the middle of the warehouse space. A heavy-set thug, wearing a blood-soaked white vest, was meticulously laying into her using brass knuckles, striking her head and body with enough force to cause pain and suffering, but not enough to knock Nadia out. Even so, the officer's face was bruised and swollen, to the point where her right eye was closed completely, while blood oozed from cuts to her arms and legs. It was clear that she'd been tortured for some time, which in Carter's mind suggested that she'd refused to give her captors what they wanted.

"Damn it, she's here because of us," Carter grunted to the others, who were also stealthily watching the gang thugs go to town on Nadia.

"We have to help her," Amaya said, hand wrapped around the grip of her rapier. "But if we storm out there, weapons raised, Nadia will get caught in the crossfire."

Carter let his mind race but given the distance between him and the white-vested torturer, he couldn't see a way to rush the gang members and avoid the lieutenant becoming collateral damage. Then the thug punched Nadia again and her head lolled to the side, her body limp. The vest-wearing goon slapped her a couple of times without a response, then gestured to one of the others in the room. The second thug removed a syringe from a box he'd been holding, injected its contents into Nadia's neck, then stood back. A few seconds later, the Union officer jolted awake and sucked in a terrified gulp of air, like she'd just emerged from a dangerously deep dive.

"That's twice now I've had to revive you," the vest-wearing thug said, gripping Nadia's jaw in his rough hand and forcing the woman to meet his eyes. "I won't bring you back a third time." The man leaned in closer, so that his lips were almost touching the woman's ear. "Just tell me where the Union survivors are hiding, and I'll let you go. Simple as that…"

Lieutenant Ozek mumbled a response, but it was little more than an incoherent slur. The thug sighed, then moved his head closer to the officer's mouth and tapped his ear.

"You'll have to speak up, sweetheart. I'm a little deaf…"

The comment elicited a ripple of laugher and jeers from the other gang members, who appeared to be enjoying the morbid spectacle like it was a public execution in Victorian Britain. The vest-wearing goon accepted their tribute then quietened down the gang members so that he might actually be able to hear Nadia's response. A few seconds later, the officer struggled to mumble two words, "Fuck… you…", and the torturer's face went red with rage. The thug stepped back and raised his fist to strike Nadia again, but Carter had seen enough. He marched around the side of the storage containers, and into plain sight, his hands held high above his head.

"Guv!" one of the goons shouted, and all the weapons in the room were suddenly turned against him.

"I'm here to talk," Carter said, eager to avoid testing how

many bullets his battle uniform was capable of repelling. "I'm the one your boss is looking for."

"Hold up, mister," the torturer said, stepping away from Nadia and pulling a gauss pistol from his waistband. Carter didn't stop walking, and the thug fired a warning shot that he heard whistle past his right ear. "I said stop fucking walking!"

Carter stopped, but he was still ten meters from the man, and he needed to get closer.

"Having a conversation would be easier if you let me get a little nearer, so we don't have to shout," Carter said, remaining calm. "It would also help if I knew your name."

"I'm not interested in a conversation, jackass, and you don't need to know my name," the thug hit back. "Now, drop your weapons on the deck, like a good boy."

"Fine, if you won't tell me your name then I'll just call you 'knuckles'," Carter said, alluding to the man's chosen weapons.

"Call me knuckles and I'll smash every last tooth out of your smarmy mouth," the man snapped. "Now put your fucking weapons on the ground!"

Carter carefully removed his 57-EX revolver and placed it on the floor, followed by his plasma cutlass, still in its sheath.

"What the fuck is that? A sword?" The thug laughed, and the others in the room joined in on cue. "Do you think you're King Arthur or something?" he added, generating even louder guffaws from his mob of lackies.

"I'm Master Commander Carter Rose of the Union Longsword Galatine, so it would be more accurate to say that I'm Arthur's nephew, Sir Gawain," Carter said.

The thug shrank back and stared at Carter like he'd lost

his mind. "Is that supposed to be a joke?" He looked at his entourage. "What do you reckon, lads? Sir Gawain, here, thinks he's a comedian!"

The lackies laughed, though with less gusto on this occasion, which seemed to sour the torturer's mood, as if Carter's pithy heckle had caused him to lose his audience.

"It's me that Javelin wants, so let Lieutenant Ozek go," Carter said, referring to Damien Morrow by his assumed moniker. He was trying hard not to let the thug rile him. He needed to remain composed, at least until Nadia was out of danger.

"You're not the one calling the shots here, Sir Gawain," knuckles replied, jabbing his pistol at him like the point of a finger. "And you're in no position to make demands."

"Just let her go," Carter repeated. "She's no use to you now that I'm here."

The man snorted and shook his head. "Tell me what to do again, and I'll shoot you in the leg," he said, pointing the gauss pistol at his right thigh. "Go on, do it. I dare you…"

Carter sucked in a deep breath and chanced another couple of paces forward, hands still raised.

"I'm trying to be reasonable…" Carter began, then the crack of the gauss pistol cut him off, and he stumbled as the slug thudded into his leg. He held up a hand, hoping to stop Amaya and Kendra from jumping to his rescue, and the silence from behind him suggested they'd taken the hint.

"I told you to stay where you are," the thug growled. "You're not very good at following instructions, are you?"

This drew another ripple of laughter from the other gang members, which seemed to please knuckles. Carter, however, was less than amused. He gripped his thigh with both hands and saw that the slug had not only punched through his battle uniform but his flesh too. Sensation blockers had numbed the pain, and Carter could see the silver-colored slug protruding from his skin like a thorn. He plucked it out but kept it in his hand, and the wound immediately began to heal. Even so, he hated getting shot, and he especially hated getting shot by loud-mouthed sociopathic bullies.

"Now, are you going be a good little boy, like I asked, or do I need to shoot you again?" knuckles said, becoming more malicious as his confidence grew. "You see, my boss doesn't care if I deliver you hurt, only that I deliver you alive."

Carter straightened to his full height, which was several inches taller than the brawny torturer, then tossed the warped bullet at the man. Knuckles caught it one-handed, and Carter enjoyed the look of sheer befuddlement that contorted the man's blood-splattered face.

"You can't hurt me," Carter said, with measured menace. "But unless you let Lieutenant Ozek go, right now, you'll find out just how much pain I can inflict on you and your men."

"What the fuck are you?" knuckles spat, tossing the bullet like it was red hot and pointing the pistol at Carter's head.

"I'm your payday, so why don't we cut the crap?" Carter replied, "Let her go, and I'll come with you, willingly."

The thug was alternating his gaze from the crumpled bullet on the floor to the now invisible wound on Carter's leg. It was dizzying to watch, but it also told him that knuckles had been rattled.

"Fine, whatever," the man said. He nodded to one of his associates then aggressively hooked a thumb toward Nadia.

"She was fucking useless, anyway, and didn't tell me a damned thing."

Carter watched the gang member free Lieutenant Ozek, feeling a sense of pride in the Union officer for withstanding her torture without giving up her colleagues. The plastic ties holding her hands and feet to the chair were cut with a switchblade, and Nadia toppled sideways onto the floor, barely able to cushion her fall with her blood-starved hands. Carter tried to go to her aid but found the torturer's pistol shoved into his face again. He stepped back and clenched his teeth, fighting the urge to take the weapon and force-feed it down the man's throat.

"Let me help her," Carter said, and the thug raised an expectant eyebrow. He sighed heavily then added, "please…" even though it physically hurt him to do so.

"Well, since you asked so nicely…" knuckles said, grinning at him and stepping aside.

Carter knelt in front of Nadia Ozek and she turned away, fearing that he was the torturer, returned to inflict more punishment, but the sound of his voice, somehow familiar in the back of her mind, encouraged her to look into his eyes.

"It's going to be okay, Lieutenant," Carter said, speaking the words with such conviction that no-one could doubt his sincerity. "Come with me, and I'll get you to safety."

Nadia nodded and tried to mouth a reply, but all that emerged from her split and swollen lips was a dribble of blood-stained saliva. Carter helped her to stand then guided her toward the rear of the warehouse, to where Amaya and Kendra would be able to take care of her.

"Just head behind those crates," Carter whispered, not wanting knuckles or his pack of fools to overhear. "My friends are waiting."

Nadia nodded again then managed to hobble away without his support. Carter was glad of this, because he had unfinished business with the gang of thugs. Suddenly, knuckles snapped his fingers, and the sound reverberated around the warehouse like a whip-crack.

"Shit, I just remembered something," the thug said. Carter felt his senses sharpen. "The boss gave me orders to kill any Union scum we find…"

Knuckles raised his gauss pistol and fired at Nadia, but Carter deflected the slug with his buckler before it could hit its target. The whirlwind pace of his movements stunned the gang's leader, and Carter quickly pulled Nadia into cover.

"Stay down," he told the woman, then he grabbed one of the barrel-sized storage containers and hurled it at the gang, scattering them like pigeons. "Amaya, Kendra, now!"

Carter ran at the leader then collected and unsheathed his sword in a single fluid motion. Knuckles barked commands at his gang and fired haphazardly in his direction, but the man's fate had already been sealed. Carter jumped and spun in mid-air, severing the man's thick neck and cutting his head clean off. Blood gushed like a geyser and this time the torturer's entourage didn't burst into fits of laughter, but instead screamed and yelled in terror and shock. Knuckles' head thudded into the deck like a lump of rotten meat, then Amaya and Kendra stormed out of cover and lit up the room with plasma fire.

A flick of a switch sent energy coursing along the blade of his cutlass, and Carter employed his inhuman speed and pent-up anger to decimate the gang in a hurricane of energized cuts and slashes. Nine lay dead within seconds, some with plasma burns pockmarking their heads and bodies, and others lying in pieces dismembered by his sword. Soon the remaining thugs were fleeing, but Carter had given the gang ample opportunity to save their skins, and they had spat it back in his face. They had thrown in their lot with the enemy and would receive no clemency. Five more were quickly put down by Amaya and Kendra, and Carter charged after the rest. His blade flashed with invisible speed and the last three gang members were cut down before they knew what hit them. Unlike knuckles, Carter did not torture the men or leave them writhing in misery, despite natural justice dictating that they deserved nothing less. His kills were quick and clean, and the fight was over in seconds.

"We're clear, boss," Kendra announced, while scanning the area with her comp-slate. "I'm not picking up any more life signs within a fifty-meter radius, though I wouldn't bet my Vinci XL100 car on there being no more of these scumbags somewhere on this level."

Carter nodded, disengaged his blade then returned to Nadia, who was sitting up on the deck. Amaya removed her long cloak and wrapped it around her semi-naked body, and she flinched at her touch, but then mumbled the words, "thank you..."

"Kendra, see if you can find a med kit in here," Carter said. He considered giving Nadia a very low dose nano-stim, but in her condition, there was a strong chance it would kill her.

Kendra scouted the room then returned with an emergency medical pack. She cracked it open and began tending to the worst of Nadia's wounds, stemming any bleeding and injecting her with medicines that would help with the swelling and pain. As his Master Engineer was treating the Union officer, Carter noticed cigarette burns on her body. A swell of rage built inside him, and even though it was unbecoming of a Union officer to think in such a way, he sorely wished he'd hadn't given the torturer such a quick death.

"Thank you, Commander," Nadia said, finally able to speak in more than garbled murmurs.

"Don't thank me, Lieutenant, it was helping us that got you into this mess," Carter grunted.

Nadia shook her head. "No, don't put that on yourself. You didn't do this." She looked toward the mass of bodies and spat in their direction. "They did..."

"It's mostly cuts, bruises, some minor burns, a dozen or so compound fractures, and a concussion, of course," Kendra said, assessing Nadia's condition on her comp-slate. "The swelling actually helped to cushion you from some of those blows, so while your face looks like a giant marshmallow, it actually saved your life."

Nadia managed a strained laugh. "I look that bad, huh?"

Kendra realized her gaff but styled it out in her usual manner. "Don't worry, I've seen worse. You should see how Commander Rose looks first thing in the morning..."

Carter scowled at his engineer, but since she was trying to comfort Nadia, he went along with it.

"I'm more interested in how you know what he looks like first thing in the morning..." Nadia answered, somehow managing to crack a joke, despite being beaten half to death.

"We're a very tight-knit crew," Kendra answered, a twinkle in her eye.

Carter laughed, taking the jibes in good humor, but as much as he wanted to do more for Nadia, they had other pressing matters. "Now you're feeling stronger, I'm afraid we have to leave," he explained to the officer.

"Leave to go where?" Nadia asked, more curious than afraid.

"The Aterniens plan to use Venture Terminal as a weapon, and we need to stop them," he replied, condensing the elaborate details of the plan down to the bare essentials. "That means we have to get to deck thirty-eight. We can guide you to an elevator, and Kendra can hack the controls to take you to a safe deck, but I'm afraid we can't escort you."

"Don't worry about me, I have people who can help," Nadia said, bracing herself on Carter and Kendra and climbing to her feet. "But if the station is in danger, I want to do something. Tell me how I can help."

Carter couldn't believe what he was hearing, and in that moment, he wished that the lieutenant was strong enough to go with them. In another time, Nadia Ozek would have made a fine Longsword Officer, he mused.

"Yes, there is something you can do," Carter said.

"Name it…"

He smiled at the lieutenant. "You can stay alive. And that is an order."

TWENTY-THREE

A PRICE TO PAY

KENDRA LED the group out of the warehouse space where Nadia Ozek had been tortured, using her comp-slate to scan ahead for Aternien infiltrators and gang members. Carter was in the middle, with Amaya at the rear, helping the lieutenant, whose injuries precluded her moving at anything more than a geriatric shuffle. They'd barely made it outside the warehouse when the lights shut off, as if the station had suffered a catastrophic power cut. Emergency generators kicked in a few seconds later and floor-level lighting provided a minimal amount of illumination; barely enough to see more than ten meters ahead, even with his enhanced vision.

"That's ominous..." Amaya said, anxiously looking around the darkened corridor, as if expecting a ghoul or poltergeist to attack her at any moment.

"It's the soliton drives," Kendra said, and Carter immediately noticed the pattern of vibrations that were rippling through the deck, almost imperceptible through the soles of his boots. "The Aterniens have started to spin them up, and they're sucking a massive amount of power from the reactor."

"How long before they can jump the station?" Carter asked.

Kendra worked her comp-slate, but the more her fingers flashed across the screen, the more her expression grew frustrated.

"The overlapping warp fields are playing havoc with my scans, so I can't get any clean data," Kendra said, tapping the screen so hard she almost broke it. "But if I had to make an educated guess, given the size and mass of this station, and the fact they need to create a perfectly synchronized field, it could be up to an hour. Worst case, we have half that."

"Then let's plan for something worse than the worst case," Carter replied, stalking ahead, cutlass in one hand and revolver in the other. "We need an exit off this level. Preferably one that can take us down to the reactor core on deck thirty-eight, and Lieutenant Ozek back to the habitat zone."

"I'm reading a bank of elevators in the dead center of this level," Kendra said, splitting her attention between the screen of the comp-slate and the darkened corridor ahead. Besides the gang-thugs they'd met earlier, the warehouse levels seemed abandoned. "There are passenger elevators leading back up to the habitat and higher, while the cargo elevators will take us where we need to go."

Carter nodded and they continued in silence, though even with Amaya practically carrying Lieutenant Ozek, progress was still impeded by their wounded cargo. Then two low chimes rang out from Kendra's comp-slate, followed by the same two-chimes a second later.

"We've got movement, but interference from the soliton drives is scrambling the readings."

"Then rely on your own senses," Carter replied, trying to tune in to his own early-warning system. "Those drives might be able to mess with our scanners, but they can't affect our minds."

Just then Carter caught of flicker of movement in his peripheral vision. His eyes snapped toward it in a near-instant, and for the briefest moment he thought he saw the flutter of a cloak, but it was gone just as quickly.

"What's up, skipper?" Amaya asked. "You look like you've just seen a ghost."

"In a funny sort of way, I think I just did," Carter grunted, thinking of the last fleeting glimpse he had of the Overseer in the computer control room. He looked at Amaya and saw that his comment had flown over her head, but he didn't have time to dwell on it. "Come on, let's keep moving."

They continued to work their way through the warehouse level, with Kendra's comp-slate double-chiming with updates every few seconds. His engineer continued her efforts to refine the data, but her frown suggested the scan readings were still no clearer. For his part, he ignored his comp-slate completely. Instinct had saved his life on too many occasions to count, and if they were going to be ambushed, he trusted his senses above any electronic replacement to warn him of the danger. By the time they had reached the bank of elevators, Kendra's comp-slate was a mess of static, and Carter's senses were not much clearer. He knew there was a threat close by, but this was as much due to the rising thrum of the deck plates from the synchronizing soliton drives, as it was the possibility of Aterniens leaping out of the darkness.

Kendra opened the passenger elevator door and moved inside to work on the control panel, while Amaya covered them. Lieutenant Ozek was propped up inside the car, a mess of cuts and bruises. The green cloak that Amaya had given her hid her face and the worst of her injuries, and she was wearing a pair of boots taken from a dead gang member to protect her feet, but she was still in a bad way, and Carter regretted having to leave her.

"Is there someone you can go to for help on the promenade?" Carter asked, while his engineer continued hacking the elevator.

"I have people, don't worry," Nadia replied, dismissing his concern with a waft of her hand. "I just wish I could come with you."

"You can't help us in your condition," Carter replied, being frank so as to dismiss any notion of Nadia taking up arms alongside them. "But once this is all over, the Union will need officers like you, so I need you to stay alive."

"Maybe you can put in a good word," Nadia said, then laughed, which she immediately regretted as the muscle spasms sent shockwaves throughout her body.

"Keep breathing until this is all over, and I will," Carter replied, offering her a quick smile. "I promise."

"I've got it," Kendra said, stepping out of the elevator, while holding open the door. "It's all set to take you to the habitat, and it won't stop en route. It's a lot easier to make these cars go up than it is to go down."

"Speaking of which, we need to make a move too," Carter cut in. He turned to the young officer, while Kendra headed onto the landing to give them extra cover. "Good luck, Lieutenant," he said, shaking the woman's hand.

"To us both, Master Commander," Nadia answered.

Carter stepped back and the door slid shut. He waited to make sure the car began to ascend then rejoined his officers. Immediately, his senses sharpened.

"Hold it right there," a voice said. "I know who you are, and what you did..."

Carter glanced to his left and saw a gang thug creep out of the shadows. The man had a powerful gauss rifle aimed at his head. It was set to automatic and his finger was on the trigger, but more importantly, the thug's hands were trembling with fear. He cursed himself for letting his guard down while saying goodbye to Lieutenant Ozek – that slip had allowed the gunman to get the jump on him.

"If you're talking about the dead men in the warehouse, they're dead because they crossed me," Carter said, keeping perfectly still, apart from the movement of his lips. "I suggest you don't make the same mistake."

"Put your weapons down, or I'll blow you away, right here!" the man shouted. He was so close to shooting that a gentle breeze would have been all it took to activate the trigger.

"I'm not here for you," Carter said, trying to talk the man off a ledge. "But me and my officers have to go down to level thirty-eight. If we don't then the entire station will be destroyed."

This bombshell seemed to stun the gunman and there was a flicker of hesitation, as if he might actually lower his rifle, then fear gripped the man again and his aim steadied. Carter knew in that moment that the thug was going to shoot.

"Bullshit, you're lying!" the gang member yelled. "You killed all those people but I won't let you kill me too!"

Carter was about to make his move when a blast of energy struck the frame of the gauss rifle, instantly reducing the barrel to molten slag. The gang member cried out in shock and pain, as the superheated metal burned his hands, then tossed the broken rifle to the deck. A second blast lit up the corridor and the man's head exploded, splattering blood and brains across the wall. Carter and the others darted into cover, aiming their weapons into the darkness, but whatever or whoever had shot the thug was nowhere to be seen.

"Kendra, talk to me!" Carter said, feeling the presence of something or someone nearby. "Where did that shot come from?"

"My scanners still can't see shit, pardon my French," Kendra replied, slapping the comp-slate like it was an ancient valve-based TV set. "The soliton drives are pumping out too much interference."

Rose closed his eyes and listened, relying on his augmented hearing in place of the scanners that were now useless. Footsteps were hurrying their way, beating a uniform pattern against the deck that only the march of organized, skilled warriors could produce.

"On your toes, people, we're about to have company…"

Aternien infiltrators wearing work overalls burst onto the landing from multiple entry points and opened fire with particle weapons. Kendra returned fire with her dual plasma pistols, mowing down the front rank like grass, before drawing and energizing her tantō, in readiness for close quarters fighting. To his right, Amaya had forgone her pistol in favor of her plasma rapier, her preferred weapon. With her speed and lightning agility, his Master Navigator made short work of the advancing imposters, but as soon as the first wave fell, more piled inside the corridor to replace them.

Carter went left, charging past the headless body of the gang thug, and firing on the move with his 57-EX. The imposters may have benefited from an Aternien skeleton and Aternien strength, but without their scale armor, their synthetic bodies were vulnerable to a bullet. Five fell in short order then Carter continued his assault with his cutlass, hacking and slashing the infiltrators with unrestrained brutality, until finally there was a let up in the assault.

"Kendra, get to the cargo elevator," Carter called out, taking cover as yet more imposters entered the fight. "We have to get off this deck!"

His Master Engineer acknowledged the order and withdrew, then Carter and Amaya met in the center of the lobby and fought back-to-back. Still the imposters came, some shooting energy pistols and some attacking with improvised weapons or even their bare fists. His sensation blockers made it difficult to count the number of hits he'd taken, but the residual effect of the nano-stim was helping to plug the holes his enemies were putting into his body. It also helped that Amaya was fighting with him. In full flow, she was a force of nature, almost impossibly fast and impossibly deadly. She whirled through the ranks of Aterniens, dispatching them with pin-point thrusts through their neuromorphic brains, or rendering their bodies lame and unable to fight, by slicing synthetic muscles and tendons in their arms and legs.

The severity of the fighting caused him and Amaya to become separated, and Carter was set upon by a dozen imposters. He reloaded his revolver and fanned off all the shots in record time, but five were still left standing. He cut one down before the others reached him but was then grabbed and restrained. An Aternien held each of his arms, while a third imposter slid behind and pulled him into a choke hold. Carter's sword was prized from his grasp and to his horror he realized that it was about to be used against him. With a lifesaving burst of strength, he shook off the Aterniens who were holding his arms, and the energized blade sliced through synthetic flesh, rather than his own. Then he elbowed the Aternien who was strangling him so hard that the imposter's face caved in like a sunken soufflé.

Carter's own sword was swung at him again, forcing him to block with his buckler, but the shield was sliced through and the blade cut into his shoulder. His sensation blockers failed him and Carter roared with pain, but this only made him stronger. With the imposter's last opportunity to kill him gone, he threw the hardest right cross he'd ever delivered in his long life, landing it cleanly and breaking the Aternien's metal neck. The imposter dropped the cutlass and he pulled the enemy fighter into a headlock, wrenching the Aternien's head from its body like twisting the cap off a beer bottle.

"Clear!" Amaya called out, returning to Carter's side, nursing a few wounds of her own. "For now, at least…"

"Kendra, report!" Carter called out, backing up next to his Master Navigator while pressing a hand to his wounded shoulder.

"I've hit a roadblock, boss," his engineer called back. "It's something we've not seen before, and I could use your insight."

Carter and Amaya ran to the cargo elevator and found Master Engineer Castle buried under a mass of wires, and with a circuit board clutched in her grasp.

"Everything is good to go, but there's a master control lock that's keeping the elevator rooted to this floor," Kendra explained, extracting herself from the tangle of wires. "It's like getting the engine of a car running, then finding out its wheel has been clamped. I've tried to bypass it, but this is tech I've never seen before."

Carter crouched beside his Master Engineer and examined the control panel. It was clearly Aternien technology, but there was something about it that was oddly familiar. There was a circular hole in the center that looked like it could be a socket designed for a physical key of some kind. Then he had a thought, and removed the blue lapis lazuli that the mysterious hooded figure had thrown at him while they were on the habitat level. Kendra watched with interest as he offered the stone to the panel and it snapped into place, like a magnet attaching to a fridge door. Aternien hieroglyphs lit up on the stone and the controls were unlocked.

"Well, fuck me sideways," Kendra said, shaking her head in amazement. "I can't believe that actually worked!"

Carter sighed loudly at his engineer, but she didn't offer an apology, and this time he couldn't blame her. Though he hadn't vocalized it, he'd had a similar reaction.

"Amaya, get in here," Carter said, rising to his full height.

The Master Navigator joined them and immediately

noticed the glowing blue stone in the control panel. "That's pretty. Where did you get it?"

"I'll explain later," Carter said, hitting the button for deck thirty-eight, power services. "First, we have some warp drives to sabotage."

The elevator car descended swiftly and arrived at its designated floor without incident. The glowing Aternien control panel pinged and the doors slid open, though while all three longsword officers were waiting with weapons ready, there was no-one there to greet them, friend or foe.

"This seems too easy," Carter said, grabbing the blue stone out of the control board before exiting the car.

"Don't knock it, boss, we could do with some good luck," Kendra replied. She then pointed to a heavy wall and an equally heavy-looking door. "The reactor room is through there, but that wall looks like a recent addition."

Carter approached and pressed his hand to the metal. It was an Aternien alloy.

"This armor looks like it belongs on the hull of a Khopesh-class destroyer," Carter said, stepping back and trying the control panel, but it didn't respond to his inputs. "We'd need a plasma cutter to get through, and even then, it would take more time than we have."

"How about trying your fancy stone?" Amaya suggested. "Is there anywhere it might fit?"

They all searched the wall and the door, looking for hidden panels or pebble-shaped indentations that might serve as a secret locking mechanism, but they found nothing. And all the while, the thrum of the soliton drives was building. Eventually, frustration overcame him and he punched the door before standing back, hands on hips.

"There has to be a way inside."

"No human can open that door…"

Carter pulled his 57-EX out of his holster and aimed it toward the source of the voice. It was the hooded figure that he'd seen on so many occasions, though this time, she was making no attempt to stay hidden.

"Only an Aternien can enter," the Overseer explained. "I will let you in, but there is a price to pay for my help."

TWENTY-FOUR

DUEL OF HONOR

THE OVERSEER APPROACHED THEM AND, to his surprise, Carter found that his senses were not seeing her as a threat, at least not yet. Kendra and Amaya both drew their weapons, but he held up his hand and his officers both stayed their blades.

"It was you in the hooded cloak all along?" Carter asked, looking into the Overseer's glowing blue eyes.

"Yes…" the Overseer replied, plainly. Her perfect Aternien features were downcast, like she had suffered a tragic loss and was in mourning.

Carter removed the blue Lapis Lazuli pebble and tossed it to the Overseer, who caught it with cat-like reflexes. "You threw this stone to warn me about the approaching gang members, but you must have known it was also a key?" Carter continued. "You must have known it was something we'd need?"

"Yes…" the Overseer said again, presenting no appearance that she was about to explain her actions.

"It was also you who killed Fleur Lambert, saving me

from Damien Morrow, and you've intervened to keep me alive on other occasions too."

"You are wanting to know why?" the Overseer asked.

Carter laughed and threw his arms out wide. "Well, of course I want to know why! Not all that long ago, it was you who was trying to kill me."

The Overseer considered the question, perhaps ruminating on how much to reveal. Secrecy was the Aternien way of life. Their culture was steeped in mystery and borrowed heavily from ancient Egyptian mythology. Almost everything about their world and society was unknown to the Union, which is how Markus Aternus wanted it. The planet that the god-king and his followers were exiled to had been the Aterniens' home for barely more than twenty years, before their entire civilization upped and left to New Aternus, the location of which remained a secret.

"I am no longer an Overseer of the Aternien Empire," the woman said. The revelation appeared to take a weight off her mind and her rod-like posture relaxed, if only by a minuscule amount. "The Grand Vizier stripped me of that title because of my repeated failures and reduced me in rank to Warden."

Though she didn't specify the exact nature of her failures, it seemed clear to Carter that she was referring to her inability to stop the Galatine, and to kill him specifically.

"I will never again attain the title, Overseer. I will never be permitted to ascend to the Aternien Royal Court. Warden is as high as I will climb, from now until my eventual death."

The Overseer paused for a moment, and Carter could see that she was wrestling with her feelings. He'd never considered the Aterniens to be an emotional people, but it was clear that the Overseer was torn up inside and fighting hard to maintain her composure.

"After more than one hundred and seventy years of service to the empire, I have been cast aside," she continued, her voice cracking as she spoke the words.

In that moment, Carter experienced something that he never imagined in his wildest dreams that he would feel for any Aternien – sympathy. "I know a little something about what it's like to be an outcast," he said, offering the Aternien a half-smile. However, the Overseer merely scoffed and threw his generosity back in his face.

"You do not understand…" the Overseer said, hissing the words with a bitter rasp. "You regained your former rank, which means your superiors still value you." She gestured to Amaya and Kendra with the flat of her hand. "And you retained the respect of your crew and were even given back the command of your old vessel." She waved the same hand at him dismissively. "You and I are nothing alike."

"Don't pretend that all this is not a situation of your own making," Carter grunted. After her outburst, the very limited sympathy he'd felt for the Overseer was rapidly eroding. "You made your choices, and you are suffering the consequences of them."

A flash of anger pulsed behind the Overseer's eyes, but it was gone a moment later, and she bowed her head, accepting his judgement. "You are correct, of course," she admitted, with unexpected grace.

"And you're wrong about me," Carter added, still looking to find common ground. "I may have regained my rank, my ship and my crew, but it's only because the Union needs us. It doesn't mean that humanity fears us any less."

"And yet you willingly serve those who distrust and

denigrate you?" She shook her head, genuinely at a loss. "You are so much more than they could ever be. You are demigods, made to serve the unworthy."

"I'm just a man," Carter replied, half-smiling again. "A little stronger and faster, maybe, but a man nonetheless."

The Overseer laughed, though it was not the cruel, unkind laugh that he was used to hearing from those in the high echelons of Aternien society, but a sympathetic one.

"Humility is a very human trait," the Overseer said. "It is one that we do not share."

Carter had found the conversation with the Overseer to be fascinating and enlightening in equal measure, but he was also acutely aware that they were on the clock, and that they had a job to do.

"Look, Overseer, or Warden, or whatever the hell I'm supposed to call you, this is all very interesting, but as I'm sure you know, this station is about to be jumped into the atmosphere of Terra Prime, where it will kill billions." He paused to let that sink in, but there was no indication that the Overseer was oblivious to this plot. "You said you'd help us, so help us."

"I also said there was a price for my help."

"So, name it," Carter said.

"You must agree to fight me, right now, one-on-one," the Overseer replied.

Carter recoiled from the Aternien. "What?"

"I will not serve the rest of my life as a mere Warden," the Overseer stated with determination. She was becoming more animated as the anger that was bubbling beneath her perfect Aternien skin started to boil. "If I cannot ascend, I would rather be nothing, so I have come to salvage what remains of my…" she paused, searching for the right word, or perhaps the kindest one, before adding, "…pride."

"But Markus Aternus won't grant you the rank of Overseer again, even if you do beat me," Carter pointed out. "You said so yourself."

The Overseer stood firm. "That is the price for my help, Master Commander Rose. I have lost my rank and status. My reputation is in ruin. At least if I defeat you, I can endure exile with my honor intact. It is something, at least."

Carter sighed and rubbed his hand through his silver hair. He looked to Amaya and Kendra for their thoughts or guidance, but both of his officers looked as dumbstruck as he felt. Certainly, 'a duel of honor with an Aternien Overseer' had not been on his to-do list for that day.

"There has to be another way," Carter finally said. "Another way to salvage your honor."

The Overseer calmly shook her head. "There is not. But, win or lose, your price is paid. Give me your word of honor as an officer that you will fight me, alone, and I will unlock the door." She paused for effect, and Carter felt the impact of her words. "Believe me, Master Commander, I am the only way that you will get inside that room."

Carter let his mind race, searching for any other option that would avoid the duel, but on this occasion, he was in a bind, and the Overseer knew it.

"Very well," Carter replied, standing tall as if to attention. "You have my word of honor as an officer of the Union that I will fight you."

"And you swear on your honor that your crew will not intervene, no matter what?" the Overseer asked.

"I swear…"

"Even, if I am about to kill you?"

Carter glanced at Kendra and Amaya to make sure they understood. "Even if the Overseer is about to kill me, my officers will not intervene."

The look Kendra shot him in response to that statement was borderline insubordinate, while Amaya just looked like she'd been given a death sentence of her own. For someone who could find the light even in the center of a black hole, this was unheard of from his Master Navigator.

"I accept your word," the Overseer said.

The Aternien then walked to the massive, slab-like door that was barring their entrance into the reactor room and pressed her hand to the surface. Hieroglyphs lit up on the metal, shimmering and shifting like unearthly projections from the Egyptian underworld, then the bolts retracted and the door unlocked. Carter nodded to Kendra and she inched the door open to peek into the reactor room.

"It's clear," she called back.

"Then wait for me inside," Carter ordered, drawing his cutlass and activating his buckler shield.

He heard Kendra mutter a coarse selection of expletives under her breath, but his Master Engineer did as he instructed. Amaya followed her, with similar reluctance. Once the two officers had gone, the Overseer removed her cloak, and set it down next to the wall, before drawing her war spear, which had been stowed along the center-line of her back. For a few seconds, the two fighters simply watched each other, pacing in circles. Carter was trying to read the Overseer, studying her stance and footwork for a clue as to her first attack, but there was a strange lack of hunger in her eyes. Though he had defeated her before, doing so had required all of his skill and determination, yet as he watched her then, her thirst for victory was missing.

"And so it begins," the Overseer said, saluting with her spear.

Rose returned the salute as a mark of respect, then engaged the plasma-edge of his cutlass and attacked first, pushing the Overseer back and forcing her to block his cuts with the shaft of her spear. It was an exploratory assault, designed to test the Overseer's defenses, but while she had an opportunity to counterattack, she instead danced out of range and began circling him again.

"You're strangely composed," Carter said, though this was a euphemism for cautious. "I expected you to come at me, hell for leather. Surely, your honor demands nothing less?"

"How I fight is none of your concern," the Overseer hissed. She flourished her war spear than darted toward him, using the weapon's greater reach to good effect. Carter deflected the thrusts using his buckler then the Overseer slashed the blade-edge of the weapon down toward his head, forcing him to parry with his sword. The attack left her open and Carter capitalized by kicking her hard in the gut. The Overseer reeled back, and pulled her spear in to a defensive posture, but he broke her guard, and she was open again. His blade crackled through the air and scored a groove across her scale armor, from shoulder to hip. If his cut had been mere millimeters closer, the Aternien would have been beaten. Ordinarily, this would have given him encouragement, but on this occasion, Carter's senses were telling him that something was wrong.

"You're out of practice," Carter said, curtailing his assault and resuming their circular dance around one another.

"Do you always talk so much?" the Overseer countered.

"I only want our duel to be civilized," Carter added,

lunging forward and testing the Overseer with a couple of sharp thrusts, which she parried, albeit half-heartedly. "After all, this could be the last conversation you ever have."

"You overestimate your skills…"

The Overseer attacked again, this time with more tenacity, thrusting high and low in a dizzying blur of strikes. His shoulder and calf were both nicked by the impossibly sharp edge of the Aternien spearhead, and Carter was forced to up his game too, parrying the next attack, and landing a counter-blow across the Overseer's back. She adjusted her stance, and he lunged but overextended the attack, leaving an opening for the Overseer to retaliate, but she did not take it, and instead withdrew.

"What are you doing?" Carter growled, also falling back so that he was out of range of her spear thrusts, not that it appeared the Overseer had any intention to strike him.

"What sort of question is that?" the Aternien woman snapped. "You know what we are doing."

Carter shook his head. "You're trying to lose."

The Overseer didn't answer, but he could see in her eyes that he was right. She looked away, shamefaced, and her jaw clenched. Her body and mind may have been synthetic, but her emotions were real, and every bit as human as his were. Suddenly, she jumped toward him and lanced the spear at his head. Carter tried to dodge but the attack was delivered with whipcrack speed and scored a deep cut across his cheek. The injury triggered his augments to flood his bloodstream with engineered hormones, amping up his strength and reaction times even further. At the same time, the Overseer followed up with a thrust to his leg, but it was delivered with far less speed and power, and again he had an opening. He punched his buckler into the Overseer's face then slashed the spear out of her grasp before throwing her against the wall and cutting deeply across her midsection. The Aternien fell to her knees in front of him, disarmed and defenseless, and Carter raised his cutlass ready to strike the killing blow, but something stopped him. He checked the swing of his sword at the last moment and held the blade of his cutlass an inch away from the Overseer's exposed neck. She raised her gaze to meet his, eyes and body trembling like she was shivering with cold, but still the woman offered no resistance.

"What are you waiting for!" she cried. "Kill me!"

"No..." Carter grunted, disengaging the plasma blade and stepping back. "I won't be your executioner."

"But you must!" the Overseer implored him, shuffling toward him on her knees, pleading. "You gave me your word."

"I promised to fight you, and I've kept my promise," Carter answered. "But you didn't come here for a duel to save your honor. You came here to die."

The Overseer's chin dropped to her chest. He might not have killed her, but it was clear that she considered mercy a worse outcome.

"I cannot bare this shame," the Overseer said, her voice barely audible over the thrum of the soliton drives battering the deck. "I cannot kill myself. If I take my own life then I will never be considered amongst the justified dead, and I will never be called upon to crew the Boat of Millions in the afterlife." She again looked into his eyes, despairingly. "You must kill me, Commander Rose. I have disabled my link to the Soul Crypt so you can give me an honorable death."

"No," Carter repeated, and sheathed his sword.

The Overseer's head fell into her hands, and Carter

crouched down beside her. His senses told him that she was no longer a threat.

"Who were you, before you ascended?" Carter asked, his tone softer.

The Overseer frowned. "What do you mean?"

"Before you were Aternien, who were you?" he asked again. "Do you even remember?"

The Overseer considered the question, her eyes flicking from side to side, as if she were trying to recover memories that were buried so deep inside her neuromorphic brain that they had almost degraded to nothing.

"We are encouraged to purge all memories of our human lives," the Overseer finally replied, an anguished expression now taking over from the frown. "There is no point in remembering."

"Humor me…" Carter grunted.

The Overseer became distant, staring blankly ahead, and for the first time Carter saw a life in her eyes that had not been there before. It was uniquely human, like an echo of her former self.

"I was born and lived in Toulouse, a city in the south of France on Terra Prime," the Overseer began, speaking as if in a trance. "I grew up there, and lived there all my life, until I began work as a computer scientist for the Aternus Corporation."

"How old were you then?"

The Overseer smiled, and it was natural. "I was twenty-two years old. I had loved computers all my life. I studied them and knew them inside and out, like code was my second language. So when Markus invited me onto his personal team, I was blown away."

"You knew Markus Aternus, back on Terra Prime?"

"Oh, yes," the woman said, still smiling. "He was transformed by then, of course, though his appearance was different; still human. He was kind to me." She exhaled softly and though there was no moisture in her eyes, she appeared tearful. "I was not a confident person, and I certainly did not believe myself worthy of ascension, but Markus convinced me. He believed in me…"

Carter sighed and stroked his beard. "How long ago was this?"

"I ascended one-hundred and seventy-three years ago, five years before we were exiled," she explained. Then the joy of the happy memory she was experiencing evaporated and a pained, mournful expression returned. "All those years and look at me now." She shook her head and stared at the shaking deck plates. "That's all I remember. Even that is too much."

Carter thought for a moment then he made a decision – a choice – that he never expected to make. "What's your name?"

The Overseer scowled at him again. "I am a Warden of the Aternien…"

"No, not that," he interrupted her. "Your real name. The name of the twenty-two-year-old computer scientist from Toulouse, France."

The pained expression returned, though this time it was because she was trying to recall a time from her distant past. "It was… Monique," she finally replied, appearing surprised that she could remember. "My name was Monique Dubois."

Carter stood up then offered the woman his hand. She stared at it then met his eyes, confused.

"The Overseer was my enemy. Monique Dubois is not."

The woman took his hand and he helped her to stand.

"I too was forsaken by those I trusted above all others, but it wasn't the end for me, Monique, and it doesn't have to be the end for you."

"The Aterniens will never take me back," Monique whispered. "What is there for me now, but an honorable death?

"How about a normal life?" Carter suggested, offering her a kindly smile. "At least think about it, before you throw in the towel."

"You're letting me go?"

"I'm giving you the freedom to choose your own path."

Monique took a moment to process everything, but Carter sensed that she was at least considering his proposal.

"I will not join you to fight the Aterniens," she said. "I have my honor too."

Carter nodded. "I'd expect nothing less." He then had a thought and wondered if this new 'Overseer' might be willing to help him understand something that had bothered him since their first encounter. "When we first met, you told me that your essence was permanently linked through a spacetime conduit to something called the 'Soul Crypt', and you mentioned it again just now. Where is this crypt?"

Monique considered the question for a moment, perhaps wrestling with her own conscience in terms of how much to reveal about her former masters.

"The Soul Crypt resides on New Aternus, in the capital city," she finally answered. Monique then regarded him with more circumspection. "You are considering whether it can be destroyed?"

Carter smiled. "Guilty as charged. I figure that doing so might cause Markus Aternus to think twice about continuing this war."

Monique's synthetic eyebrows raised by the slightest amount. "More than you could possibly know…"

The former Overseer then picked up the cloak she'd placed on the deck earlier and pulled it on. She met Carter's eyes again, and seemed to consider saying something, but instead turned to leave. At the entrance to a darkened corridor, she stopped and looked back. The blue stone was in her hand, but it was flashing with golden Aternien hieroglyphs, as if she was reprogramming it.

"This is yours now…" Monique said, tossing the stone to Carter. He caught it and watched the hieroglyphs fade. "You may find that it unlocks many doors. Doors that were once closed to you."

Then she pulled up her hood and was gone.

TWENTY-FIVE

FORCED ALLIANCES

CARTER ENTERED THE REACTOR ROOM, and it was like he'd stepped onto a different planet. The Aterniens posing as work crews had transformed the space so that little of the original Union technology remained. The modifications were so extensive that he had to glance back through the open door to make sure he hadn't inadvertently walked through a fold in space and ended up inside an Aternien Solar Barque.

"You're alive, so I take it you won?" Amaya said, jogging over to meet him. She touched a finger just below the cut on his cheek, which was still healing. "Though not without a few extra scrapes and bruises, I see."

"I won, though it wasn't much of a contest," Carter replied.

Amaya raised her eyebrows at him. "Really, skipper? That must be the first time I've ever heard you brag!"

"It wasn't a brag, trust me," Carter said, hands on hips. "Let's just say that Monique Dubois had an ulterior motive for wanting to cross swords."

The Master Navigator's surprised expression morphed quickly into one of confusion, before she connected the dots in her own mind.

"The Overseer told you her real name?" she asked.

Carter nodded. "As crazy as it sounds, she had a crisis of the heart, or whatever it is that pulses inside their synthetic chests. She was looking for an execution, not a duel."

Amaya's eyebrows shot up again. "And did you grant her wish?"

"No, I didn't..." Carter glanced through the open door again, half-expecting to see the Overseer sneaking up on him, spear in hand. "But I don't think we'll see her again. If we do, I hope it won't be as enemies."

He tried to put Monique Dubois out of his mind and focused his attention on the Aternien contraption in front of them. The original reactor core of the station was barely visible, shrouded on all four sides by the soliton warp drive assemblies that had been tied together in order to warp the station into Terra Prime's atmosphere. The drives were all spinning rapidly, but from the off-canter beat through the deck plates, he could tell that they had yet to fully synchronize. The other reason he knew this was because if the drives had been spooled up, ready to jump, they'd already be dead.

"Has Kendra figured out how to shut that down?" Carter asked, nodding toward the quartet of warp drives. The modified machine occupied a full half of the total deck area and stretched forty meters toward the ceiling. Standing in front of the contraption, Kendra looked minuscule.

"I just fly things, skipper, and have no idea what makes them fly," Amaya shrugged.

Carter shared his Master Navigator's sentiment and

resolved to get his answer from his Master Engineer. However, Kendra was so enraptured with the device, and the scan data she was compiling on her comp-slate, that she barely noticed him arrive.

"This is blowing my freaking mind, boss," Kendra said, for once remembering to substitute an actual f-bomb for a fake one. "The technical knowledge and engineering precision required to synchronize four drives is staggering. I could spend days in here trying to figure out how this works, and barely scratch the surface of the basic science."

"Kendra, I need you to shut it down, not figure out how it works."

"I know, I know," Kendra hit back, patently irritated by this fact. "It's a crying shame, is all. Busting this up would be like defacing the Mona Lisa or smashing the statue of David."

"If taking a hammer or a sword to this contraption is what it takes to shut it down, then so be it," Carter added. "But one way or another, we have to stop it, or we'll end up free-falling toward New London without a parachute."

"I understand, boss, and believe me, I'm on it, but it's just not that simple." Kendra was frantically working her comp-slate while she was talking, ploughing through reams of equations and simulations using the data she'd gathered from her scans. "If we forcibly stop any one of these drives, power will spike to the others and they'll spin out of control. We risk creating a spacetime distortion that would, at best, tear the station apart and, at worst, create a singularity."

Carter considered this, dredging up memories of his physics classes from longer ago than he could remember.

"By a singularity do you mean a black hole?" he asked, hoping he'd remembered incorrectly.

"Not necessarily, but we might get one of those as well," Kendra replied, though her answer did nothing to help Carter understand the situation any better. "Like I said, I'm on it. I don't want to be ejected into Terra Prime's stratosphere, any more than you do..."

Carter nodded then suddenly felt his senses climb. He glanced at Amaya and saw that she had detected a presence too, and spun around, fingers wrapped around the grip of his revolver. He expected to see the Overseer staring back at him, returned to make another attempt to salvage her honor, but instead, he saw Damien Morrow, accompanied by the walking slab of muscle that was Rollo Jay.

"Keep at it, Kendra," Carter said, noticing that his engineer had also been distracted by the entrance of the traitor Longsword officers. "Let Amaya and I deal with these two."

"Be my guest, I hate those assholes..." Kendra replied, and returned to work. "But shout if you need me..."

Carter paced toward Morrow and Jay with his Master Navigator at his side, but neither of the men were focused on him, and were instead gawping at the warp drive contraption like it had cast a spell on them. Morrow, in particular, was wide-eyed and visibly disconcerted.

"What the fuck is going on?" Morrow said, bizarrely directing the question to Carter, who returned an equally stunned response.

"Why the hell are you asking me? This is your doing, or at least it's the handiwork of your benefactor, Aternus."

"The energy density is much too high," Morrow added. The man was now accessing a pocket comp-slate in his hand, while Jay watched Carter closely to make sure he didn't try anything. "The warp field is only supposed to encapsulate the contents of the warehouses, but if this synchronizes then the entire station could jump." The traitor pushed his comp-slate into a pocket and stared at Carter, accusingly. "What have you done to it?"

"What have *I* done to it?" Carter hit back, suddenly wondering if the door they'd walked through had actually sent them to a different dimension. "Are you out of your mind, Morrow? This is how it was set up, in order to warp Venture Terminal into orbit of Terra Prime and use the station as a vehicle to disperse the super-aerosol." He clicked his fingers, trying to remember the term that Doctor Rauscher had used, then it came to him. "Stratospheric Aerosol Insertion."

"I know the plan, but this isn't it!" Morrow snapped, hustling to a control console that was Aternien in design. "It's only supposed to be the aerosol vats that jump, not the entire fucking station."

Jay remained by Damien's side as the man frantically worked the console, punching in hieroglyphs in sequences that made no sense to Carter. While Morrow appeared to comprehend the Aternien language, the console did not respond to his inputs. In Carter's mind, there was only one rationale that could explain Morrow's reaction, and it was beautiful in its irony.

"Your god-king has betrayed you, Damien," Carter said, using Morrow's given name to allow the revelation to have a more personal impact. "He lied to you about this device, so that you'd die on this station too."

"That's bullshit, I've done everything Aternus asked!"

Carter shook his head. "You failed him on Terra Six and on Terra Eight, which is why I'm still alive. And the god-king does not reward failure."

"Shut the fuck up!" Morrow snapped, shaking a fist at him.

For a moment, Carter thought that the traitor was going to draw his cutlass and charge, but the man's instinct for self-preservation overcame his rage.

"Boss, we've got about two minutes before we're skydiving," Kendra called out, causing Morrow's gaze to snap toward her. Up until that moment, he apparently hadn't noticed Carter's Master Engineer. "I think I know a way to stop it, but these are Aternien systems, and even if I could read their gobbledygook letters, I don't have the right tools with me."

Carter nodded then looked at Morrow, who looked back at him. He knew that they'd both had the same idea, and that they were both struggling to propose it, though for different reasons. The stalemate continued, but if Morrow wasn't prepared to swallow his pride, then he would.

"We need to call a truce," Carter said, taking a few steps closer to the turncoat master commander. Jay met his advance, hand wrapped around the handle of his claymore, but he ignored the brute. "You and Kendra have to work together to fix this. If you give her access, and the ability to translate the Aternien user interface, she'll shut it down."

"I'm not giving her access to the Aternien computer system..."

"We don't have time for this!" Carter yelled, cutting across him. "You either do it or we all die."

Morrow clenched his teeth then cursed into the air. "Alright, dammit!" He turned to Jay and jabbed a finger into his barrel chest. "Watch them, and if they try any shit, cut them in half."

"It would be my pleasure," Jay grunted, drawing his

claymore and squaring off against himself and Amaya, like an ancient King's Guard protecting his liege.

Morrow ran toward Kendra then jumped onto the enclosure of the first soliton drive. Kendra backed away, gripping the handle of her tantō, but Morrow raised his hands to indicate he wasn't a threat.

"It's okay, Kendra, let him help," Carter said.

Kendra reluctantly released her short-sword then Morrow took his comp-slate back out of his pocket. He unfurled a golden cable from the computer then grabbed Kendra's forearm and attached it to the universal input port of her device. His Master Engineer came close to decking Morrow, but she managed to keep her cool, and allowed the traitor to work. At the same time, Jay had taken several measured paces toward him. Amaya drew her rapier, but Jay merely laughed at the weapon, then laughed at his Master Navigator.

"What are you going to do with that, sweet pea? Pick food out of my teeth?" Jay laughed again, and the booming sound carried even over the racket of the soliton drives.

Amaya energized the blade and stepped toward the hulking figure, but Carter held up a hand. Jay wanted to rile her up and goad her into attacking first, but even with Amaya's speed and pinpoint precision with her blade, the odds were against her. Jay had been a Master-at-arms for good reason. The man knew how to fight, and that included getting inside the minds of his enemies. He would allow Amaya to think he was clumsy and oafish, then before she knew it, she'd be dead.

"It's okay, Amaya, Rollo is just being friendly, isn't that right, Rollo?" Carter said, playing the man at his own game.

"What sort of name is Rollo, anyway? Did your mom name you after the family dog?"

"We did have a family dog, but I was always a big kid, and I broke its neck and killed it," Jay replied, still grinning at Amaya. "Have you ever heard a dog's neck snap, sweet pea? It sounds like stepping on a twig."

The man then made a harsh clicking noise with his tongue and throat, while simulating strangling the neck of a small creature. By this time, Amaya was fizzing with rage, but Carter made sure that his Master Navigator didn't do anything foolish, by stepping to Jay himself.

"Don't get too close, Commander," Jay said, his smile now turned upside down. "I bite, you see…"

Carter wanted to spear the man like a fish, but he held his nerve and returned Jay's smile.

"It's a shame that you were never placed under my command," Carter said, facing down the man. "I would have taught you some respect."

Jay moved closer, and hissed, "You're still welcome to try."

"We almost have it!" Kendra called out, needing to shout to be heard over the din of the surging soliton drives. "But the drives are almost synchronized, so be ready for things to get a little weird…"

Carter was about to ask what his engineer meant by 'weird', when the reactor room began to shake violently and spacetime distortions rippled through the station like shockwaves. Suddenly, his head felt like it was about to explode, and he staggered back from Jay, hands pressed to his temples. His sensation blockers did nothing to ease the agony he was experiencing, and he cried out. Then everything was silent and his eyes went dark. A second later, he found himself standing on the forest moon of Terra Nine, looking out toward his log cabin in the woods. Everything seemed perfectly real, from the air temperature, to the earthy, damp aroma that was laced with a hint of wood smoke from his cabin's burner. Then the scene shifted again and his cabin was gone, razed to the ground, along with the forest surrounding it. He found himself wandering aimlessly, and soon he was in the middle of Ridge Town, but the buildings were rubble, and bodies lay in the streets, bleeding from their eyes.

Pain returned and he blacked out for a second time, only to then find himself outside Union Headquarters in New London on Terra Prime. It was a beautiful summer's day, without a cloud in the sky. Market stalls peddled their wares, and the air was heady with the scent of street food. Couples were walking arm-in-arm, laughing and chatting in their chiffon dresses and cool linens – the current summer fashion in the city. Then the air shook and the windows of Union HQ blew out. People screamed and pointed to the sky. Carter peered up to see Venture Terminal plummeting toward him, whirling like a spinning top. People ran, cars crashed and flyers collided, but there was no escape. The station detonated, and thousands of aerosol vats were ejected, popping open like corn kernels when exposed to the rarified gases in the stratosphere.

The sky began to blacken above the city, as if the hot summer sun had been doused with a celestial bucket of water. The veil of darkness expanded outward like a giant ink blot and soon stretched all the way to the horizon. Time accelerated and Carter watched as a permanent night fell across not only the city, but the entire planet, which then froze into a lifeless wasteland. Unable to intervene, he was forced to witness the city's once great buildings and monuments crumble to dust and be consumed by ice. The only light came from the luminescence of his battle uniform, but even that was beginning to wane. He felt the cold seep into his bones, and his skin turned blue. Then, as the light from his uniform failed, darkness weighed down on him like a lead-lined blanket, until the snow and ice consumed him too. He tried to scream, but his jaw was frozen shut. The oxygen in his super-human cells was somehow keeping him alive, but it was a curse that spared him the mercy of death. He couldn't move or even breathe, but his mind remained as sharp as his cutlass. In that moment, Carter Rose was the only living thing on Terra Prime, then, like a candle flickering as it reached the end of its wick, he was gone too.

For a time, he seemed to exist without a body, floating through the cosmos as pure energy and thought. Then the universe exploded into existence around him, and he was back in the reactor room on Venture Terminal. He fell to his knees, gasping for air. His head still throbbed viciously, and his vision was a blur, but he could feel the cold metal deck plates beneath his hands, and the vibrations were rapidly diminishing. Shaking his head, he tried to look at the soliton drive assembly. The room was no longer shaking, and steadily his focus returned. Amaya was down, dazed and disorientated, and Jay was bent double, bracing himself on his knees. Over on the warp drive enclosure, he could see that Morrow and Kendra were clinging on to one another, like survivors of a shipwreck who were being tossed around in a life raft on rough seas. Their comp-slates were still tethered by the golden cable.

Carter forced down a dry swallow then checked his own comp-slate. The warp fields were collapsing and all four soliton drives were spinning down in a controlled manner. He felt suddenly elated. Kendra had done it! Then his elation was devoured by a dread sense of foreboding. He turned to Amaya, and saw Jay in front of her, Claymore in hand, but his Master Navigator was on her knees, still dazed and unable to defend herself.

"Amaya, move!" he called out, but it was too late, and Jay thrust the broad blade of the Claymore through Amaya's gut and out of her back, driving the mighty sword through her flesh all the way to the hilt.

TWENTY-SIX

I'M READY

CARTER CRIED out with incoherent rage and charged at Jay, drawing and firing his 57-EX on the move, but his bullets merely chased the turncoat Master-at-arms into cover. Dropping the revolver, he drew and energized his cutlass, and was prepared to follow Jay to the gates of hell if required, when a sick feeling gripped him again. He looked to his Master Engineer and saw Morrow beside her, the golden cable from his comp-slate wrapped around her neck and pulled tight.

Kendra clawed at Morrow's fingers and thrashed her legs, but the traitor was the stronger of the two. Suddenly consumed with despair at possibly losing not one but two of his colleagues and friends, Carter abandoned his pursuit of Jay and ran to his engineer's aid, but particle blasts intercepted him and he was knocked off his feet. He extended his buckler and ducked behind it as more blasts from Jay's particle pistol thudded into the shield, weakening his defenses with each shot. The next blast collapsed the buckler and he was struck to the chest and floored. Jay appeared above him, energized Claymore sword held high, with Amaya's blood still staining the flat of the blade.

"You lose, Master Commander…" Jay spat, speaking Carter's rank with disdain.

The sword came crashing down, but the blade was blocked by an energized katana. Carter gasped with relief as he saw his own Master-at-arms standing over him, sword in hand. Brodie Kaur hammered the back of his fist into Jay's face and drove the man back, his anger burning so hot that the man's footsteps almost set the deck alight. Jay recovered then swung the Claymore, but Brodie parried and punched the man again, caving in the traitor's teeth like smashing pottery with a hammer. Jay tried to defend, but Brodie was now an unstoppable force. He slashed the traitor's arms and chest, cutting to the bone, then plunged the katana into the man's heart, burying it hilt-deep, as Jay had done to Amaya. The turncoat dropped to his knees, staring at the sword in his chest with disbelief, then Brodie stole the traitor's energized Claymore, and held it in two hands, while fixing Jay with a vengeful stare.

"This is for Amaya, you piece of shit!"

The Claymore flashed through the air and Jay's head hit the deck a second later.

"Brodie, help Amaya," Rose called out, as his Master-at-arms stowed the enormous sword on his back scabbard. "There might still be time to save her."

Brodie nodded then ran to Amaya, who was splayed out on the deck a few meters away. Her eyes were scrunched tight and teeth clenched, bearing down against the pain, but she was alive.

"Give her this," Carter called out, tossing a nano-stim capsule to his officer. "Whatever dose you think she needs."

Brodie caught the stim, adjusted the dial and applied it directly to the sword wound in Amaya's gut, before holding the woman tightly to his own body to help her bear down against the pain. Her screams were the stuff of nightmares, but Rose couldn't concern himself with his Master Navigator yet, because another of his officers was in grave danger.

"I gave her a high-dose, which is kicking her ass, but she's strong and she'll make it," Brodie called out. Carter listened while collecting his weapons but he could no longer see Kendra or Morrow, and not knowing his engineer's fate was killing him. "The sword perforated her stomach and right kidney, but it missed her spine," Brodie added. "She was actually kinda lucky."

"Will she die, Brodie?" Carter asked, eyes still scouring the reactor room for the traitorous master commander.

"Not a chance in hell, not on my watch," his Master-at-arms replied, without any shred of doubt. "I won't let her."

Rose grunted an acknowledgment. "Then stay with her, Brodie. I need to find Kendra."

His Master-at-arms looked toward the soliton warp drive enclosures, and he could see the unease in the man's kind brown eyes.

"Go get that piece of shit, MC," Brodie said, still immobilized by Amaya's writhing convulsions. "We'll both be here when you get back."

Carter nodded then marched toward where he'd last seen his engineer, feeding off his senses and trusting them to tell him where his enemy was hiding.

"Come out, Damien," he yelled, knowing instinctively that the traitor was close by. "It's over. You lost..."

"It's not over..." Morrow called back, but the sound of the man's voice echoed around the reactor room, making it impossible to pinpoint his location. "Do you think this is the only plan we have to destroy Terra Prime? You've not beaten us, Carter, you've just delayed the inevitable."

Carter continued ahead, plasma light from his cutlass creeping into the dark corners of the reactor room, which had fallen silent after the deactivation of the soliton drives.

"Who's 'us', Damien?" Carter called back. "Aternus was about to let you burn along with everyone else on this station. You're not special to him. You're just another disposable tool in his grand plan."

"That's a lie!"

Carter stopped and listened as Morrow's voice bounced off the walls and surfaces, allowing his augmented mind to process the reflections and calculate the source. It all happened as unconsciously as breathing, but still the traitor's location remained shrouded.

"Don't be naïve, Damien," Carter said, trying to keep the man talking. "Aternus doesn't give a damn about you. He played you for a fool, and our brothers and sisters in arms paid the price. Marco, Fleur, Shime and now your bulldog, Jay. All dead, because of you."

The silence that answered him was telling. As a Master Commander, Morrow prided himself on his ability to lead, and to keep his people safe. That was his duty, just as it was Carter's. And Morrow had failed.

"I'm not the only one who failed their crew, Carter..." Morrow finally replied. The words struck him like a bolt of lightning. "But you forced my hand. Her death is on you, not me."

Carter worked his way behind one of the warp drive enclosures, then he saw her. Kendra Castle was on the floor, with the golden cable still bound around her neck, buried into her flesh like a garrote. He rushed to her side and unwound the cable, having to break skin that had partially healed around it. Her throat was cut and Carter could see damage to the vertebrae in her neck, but she was still alive, if only barely.

"Relax, Kendra, I've got you," Carter said, popping the cap off his final nano-stim and setting the dosage to maximum.

He knew this was a terrible risk so soon after his Master Engineer had received another high-dose, but he had no choice. If he didn't treat her, she'd be dead within seconds. Pushing the stim deep into the cut in her neck, he depressed the plunger and the invisible nano-machines immediately set to work, rebuilding bone, muscles, cartilage and skin as if by magic. Her sensation blockers were useless against the raw agony of having her body rebuilt at a cellular level while still conscious, and Kendra's screams were even more harrowing than Amaya's. Her fingers burrowed through his armored uniform and bit into his skin as she bore down, but he didn't flinch. He simply held his Master Engineer close and hoped that he'd found her in time.

Finally, her convulsions began to subside, but she was pale and weak. Carter shuffled her body in his arms so that he could read his comp-slate and ran a medical scan, but the bio-readouts contained so much red that he had to turn it off and look away. The nano-machines had repaired her flesh, but they had also overloaded her augments, and her systems were crashing, one after another, in an unstoppable cascade. Perhaps if he'd had a Master Medic and the Galatine nearby, there might have been something more he could do, but without either, Kendra was finally at the mercy of her human biology.

"Hey, don't worry, it's only a flesh wound," Kendra said, her voice hoarse. Carter had been so distracted by the medical scan that he hadn't noticed her open her eyes. "I've had worse..."

"You're dying, Kendra. Now isn't the time for your bullshit," Carter replied, firmly, but also with compassion. He knew that there was no point trying to offer her false comfort because she knew better than anyone what was happening to her body.

"Now is the perfect time for my bullshit, boss," Kendra replied, smiling. "What other chance will I get?"

"I'll give you another nano-stim," Carter said, reaching for a capsule, before remembering that he'd already used his last one. "Shit, I can get one from Amaya..."

He was about to leave her when Kendra grabbed his shoulders and trapped him. "Save it, Carter," she said, softly. "Save it for someone who needs it."

"*You* need it," Carter shot back, angry at his engineer for stopping him. "You're the toughest person I know, Kendra. If anyone can handle another dose, it's you."

"It's okay, Carter," Kendra replied. She moved her hands to his face and pressed her fingers into the thick bristles of his silver beard. "I've had a long life, and a good life. I have no regrets, and that includes coming back to serve on the Longsword Galatine one last time. Being with you, Amaya and Brodie again has meant more than you could ever know."

Kendra's comp-slate began ringing out a strident alert, and the screen flashed on, showing that her blood pressure and heart rate were critical. Her chest was barely rising and falling and her eyelids had begun to flutter.

"I'm ready," Kendra whispered. She smiled at him.

"Thank you, Carter, for being my friend. I never told you, but I loved you like a brother."

Carter clenched his jaw shut and felt tears well in his eyes but he forced them back. He did not want the last thing that Kendra saw to be him weeping. Instead, he took her hand, and pressed it more firmly to his face, and smiled back at her.

"That means everything to me, Kendra," he said, letting his guard down just enough to allow the human side of Carter Rose to bleed through. "You mean everything to me."

She winked and managed to pat his cheek. Then a long, low tone emanated from her comp-slate, and Carter could no longer hear the beat of her heart.

"Go get him, boss…" Kendra said, forcing the words out with her last breath.

Then Kendra Castle's hands fell from his face and thudded into the deck, and her eyes went glassy. The tears that he'd held back now flowed freely and he rested his head on her chest, willing her heart to start beating again, but he knew it wouldn't. She was dead. Damien Morrow had killed her, and so help him God, he would make the traitor pay.

TWENTY-SEVEN

ATERNUS IS IMMORTAL

CARTER WIPED his eyes with the back of his hand then clawed the remaining wetness off his face, scratching lines into his skin as he did so. By the time his tears had dried those marks had already faded, but he remained scarred on the inside. The mind was the one organ that his augmented powers of healing couldn't touch. Whatever damage was done there remained, forever.

He arranged Kendra's body into a funerary position then removed her tantō, and placed it into her hands, blade pointed toward her feet. Longsword officers didn't follow any specific customs when it came to honoring their fallen, and Carter was not a man of words, anyway. He simply stood over the body of his Master Engineer and vowed to obey her final wish. *"Go get him, boss,"* she had told him, and he intended to do just that.

Energized cutlass in hand, Carter reached down and picked up the golden cable that Morrow had used to garrote his Master Engineer and coiled it around his scabbard. Then he took one final look at Kendra's face – strangely peaceful, in a way that he'd never seen before – and walked away, willing his senses to lead him to his friend's murderer. *But you forced my hand,* Morrow had told him. *Her death is on you, Carter, not me...* His anger swelled and he allowed it to fill him up. That Morrow had the audacity to blame him for Kendra's death made him want to tear the station to pieces with his bare hands, but he needed that fury contained, ready to explode at a moment's notice when he finally caught up with the traitor and enacted his vengeance upon him. Perhaps it wasn't the honorable thing to do, he considered, but this time Carter didn't care. Damien Morrow was going to perish by his hand, or he'd die trying.

Suddenly, he heard the sound of metal grinding against metal coming from somewhere in the dark corner of the reactor room. He accelerated toward the noise and discovered Damien Morrow, forcing open a panel in the wall so that the traitor could flee into the void spaces. *Not this time...* Carter told himself. *This time, you don't get away...* He drew his 57-EX and fired a single shot that punched through the back of Morrow's hand. The man cried out and cursed, more from surprise than from any pain he might have felt, then dropped the wall panel before cradling the injured hand to his chest.

"Going somewhere?" Carter asked, before firing another shot and forcing the traitor to dive away from the gap in the wall and roll into cover.

He had never intended the bullet to kill or injure Morrow, only to keep him from escaping. A bullet was too good for him. Too easy. Too quick. Damien Morrow would fall at the edge of his sword and die staring into his eyes.

"You forced my hand, Carter," Morrow called out, hidden behind a bank of power distributors. "I wanted us to work together as a team, but your misplaced loyalty to the Union blinded you."

"We were already a team," Carter growled, furious that Morrow was peddling the same old story, like a stuck record. "It was you who was blind to what Markus Aternus really is."

Carter could just see the top of Morrow's left shoulder poking over the power distributors, and he aimed and fired, shaving off a sliver of the traitor's scale armor, and chipping his bone. Morrow cursed again and utilized his inhuman speed to run for deeper cover, but Carter was faster, and he shot the man's left calf, causing Morrow to tumble heavily across the deck, like a bolder rolling out of control down a hill. The traitor quickly righted his fall and dragged himself into concealment. Despite the speed of the man's recovery, Carter could have still shot him again if he'd wanted, but he didn't. He was toying with his prey, like a cat with a mouse.

"It doesn't matter what you think of me," Morrow called back. His words were more strained; the physical pain from his injuries were starting to assert themselves. "What matters is that I'm right. The Union can't win this war. Why fight for a losing side?"

"We already chose our side, a very long time ago," Carter said, stalking toward the sound of the turncoat's voice. "It doesn't matter if they deserve our help or not, we took an oath to defend the Union. That's all that matters."

Morrow laughed. "Suit yourself, Carter, but I won't die fighting a hopeless cause."

"No," Carter snarled. "You'll die fighting me."

Morrow darted out of cover and opened fire with his particle pistol, but Carter dodged and weaved, blocking the on-target shots with his already damaged buckler. The traitor then made a run for the exit, risking being shot in the back, but Carter didn't need to waste another round from his 57-EX, because he already knew there wasn't a chance in hell that Morrow could get away. It took the former master commander a couple of seconds to realize that Brodie was standing guard at the door, energized Scottish Claymore in one hand, and Rollo Jay's particle pistol in the other. Morrow put on the brakes and raised his weapon, but Brodie blasted the pistol out of his hands with a shot that would have put Annie Oakley to shame. Cursing bitterly, Morrow drew and energized his cutlass, but Brodie simply shook his head at the man.

"As much as I'd love to be the one who hacks you to pieces, my job is only to stop you from leaving," Brodie said, his words dripping with restrained menace. He then aimed the energized Claymore at Morrow like the barrel of a cannon. "And if that means I have to cut off your feet to keep you here then I will."

"This is as far as you go, Master Commander Morrow," Carter said, steadily pacing toward his enemy, cutlass crackling like thunder.

Morrow spun around to face him, gripped by panic, like a cornered animal.

"So, is this how it ends?" Morrow answered, struggling hard to conceal his fear. "You two are going to take me down together. Mob justice, is that it?"

Carter slowly shook his head. "No, Damien, there can be no justice for what you've done," he said, voice booming like it had been spoken from the heavens. He then raised his sword and adopted a guard position. "But there can be vengeance."

With nowhere to run, Morrow bared his teeth then

charged, swinging his cutlass at Carter's neck. He parried and the impact of the two blades clashing sent shockwaves through his bones and rattled his teeth. He pushed Morrow away, and the traitor took a step back before swinging again, first at his legs, then at his chest. Carter dodged the first attack and deflected the second, before countering by slicing open the chest scales of Morrow's Aternien armor. Undeterred, Morrow launched another flurry of strikes, and scored a glancing blow to his leg. A swift left jab then stunned Carter and the traitor drew the blade of his energized cutlass across his chest, splitting open his battle uniform and cutting a groove into his flesh, to match the one Carter had given to Morrow. Sensation blockers numbed the pain, but Carter was so amped up, he doubted he would have felt anything even without his augments. Morrow came at him again, trying a similar combination of blows, but Carter parried then closed the distance between them and pummeled Morrow's face with the guard of his cutlass, before dragging the blade across his gut.

The traitor's blood spilled onto the deck, and Morrow reeled back, clutching his hand to the wound. The cut began to heal, but the damage was done, both physically and psychologically. Carter waited for his former comrade to meet his eyes, and he reveled in the terror he saw behind them. Upping the tempo of his assault, Carter darted forward and flashed his cutlass high and low, wounding Morrow to the arm and hip. His opponent counterattacked and Carter absorbed a strike to the shoulder, but in the process, he cut deeply across the traitor's side, spilling yet more of his blood onto the deck. Morrow wheezed with pain and attacked again, but Carter dodged and deflected the ever more frantic swings of the man's cutlass, before landing a powerful strike that split Morrow's thigh, down to the bone. The man cried out and collapsed to one knee, then reached for a nano-stim, but Carter slapped the capsule out of Morrow's hand and sent it skidding into the darkness. Then he swung his sword and severed the traitor's hand clean off at the wrist. Morrow clutched his cauterized stump and bit down so hard his front teeth shattered.

"Stop, you've won!" Morrow yelled, spitting bits of teeth onto the deck, like broken pottery. "But killing me won't change a thing. You can't believe you have a chance?"

Carter looked the man in the eyes and raised his cutlass. "I'll tell you what I believe, Damien," he said, face half in shadow from the glow of the energized blade. "I believe in fighting until I can't. And while I still draw breath, Markus Aternus will never be safe."

Morrow snorted and shook his head. "Go on then, do it," he said, speaking to Carter with disdain.

He moved behind Morrow and the traitor maintained his posture, determined to meet his end with some semblance of dignity, but Carter had no intention of giving the man a clean death. After what he'd done to Kendra, he didn't deserve it. Carter swung the cutlass, but instead of the blade severing Morrow's head from his neck, it cut deeply into the deck plates, where it remained, like Excalibur in the stone. Morrow turned to look at him, his face warped with confusion, then Carter unhooked the golden cable that the traitor had used to kill his Master Engineer and wrapped it around the man's neck. Morrow struggled, but Carter's will was unconquerable. He pulled the cord tight, then dragged Morrow, kicking and thrashing, to the warp drive enclosure where Kendra lay dead. Tossing one end of the cable over an upright, he hauled Morrow up and held him there, feet dangling inches off the deck. The traitor continued to kick and thrash, his eyes bulging and skin turning blue, but Carter stood firm and watched the man hang.

"Aternus may be Immortal, Master Commander Morrow," Carter growled. "But you are not..."

TWENTY-EIGHT

THE AFTERMATH

CARTER FELT numb as he watched two Union medics from the Battleship Dauntless wheel the casket containing the remains of Kendra Castle out of Venture Terminal's morgue. Her body was to be loaded onto the Galatine at his request, though quite what he intended to do with the remains of his oldest friend, he wasn't yet sure. Longsword officers had no funerary rituals, and Kendra had not left a last will and testament, or any instructions for how to dispose of her body. As such, he'd taken it upon himself to make those arrangements. He knew that it was sentimental, and that the casket contained nothing but an empty shell, but he'd be damned if Kendra would be left on Venture Terminal to be incinerated like trash.

"I'm sorry for your loss," said Lieutenant Nadia Ozek. The officer was a few hours post-op and was still in her surgical gown, with a clinical white robe over the top. Considering her ordeal, she looked strong.

"Thank you, Lieutenant," Carter replied, offering her a grateful smile.

"It's such a waste," Nadia continued, arms folded across her chest. "There are so few of you left."

"Kendra lived a long life, far longer than most people get to enjoy." Carter was determined not to be maudlin, since he knew Kendra would have hated that. "And she died doing her duty, which is all that any Longsword officer can hope for."

Nadia looked at him, uncertainly. "Surely, there's more to your lives than duty?"

Carter shook his head. "Normal lives are for normal people like you, Lieutenant."

"But don't you have family?" Nadia continued. "I don't know quite how old you are, but I'm guessing it's old enough that you should have grandkids, at least?"

Carter huffed a laugh and smiled at Nadia. It was easy to forget that more than a century had passed since he had been in the company of regular human beings, or 'normies' as Kendra had liked to call them. In that time the Longsword officers had passed into myth, much like the stories of Arthurian legend that their ships were named after.

"I'm quite a bit older than you probably realize," he replied, though in a kindly manner. "And I can't have children. I can't have a family. It's not what I was made for."

To his surprise, Lieutenant Ozek snorted with derision. "Well, that's bullshit, if you ask me. You deserve a life, the same as everyone else. Hell, if you ask me, you deserve it more, because most of us would have never been born if it wasn't for the Longswords. And I'd be dead now, if you hadn't rescued me from that gang."

"You and Kendra would have gotten along, I think," Carter replied, recognizing some of his Master Engineer's straight-talking fire in the young lieutenant. "And for what it's worth, I think you would have made a fine Longsword officer."

Lieutenant Ozek swelled with pride at this comment. "That actually means a lot, thank you, sir."

Carter grunted. "Don't be so certain; this is a curse, not a blessing. You should be thankful for what you are."

The door to the medical ward swooshed open and Admiral Clara Krantz marched in, flanked by a quartet of personal bodyguards. She raised a hand to the armed soldiers and they held back, watchfully guarding both the entrance and the admiral. Krantz had arrived at Venture Terminal a few hours earlier on the newly-revamped Battleship Dauntless. After he'd gotten word to the admiral about what had transpired on the station, she'd sent a taskforce to immediately recapture Venture Terminal, and deal with its criminal infestation. In truth, most of the gang members had surrendered without much of a fight. Damien Morrow had been the architect of the takeover, under the assumed identity of crime kingpin, 'Javelin', and with him gone, the organization quickly unraveled. The only real trouble had come from the remaining Aternien infiltrators, but even they had not put up much of a fight, largely on account of the fact that Carter and his officers had already killed most of them.

"Master Commander Rose," Krantz said, approaching him with a respectful nod.

"Admiral," Carter grunted in reply.

Carter then noticed that Lieutenant Ozek had straightened up like a beanpole and gone just as rigid. She threw up a stiff salute, almost knocking herself out in the process. It was endearing and made him like her even more.

"Admiral Krantz, ma'am," Nadia said, holding her salute.

Krantz almost rolled her eyes, but didn't, and quickly returned the salute. "At ease, Lieutenant, before you pop your stitches."

Nadia lowered her salute and adopted the at ease position. In her surgical gown and white robe, she looked comical, and Carter choked down a laugh.

"Ma'am, with your permission I'll return to my bay, and leave you two to talk," Nadia said. The officer was self-aware enough to realize that whatever he and the admiral were about to discuss was above her pay grade, and that she needed to make herself scarce, before being asked to. However, Krantz had other ideas.

"Permission denied, Lieutenant, you are not dismissed," Krantz said.

Nadia was already leaving, and the admiral's order caught her by surprise. She swiftly snapped back into the at ease position, eyes wide.

"Don't forget to breathe, Lieutenant," Carter said, noting that the woman had gone so still that her chest wasn't even rising and falling. "I don't want to have to call a crash trolley to resuscitate you."

"Yes, sir," Lieutenant Ozek squeaked, literally forcing herself to breathe, as if the autonomic part of her nervous system had collapsed under the stress of Krantz's intimidating presence.

"Not that I'm ungrateful for what you've done here, Master Commander, but aren't you supposed to be… elsewhere?" Krantz said. She had referred to his mission to find Nathan Clynes in deliberately vague terms due to the presence of Lieutenant Ozek.

"I was 'elsewhere', when we received a coded message from Brodie Kaur, my old Master-at-arms," Carter explained. He took Krantz's brusqueness for what it was – simply a busy woman getting to the nub of things. "I figured if we could pick up Brodie on the way then another Longsword officer would be an asset in the mission ahead."

Krantz watched the casket finally leave the ward and turn left along the corridor. "It seems that you've gained an officer and also lost one," she added. "My condolences."

"I didn't *lose,* anything." He felt that Krantz had been brusque to the point of being uncaring. "Damien Morrow murdered her, but only after Kendra shut down the warp drives, preventing this station from jumping into the atmosphere of Terra Prime and triggering a never-ending ice age that would have killed every living thing on the planet…"

Krantz raised an eyebrow at him. "I have offended you, Commander?"

"A little," Carter grunted.

"Then I am sorry," Krantz replied, bowing her head slightly. "Though don't misunderstand me. For her actions and sacrifice, Kendra Castle will receive the Union's highest military honor."

"You can save the medal, Admiral, she wouldn't give a shit," Carter cut in, perhaps unwisely. The narrowing of Krantz's eyes seemed to confirm this, though she let it slide, and chose to move the discussion on.

"Was your special assignment a success, Commander?" Krantz asked, continuing to speak in riddles. "Both aspects of it?"

The two aspects that Krantz was referring to were enlisting Nathan Clynes's help to produce a tech virus to attack the Aterniens, and saving the life of Major Carina Larsen, the admiral's niece. However, from the way her laser-cutter stare had softened, and how she had pressed her hands together at the small of her back to stop from fidgeting, he knew that it was the second aspect that Krantz was most keen to hear news about.

"The first part was a bust, I'm afraid," Carter replied, choosing to speak plainly, as Krantz had done. "The second is a work in progress."

Carter saw the admiral swallow hard and felt her pulse quicken.

"What are the chances of success?" Krantz asked.

To Nadia Ozek and any other regular human listening, the admiral's question would have sounded perfectly normal, but Carter's augmented hearing could detect the minute vacillations and shudders that betrayed her inner turmoil.

"I won't know until I return," Carter admitted, not wanting to give Krantz – or himself – false hope. "But believe me when I say that I made it very much in our contact's interest to succeed."

Krantz accepted his explanation without asking Carter to elaborate, perhaps understanding that such an elaboration might have been self-incriminating. Carter wasn't sure on the legalities of exposing a former-Union citizen to a deadly virus, but he expected that the practice would have been frowned upon. He then accessed his comp-slate, found the relevant files and mission logs, which he'd prepared earlier, and requested a secure-link to the admiral's device. Krantz raised her arm, then her eyebrow, and accepted the peer-to-peer secure link.

"Everything you need to know is in these files," Carter

said, transmitting the data. "I'll let you decide quite how much of it to reveal to the senior commanders and the president."

"Thank you for giving me your permission," Krantz replied, sarcastically. She skimmed the files and her eyes widened a little. "I shall study these in detail when I have a moment."

One of Krantz's guards approached and spoke into her ear. The officer had kept his voice low, though Carter could still hear every word, and was relieved to discover that the man was simply reminding her of an imminent appointment she needed to keep. Krantz acknowledged the reminder but made no attempt to leave.

"Since your primary objective was unsuccessful, what is your next move, Commander?" Krantz asked. "Because we could sorely use the Galatine back on the front lines."

Up until his encounter with the Overseer, Rose hadn't had a next move, but Monique Dubois had given him an idea that was even more audacious than his plan to develop a tech-virus. He knew he couldn't defeat Markus Aternus in battle – the god-king's forces were too strong – but he could do something arguably even more devastating. He could destroy the Soul Crypt – the repository of Aternien minds – and take away their immortality.

"It's all in the file, Admiral," Carter replied, pointing to Krantz's comp-slate. "But I'm going to need to ask for little more latitude. Having the Galatine on the front line will only delay our inevitable defeat, but if what I have in mind works, it could end this war in a heartbeat.

Krantz was suitably intrigued. "Then I look forward to reading your report."

The same member of the admiral's security detail

approached again, and this time she acknowledged the man before he even spoke a word.

"I'm afraid that duty calls, Master Commander," Krantz said, with a half-smile. "Please keep me updated, in particular about your XO."

"As soon as I know anything, I'll send a message through the warp buoys, for your eyes only."

"That would be very much appreciated, Commander," Krantz replied, suddenly speaking as Carina's concerned aunt, rather than her superior officer. The admiral turned to leave then locked eyes with Lieutenant Ozek, who looked like she'd been blasted with a freeze ray. "Well, Lieutenant, don't just stand there," Krantz said.

"Yes, ma'am, of course, ma'am." Nadia stepped away from the admiral, then hesitated and stepped back. "Excuse me, ma'am, what is it that you want me to do?"

"For starters, you are out of uniform," Krantz snapped, leaning into her role as the terrifying flag admiral of the Union. "Dressing gowns may have been permitted on Venture Terminal, but all officers serving aboard my ship are expected to adhere strictly to the uniform code."

Lieutenant Ozek looked so uncomfortable and out of sorts that Carter wanted to throw his arm around her and tell her it was going to be okay. He'd done his fair share of intimidating junior officers in his time, but now he found it excruciating to watch, like an episode of a reality TV series that exposed the ineptitude of its participants.

"Ma'am, I do not serve aboard the Dauntless," Lieutenant Ozek replied, though she was in such a muddle that she appeared to doubt her own assertion.

"You do now, Lieutenant," Krantz said, sternly. "I am down a bridge operations officer, and Master Commander

Rose told me of your bravery during this incident. If the Master Commander recommends you then that is good enough for me."

"Yes, ma'am," Lieutenant Ozek said, still like a rabbit in headlights.

"Get dressed and report to the Dauntless in one hour," Krantz continued, before turning back to Carter, again as if Nadia was invisible. "Good hunting, Commander. And, once again, thank you."

Carter grunted an acknowledgment then Krantz bustled away, protected by her heavily-armed entourage. He was also about to leave when he realized that Lieutenant Ozek was still flash-frozen at his side.

"Her bark is worse than her bite," Carter said, smiling. He then shrugged. "But not by much."

"Did that just happen?" Nadia asked. She looked like she'd just been roused from a deep sleep and was unsure whether she was awake or still dreaming.

"Yes, it did, so if I were you, I'd get into uniform and haul ass to the Dauntless, before it leaves without you." He paused, considering her injuries. "Assuming, you're up to it, of course?"

"I have the worst headache, but otherwise I'm cleared for duty." She then smiled and tapped a nano-stim canister attached to Carter's belt. "Though feel free to give me one of those, and turn me into a super-human Longsword officer, like you."

Carter laughed. "That's not how it works, and one of these is as likely to kill you, as make you stronger."

The young officer accepted that. "Then I guess I'll stick to aspirin."

"Probably wise," Carter said, continuing their little game

of parry-riposte.

Lieutenant Ozek's expression then became serious. "Thank you for putting a word in, sir. Serving on the flagship is everything I've ever wanted."

Carter accepted her gratitude graciously, though he always felt self-conscious when anyone gave him praise.

"You earned it, Lieutenant. I meant it when I said you'd have made a good Longsword officer, but since that isn't possible, the Dauntless is a worthy second best."

Nadia beamed a smile at him, and Carter felt his cheeks flush hot with embarrassment. He tapped his comp-slate, in the same way that people tap their watches to indicate a pressing appointment.

"Don't keep the admiral waiting…"

"Yes, sir," Lieutenant Ozek said, saluting in her dressing gown.

Carter returned the salute and the officer hustled away. He smiled as he watched her hurry past nurses and other patients with the giddy excitement of someone who'd just won the lottery. Then, when she was out of sight, the reality of what was to come next hit him like a shotgun blast to the chest, and a crushing darkness enveloped him.

TWENTY-NINE

GOODBYE, KENDRA

AMAYA AND BRODIE were waiting for him on the Galatine, ready to participate in the funeral for their shipmate and friend. Thanks to the quick actions of his Master-at-arms, Amaya had survived being stabbed through the gut, and was already rapidly on the road to recovery. That in itself had been a miracle, so to have expected Kendra to have also survived was perhaps a wish too far. Though as he walked through Venture Terminal's cold corridors on the way back to his ship, he would have given anything, even his own life, to have her back.

Seizing on any available opportunity to delay his return, Carter stopped at a viewing window and watched three freighters depart from the upper pylons, carrying with them some of the refugees from Terra Seven. A security transport filled with what was left of the criminal gangs was also leaving, though its passengers were on-route to jail, rather than another of the colony worlds or habitats. Ordinarily, he would have taken some satisfaction from that, but the truth was that it made little difference where the various transports were headed, because all of humanity had been given a death sentence by Markus Aternus. If the god-king wasn't stopped then nowhere in the Union was safe.

Finding a cure to the Aternien biogenic virus was the first step to thwarting the Aterniens' plans, which meant that Carter had to perform his unhappy duty quickly, so that they could get back underway. After that came something arguably much more difficult, and unlikely to succeed, but that was for another time. First, he had to say goodbye to Kendra Castle. Then, he hoped, he could say hello again to Carina Larsen. He didn't want to contemplate the possibility that his XO was already dead, waiting in a casket not unlike the one Kendra had been shipped out in, and unceremoniously dumped in Nathan's warehouse of Frankenstein creations. Yet, he had to accept that this was a possibility. Perhaps, it was even the most likely outcome.

The closer Carter got to the Galatine, the more the weight of the responsibility pressed down on his shoulders. He still didn't know what he was going to say, because how could any combination of words do justice to all that Kendra had achieved in her long life? Perhaps it didn't matter what he said, he reasoned. Perhaps all that mattered was that they gathered together to remember her.

"ADA, prepare to detach from Venture Terminal then ahead slow in the direction of Gliese 832," Carter said, speaking to Amaya's gopher over the internal comm channel.

The bot cheerfully bleeped a confirmation, then Carter closed the hatch and continued through the long corridors of the Galatine, in the direction of the shuttle bay. As he was walking, he felt the docking clamps release, followed by the thrum of the main engines as the ship pulled away from

Venture Terminal. By the time he reached the door to the shuttle bay, they were well under way, and clear of the station and its traffic. He paused to collect his thoughts, which were still a chaotic muddle of memories and words, then entered.

Brodie and Amaya were chatting in the relaxed, casual manner that they always had done, like two firm friends who, no matter how long they had spent apart, could always slip back into their old groove. They straightened up as Carter approached, then moved to a small table that had been set up next to shuttle pad two. Pad one was occupied by the combat shuttle that Nathan Clynes had shot down on Gliese 832-e. Kendra had already made a start on repairing it but now, like his Master Engineer's body, it would forever remain broken and inert.

"I picked up a bottle of grappa from the station stores, before I embarked," Brodie said, as Carter approached the table. "I remember that Kendra used to sip this after a meal. It's kinda like brandy, I think."

"I wouldn't know," Carter grunted, picking up the nondescript-looking bottle and examining the label, which was written in a language as indecipherable to him as Aternien hieroglyphs. "But good idea, Brodie, thank you."

Over the top of the bottle, Carter could see the casket sat in the middle of shuttle pad two. He'd been aware of its presence as soon as the door to the shuttle bay had slid open, but he'd not allowed himself to look at it properly until that moment. With a resigned sigh, he uncorked the grappa and poured an amount into each of the three waiting glasses. He had no idea how much to pour, so he filled them to the half-way mark. From the wide-eyed looks on the faces of his two officers, he guessed that his measures were generous.

"As you know, I'm not very good at this sort of thing," Carter said, picking up one of the glasses, and waiting for Amaya and Brodie to collect theirs. "We had so many close scrapes during the war but we somehow always managed to walk away, and I got used to the idea that you were all invincible. I suppose that was wishful thinking."

He sighed again then turned to face the casket, though he would have rather faced in any other direction, even if that meant staring into the fires of hell.

"By any metric, Kendra Castle was a genius, who could be as annoying as she was brilliant." Brodie and Amaya both gave each other knowing smiles. "Loud and regularly foul-mouthed, she had her own code and her own way of doing things, which often deviated from the strict center-line that the Union likes us all to stick to, though we rarely do." Both huffed laughs at this. "She used to say that 'regulations are for normies', and she certainly adhered to that creed." He allowed himself a muted chuckle, then the sight of the casket sobered him again, and he raised his glass. "Above all else, Kendra was loyal and faithful to her oath and to her crew – her family – right to the bitter end. And most importantly of all, she was our friend."

"To Kendra," Brodie said, softly.

"To Kendra," he and Amaya repeated.

They drank their grappa, which had a surprisingly sweet berry flavor, and an even more surprising kick. Like his Master Engineer, Carter wasn't much of a drinker, but he could appreciate why Kendra had liked the alcoholic spirit.

"Hey, does anyone know where Kendra was from?" Brodie asked. He'd sunk his grappa in one and was refilling his glass. "Originally, I mean?"

Carter sucked in a breath, which only seemed to intensify

the rich alcoholic flavor of the beverage, then searched the crevices of his mind.

"I think she was from Chicago, on Terra Prime, though she was born somewhere in Europe." He shrugged. "It must have been in her file, but I never really paid much attention to that stuff, or anything in the Longsword trial records."

Amaya seemed surprised by this. "Then how did you go about selecting us as your crew? You were the first Longsword Master Commander ever commissioned, so you must have had the pick of all the officers who passed the trials."

"I did," Carter grunted.

"So..." Brodie cut in, also clearly interested in the answer.

Carter had always been very secretive about the early days of the Longsword program, and his involvement in it. Part of the reason for this was Nathan Clynes, and the experiments that the scientist had performed, none of which Carter had sanctioned, or agreed with, but he knew enough to know they were unethical. Mainly, however, it was simply because he was a private man, who kept himself to himself.

"I didn't read your trial records," Carter admitted, shocking them both. "I interviewed every candidate who passed selection, which as you know was quite a short list, and made my decision based on that."

Brodie snorted a laugh. "Come on, MC, you're saying you didn't look at our service records, or psych evaluations, or read any of the results from our trials?"

Carter shook his head. Now that he thought about it, his method of selecting his officers did seem somewhat slapdash to an outside observer. However, he knew better.

"They wouldn't have put you in front of me if your

records and trial results hadn't indicated you were up to the job," Carter explained. "To be honest, the part that mattered most was the medical assessment as to whether you'd survive the augmentation process or not."

"So how did you choose?" Amaya asked again, since he'd still glossed over that part.

Carter shrugged. "I followed my gut. I wanted to get a sense for the person each of you was. I knew that as post-humans we'd be feared and vilified, as I'd already experienced some of that bigotry, so it was important that your character was as strong as your performance. For better or worse, we would be like family to one another, so I chose the people I wanted to be with the most."

The revelation seemed to hit Brodie and Amaya like a particle cannon to the face, and for a time neither of them said a word. Then Amaya set down her glass, and to his surprise she pulled him into an embrace, hugging him so tightly that it squeezed the air from his lungs.

"I wish Kendra could have heard you say that," Brodie said. He was looking at the casket, arms folded across his broad chest. "It would have made her cringe so bad that I reckon she'd have actually puked."

Carter laughed, or at least tried to, considering the wrench-like grip Amaya still had on him. Then his Master Navigator stepped back, wiped a tear from her eye and turned to face the casket too. They all knew what came next.

"We have to say goodbye now," Carter said, accessing the shuttle bay control systems on his comp-slate. "But so long as we remember her, then Kendra Castle will never truly die."

He was about to tap the button to lower the docking pad, and the casket, into the launch tube, when his senses told him to wait. Finger hovering above the screen, he looked around the shuttle bay then spotted what had triggered his sixth sense. RAEB, Kendra's gopher, was lurking in the corner of the room, his red eye dimly visible in the shadows, with JACAB by his side. The engineering assistant bot had gone AWOL ever since hearing about his keeper's death, and Carter had allowed Kendra's gopher time to grieve and come to terms in his own unique way.

"Come on, buddy," Carter called out to RAEB, waving him over. "She'd want you to be here."

RAEB moved out of the shadows, his eye narrow and dim, while JACAB remained in the corner of the room, the darkness enveloping him like a blanket of sadness. RAEB couldn't look at the casket, and after a slow, funerial procession, the bot finally arrived and Carter gently put his arm around him.

"You can do it, if you like, buddy," Carter said, holding out his comp-slate, which was pre-configured to trigger the docking pad, and jettison the casket into space. "But it's okay if you can't."

RAEB quivered and rocked from side to side, like someone shaking their head.

"That's okay, buddy, I understand."

Carter looked at Amaya and Brodie and saw that they were both ready. Then he slid his hand off RAEB and tapped the button to activate the sequence. The docking pad started its descent into the launch tube, and the pressure doors began closing to seal the hole it had left behind. Suddenly, RAEB darted forward and flew into the launch tube, taking Carter completely by surprise. He dropped to his knees at the edge of the bay, only to see that the bot had landed on the casket and magnetized himself to it.

"RAEB, come on, you don't have to do this!" Carter called out, but the bot merely looked at him with his sad red eye and didn't answer.

Cursing, Carter accessed his comp-slate and tried to override the launch sequence, but he was denied. Cursing for a second time, he repeated the commands, but was again blocked. Then he realized why. RAEB had been the one to lock him out.

"MC, I can't cancel the launch sequence," Brodie said, also attempting to halt the launch from a console in the shuttle bay.

"My comp-slate isn't working, either," Amaya said.

Carter got to his feet and turned to JACAB, but the bot hadn't moved so much as a maneuvering fin. He was about to call out to his gopher to help but he instinctively knew that JACAB didn't want to. Because of the unique bond between gopher and keeper, Carter suddenly understood what was happening. JACAB wouldn't intervene, because RAEB had asked him not to, and Carter was not about to order his gopher to break his promise.

"It's okay," Carter said, and the unheard-of softness of his voice made Brodie and Amaya take note. "RAEB knows what he's doing. It's his choice."

The two other officers ran to his side in time to catch a glimpse of the engineering bot before the pressure doors closed and locked. A warning alarm sounded then the outer bay door was opened, and the casket containing the body of Kendra was ejected into space, along with her faithful gopher, RAEB. Carter, Amaya and Brodie stood for a time in solemn reflection, before the sobering reality that they still had a mission to complete made them turn their thoughts to the future. Carter led the way, but as he reached the door leading out of the shuttle bay, he stopped.

"Everything okay, skipper?" Amaya asked. "All things considered, I mean?"

"I'm fine, Amaya," Carter said. "You two go ahead to the bridge and get the ship ready to jump to Gliese 832-e. I'll follow along in a minute."

Amaya nodded then she and Brodie left the shuttle bay, leaving Carter alone with his thoughts, and with the ghost of Kendra Castle. The last week had gone by in a blur and had been characterized by a sequence of surprising victories and soul crushing defeats. They'd foiled a plot to wipe out Terra Prime, and in the process, he'd added to his crew and lost a dear friend. He knew it was bad math to weigh billions of lives against just one, but he still felt like he'd lost more than he'd gained.

Carter Rose now dreaded returning to Gliese 832-e more than ever. It was easier to not know – to pretend that Carina Larsen was alive and kicking and driving Nathan Clynes up the wall. The easier choice was to continue his mission without her, but that was not only cowardly, it was also unfair on his XO. In any case, he had no choice, because there was something else he needed from Gliese 832-e – something that wouldn't be extracted without a fight. To defeat Markus Aternus he had to strike at the core of the god-king's empire. He had to find New Aternus and show its people that they were not immortal. He had to show them that their god was false. And to do that he needed Nathan Clynes, whether the man liked it or not.

Carter took one last look at the shuttle bay, as empty in that moment as his heart was, then walked through the door and into the long corridor that led to the bridge of the

Galatine. The great Longsword-class battleship would strike once more, this time at the heart of their enemy. For him, at least, the battle in Union space was finished. Now, the battle for New Aternus would begin.

The end (to be concluded).

ALSO BY G J OGDEN

Sa'Nerra Universe

Omega Taskforce

Descendants of War

Scavenger Universe

Star Scavengers

Star Guardians

Standalone series

The Contingency War series

Darkspace Renegade series

The Planetsider

Audible Audiobooks

Star Scavengers - click here

The Contingency War - click here

Omega Taskforce - click here

Descendants of War - click here

The Planetsider Trilogy - click here

G J Ogden's newsletter: Click here to sign-up

ABOUT THE AUTHOR

At school, I was asked to write down the jobs I wanted to do as a "grown up". Number one was astronaut and number two was a PC games journalist. I only managed to achieve one of those goals (I'll let you guess which), but these two very different career options still neatly sum up my lifelong interests in science, space, and the unknown.

School also steered me in the direction of a science-focused education over literature and writing, which influenced my decision to study physics at Manchester University. What this degree taught me is that I didn't like studying physics and instead enjoyed writing, which is why you're reading this book! The lesson? School can't tell you who you are.

When not writing, I enjoy spending time with my family, walking in the British countryside, and indulging in as much Sci-Fi as possible.

Printed in Great Britain
by Amazon

37309173R00192